# *Classic*
# WAR STORIES

# Classic
## WAR STORIES

EDITED *by*

# LAMAR UNDERWOOD

THE LYONS PRESS
GUILFORD, CONNECTICUT
AN IMPRINT OF THE GLOBE PEQUOT PRESS

The Lyons Press is an imprint of
The Globe Pequot Press.

10 9 8 7 6 5 4 3 2 1

Printed in the United States of America

Designed by Claire Zoghb

ISBN 1-59228-058-7

Library of Congress Cataloging-in-Publication
Data is available on file.

# Contents

# CONTENTS

# Introduction

> The tumult and the shouting dies;
> The captains and the kings depart;
> Still shines Thine ancient sacrifice,
>  An humble and contrite heart.
> Lord God of Hosts, be with us yet,
> Lest we forget—lest we forget!
> > Rudyard Kipling
> > *Recessional*

Even though he wrote *Recessional* before the death of his son in the First World War, Rudyard Kipling knew a thing or two about the pain of war and the drama of war stories. He knew, for instance, that the "captains and kings" would command center stage as much as the troops who fought the battles, and that afterwards the bloodshed and losses would be horrible to contemplate without linking them to some Almighty purpose.

Today, such reflections continue, just as the battles themselves continue, followed by the accounts and journals of what happened on the fields where victories and defeats were forged. News of the outcomes is not enough. The details, the exact history, the stories of the men in uniform—these accounts go on for decades, or, as in the case of some battles, for centuries. It would seem from the popularity of war literature that once a certain amount of interest is created by a particular battle or campaign, there will always be readers on the hunt for accounts and stories that put them in the very flames of the battle itself. They search to know and feel: What was it like?

What was it like at Waterloo, or Gettysburg, or the Marne. What was it like to maneuver the armies, carry the weapons and face the enemy? What was it like to feel the pain and loss?

So many of mankind's most talented authors have tackled this amazing subject so many times for the simple reason that for many, many people the material is endlessly fascinating. When it comes to war, whether the scenes depicted are of bravery and glory or tragedy and defeat, many of us avid readers are drawn irresistibility to the pages, like rubberneckers staring at the site of an accident.

The war stories I personally feel qualify for the exalted title "Classic" have earned their way onto my list by being sources of great reading reward for many years. In my mind they are not "Classics" because the gurus and high priests of literature have deemed them so, but because they are enduring as great pleasures to read. Considering the authors who have penned these tales, one can hardly be surprised by their quality and staying power. Hugo, Tolstoy, Crane, Kipling . . . several others. These are not exactly one-book celebrities. These gentlemen were drawn to war as a colossal canvas because they had plenty to say about the subject and the talent to back up their ambitions. We readers are truly blessed by their efforts.

The timeline for this volume of stories goes only as far as the First World War. Obviously, scores and scores of stories that might already justifiably be called "Classic" have been written since then, as the Twentieth Century was replete with conflicts, including the biggest of them all, World War Two. But such a collection is beyond the scope of this somewhat modest anthology, which endeavors to present the editor's choices of the older and mellower "Classics."

In rereading many of these tales, I am often struck by the vividness and intensity of the scenes the prose evokes. The great writers did not settle for dry reportage of facts and events. Their pages instead capture mood and atmosphere, while crackling along with the pace and exhilaration of action unfolding. The pages of the aforementioned Victor Hugo on Waterloo, or Tolstoy on Borodino, or Stephen Crane on a Civil War battle become some kind of magical widescreen film in my mind. I can see, hear and feel the tumult of the battle. It is the best way to go to war.

I personally have been a war literature and history junkie, if you will, for so long that I cannot remember a time-span in my life when I wasn't engrossed in some work of fiction or non-fiction from military history. One of the peculiar fascinations I find in reading about the battlefields of the past is the way both fate and individual acts create a certain randomness at the scene—a seemingly unorchestrated panorama in which the unlucky can fall as quickly as the unprepared, and pure chance is dealing a lot of the cards. Indeed, I am far from alone in my observation. The noted military historian S.L.A. Marshall put the subject far more eloquently in one of his many books, *Ambush: The Battle of Dau Tieng:*

"As I have written many times, most battles are more like a schoolyard brawl in a rough neighborhood at recess time than a clash between football giants in the Rose Bowl. They are messy, inorganic, and uncoordinated . . .

"Although the clash may be widespread and immediate, what happens in any one sector is all too often almost unrelated to the action of any other . . .

"Within a given company, each platoon may have its own fight virtually in isolation, and within one battalion, each company may get the feeling that it is standing at Armageddon and battling pretty much alone for the Lord."

It is not, in my opinion, too much of a stretch to imagine that the fears expressed by Marshall about our Vietnam battalions and companies were experienced by Caesar's legions and the armies which opposed them. So be it throughout history. Weapons and tactics may change, bringing new "captains and kings" to the battlefield. But for the men bearing the brunt of the action, the fears, expectations and sometimes despair are no doubt timeless emotions. And these have been captured timelessly, by the great writers in works which are included in the pages reprinted here.

—Lamar Underwood
June, 2003

# Carrying the Flag

[ STEPHEN CRANE ]

The youth stared at the land in front of him. Its foliage now seemed to veil powers and horrors. He was unaware of the machinery of orders that started the charge, although from the corners of his eyes he saw an officer, who looked like a boy a–horseback, come galloping, waving his hat. Suddenly he felt a straining and heaving among the men. The line fell slowly forward like a toppling wall, and, with a convulsive gasp that was intended for a cheer, the regiment began its journey. The youth was pushed and jostled for a moment before he understood the movement at all, but directly he lunged ahead and began to run.

He fixed his eye upon a distant and prominent clump of trees where he had concluded the enemy were to be met, and he ran toward it as toward a goal. He had believed throughout that it was a mere question of getting over an unpleasant matter as quickly as possible, and he ran desperately, as if pursued for a murder. His face was drawn hard and tight with the stress of his endeavor. His eyes were fixed in a lurid glare. And with his soiled and disordered dress, his red and inflamed features surmounted by the dingy rag with its spot of blood, his wildly swinging rifle and banging accoutrements, he looked to be an insane soldier.

As the regiment swung from its position out into a cleared space the woods and thickets before it awakened. Yellow flames leaped toward it from many directions. The forest made a tremendous objection.

The line lurched straight for a moment. Then the right wing swung forward; it in turn was surpassed by the left. Afterward the center careered to the front until the regiment was a wedge-shaped mass, but an instant later the opposition of the bushes, trees, and uneven places on the ground split the command and scattered it into detached clusters.

The youth, light-footed, was unconsciously in advance. His eyes still kept note of the clump of trees. From all places near it the clannish yell of the enemy could be heard. The little flames of rifles leaped from it. The song of the bullets was in the air and shells snarled among the tree-tops. One tumbled directly into the middle of a hurrying group and exploded in crimson fury. There was an instant's spectacle of a man, almost over it, throwing up his hands to shield his eyes.

Other men, punched by bullets, fell in grotesque agonies. The regiment left a coherent trail of bodies.

They had passed into a clearer atmosphere. There was an effect like a revelation in the new appearance of the landscape. Some men working madly at a battery were plain to them, and the opposing infantry's lines were defined by the gray walls and fringes of smoke.

It seemed to the youth that he saw everything. Each blade of the green grass was bold and clear. He thought that he was aware of every change in the thin, transparent vapor that floated idly in sheets. The brown or gray trunks of the trees showed each roughness of their surfaces. And the men of the regiment, with their starting eyes and sweating faces, running madly, or falling, as if thrown headlong, to queer, heaped-up corpses—all were comprehended. His mind took a mechanical but firm impression, so that afterward everything was pictured and explained to him, save why he himself was there.

But there was a frenzy made from this furious rush. The men, pitching forward insanely, had burst into cheerings, moblike and barbaric, but tuned in strange keys that can arouse the dullard and the stoic. It made a mad enthusiasm that, it seemed, would be incapable of checking itself before granite and brass. There was the delirium that encounters despair and death, and is heedless and blind to the odds. It is a temporary but sublime absence of selfishness. And because it was of this order was the reason, perhaps, why the youth wondered, afterward, what reasons he could have had for being there.

Presently the straining pace ate up the energies of the men. As if by agreement, the leaders began to slacken their speed. The volleys directed against them had had a seeming windlike effect. The regiment snorted and blew. Among some stolid trees it began to falter and hesitate. The men, staring intently, began to wait for some of the distant walls of smoke to move and disclose to them the scene. Since much of their strength and their breath had vanished, they returned to caution. They were become men again.

The youth had a vague belief that he had run miles, and he thought, in a way, that he was now in some new and unknown land.

The moment the regiment ceased its advance the protesting splutter of musketry became a steadier roar. Long and accurate fringes of smoke spread out. From the top of a small hill came level belchings of yellow flame that caused an inhuman whistling in the air.

The men, halted, had opportunity to see some of

their comrades dropping with moans and shrieks. A few lay under foot, still or wailing. And now for an instant the men stood, their rifles slack in their hands, and watched the regiment dwindle. They appeared dazed and stupid. This spectacle seemed to paralyze them, overcome them with a fatal fascination. They stared woodenly at the sights, and, lowering their eyes, looked from face to face. It was a strange pause, and a strange silence.

Then, above the sounds of the outside commotion, arose the roar of the lieutenant. He strode suddenly forth, his infantile features black with rage.

"Come on, yeh fools!" he bellowed. "Come on! Yeh can't stay here. Yeh must come on." He said more, but much of it could not be understood.

He started rapidly forward, with his head turned toward the men. "Come on," he was shouting. The men stared with blank and yokel-like eyes at him. He was obliged to halt and retrace his steps. He stood then with his back to the enemy and delivered gigantic curses into the faces of the men. His body vibrated from the weight and force of his imprecations. And he could string oaths with the facility of a maiden who strings beads.

The friend of the youth aroused. Lurching suddenly forward and dropping to his knees, he fired an angry shot at the persistent woods. This action awakened the men. They huddled no more like sheep. They seemed suddenly to bethink them of their weapons, and at once commenced firing. Belabored by their officers, they began to move forward. The regiment, involved like a cart involved in mud and muddle, started unevenly with many jolts and jerks. The men stopped now every few paces to fire and load, and in this manner moved slowly on from trees to trees.

The flaming opposition in their front grew with their advance until it seemed that all forward ways were barred by the thin leaping tongues, and off to the right an ominous demonstration could sometimes be dimly discerned. The smoke lately generated was in confusing clouds that made it difficult for the regiment to proceed with intelligence. As he passed through each curling mass the youth wondered what would confront him on the farther side.

The command went painfully forward until an open space interposed between them and the lurid lines. Here, crouching and cowering behind some trees, the men clung with desperation, as if threatened by a wave. They looked wild-eyed, and as if amazed at this furious disturbance they had stirred. In the storm there was an ironical expression of their importance. The faces of the men, too, showed a lack of a certain feeling of responsibility for being there. It was as if they had been driven. It was the dominant animal failing to remember in the supreme moments the forceful causes of various superficial qualities. The whole affair seemed incomprehensible to many of them.

As they halted thus the lieutenant again began to bellow profanely. Regardless of the vindictive threats of the bullets, he went about coaxing, berating, and bedamning. His lips, that were habitually in a soft and childlike curve, were now writhed into unholy contortions. He swore by all possible deities.

Once he grabbed the youth by the arm. "Come on, yeh lunkhead!" he roared. "Come on! We'll all git killed if we stay here. We've on'y got t' go across that lot. An' then"—the remainder of his idea disappeared in a blue haze of curses.

The youth stretched forth his arm. "Cross there?" His mouth was puckered in doubt and awe.

"Certainly. Jest 'cross th' lot! We can't stay here," screamed the lieutenant. He poked his face close to the youth and waved his bandaged hand. "Come on!" Presently he grappled with him as if for a wrestling bout. It was as if he planned to drag the youth by the ear on to the assault.

The private felt a sudden unspeakable indignation against his officer. He wrenched fiercely and shook him off.

"Come on yerself, then," he yelled. There was a bitter challenge in his voice.

They galloped together down the regimental

front. The friend scrambled after them. In front of the colors the three men began to bawl: "Come on! come on!" They danced and gyrated like tortured savages.

The flag, obedient to these appeals, bended its glittering form and swept toward them. The men wavered in indecision for a moment, and then with a long, wailful cry the dilapidated regiment surged forward and began its new journey.

Over the field went the scurrying mass. It was a handful of men splattered into the faces of the enemy. Toward it instantly sprang the yellow tongues. A vast quantity of blue smoke hung before them. A mighty banging made ears valueless.

The youth ran like a madman to reach the woods before a bullet could discover him. He ducked his head low, like a football player. In his haste his eyes almost closed, and the scene was a wild blur. Pulsating saliva stood at the corners of his mouth.

Within him, as he hurled himself forward, was born a love, a despairing fondness for this flag which was near him. It was a creation of beauty and invulnerability. It was a goddess, radiant, that bended its form with an imperious gesture to him. It was a woman, red and white, hating and loving, that called him with the voice of his hopes. Because no harm could come to it he endowed it with power. He kept

near, as if it could be a saver of lives, and an imploring cry went from his mind.

In the mad scramble he was aware that the color sergeant flinched suddenly, as if struck by a bludgeon. He faltered, and then became motionless, save for his quivering knees.

He made a spring and a clutch at the pole. At the same instant his friend grabbed it from the other side. They jerked at it, stout and furious, but the color sergeant was dead, and the corpse would not relinquish its trust. For a moment there was a grim encounter. The dead man, swinging with bended back, seemed to be obstinately tugging, in ludicrous and awful ways, for the possession of the flag.

It was past in an instant of time. They wrenched the flag furiously from the dead man, and, as they turned again, the corpse swayed forward with bowed head. One arm swung high, and the curved hand fell with heavy protest on the friend's unheeding shoulder.

When the two youths turned with the flag they saw that much of the regiment had crumbled away, and the dejected remnant was coming back. The men, having hurled themselves in projectile fashion, had presently expended their forces. They slowly retreated, with their faces still toward the spluttering woods, and their hot rifles still replying to the din. Several officers were giving orders, their voices keyed to screams.

"Where in hell yeh goin'?" the lieutenant was asking in a sarcastic howl. And a red-bearded officer, whose voice of triple brass could plainly be heard, was commanding: "Shoot into 'em! Shoot into 'em, Gawd damn their souls!" There was a *mêlée* of screeches, in which the men were ordered to do conflicting and impossible things.

The youth and his friend had a small scuffle over the flag. "Give it t' me!" "No, let me keep it!" Each felt satisfied with the other's possession of it, but each felt bound to declare, by an offer to carry the emblem, his willingness to further risk himself. The youth roughly pushed his friend away.

The regiment fell back to the stolid trees. There it halted for a moment to blaze at some dark forms that had begun to steal upon its track. Presently it resumed its march again, curving among the tree trunks. By the time the depleted regiment had again reached the first open space they were receiving a fast and merciless fire. There seemed to be mobs all about them.

The greater part of the men, discouraged, their spirits worn by the turmoil, acted as if stunned. They accepted the pelting of the bullets with bowed and weary heads. It was of no purpose to strive against walls. It was of no use to batter themselves against granite. And from this consciousness that they had attempted to conquer an unconquerable thing there seemed to arise a feeling that they had been betrayed. They glowered with bent brows, but dangerously, upon some of the officers, more particularly upon the red-bearded one with the voice of triple brass.

However, the rear of the regiment was fringed with men, who continued to shoot irritably at the advancing foes. They seemed resolved to make every trouble. The youthful lieutenant was perhaps the last man in the disordered mass. His forgotten back was toward the enemy. He had been shot in the arm. It hung straight and rigid. Occasionally he would cease to remember it, and be about to emphasize an oath with a sweeping gesture. The multiplied pain caused him to swear with incredible power.

The youth went along with slipping, uncertain feet. He kept watchful eyes rearward. A scowl of mortification and rage was upon his face. He had thought of a fine revenge upon the officer who had referred to him and his fellows as mule drivers. But he saw that it could not come to pass. His dreams had collapsed when the mule drivers, dwindling rapidly, had wavered and hesitated on the little clearing, and then had recoiled. And now the retreat of the mule drivers was a march of shame to him.

A dagger-pointed gaze from without his black-ened face was held toward the enemy, but his greater hatred was riveted upon the man, who, not knowing him, had called him a mule driver.

When he knew that he and his comrades had failed to do anything in successful ways that might bring the little pangs of a kind of remorse upon the officer, the youth allowed the rage of the baffled to possess him. This cold officer upon a monument, who dropped epithets unconcernedly down, would be finer as a dead man, he thought. So grievous did he think it that he could never possess the secret right to taunt truly in answer.

He had pictured red letters of curious revenge. "We *are* mule drivers, are we?" And now he was compelled to throw them away.

He presently wrapped his heart in the cloak of his pride and kept the flag erect. He harangued his fel-lows, pushing against their chests with his free hand. To those he knew well he made frantic appeals, beseeching them by name. Between him and the lieutenant, scolding and near to losing his mind with rage, there was felt a subtle fellowship and equality. They supported each other in all manner of hoarse, howling protests.

But the regiment was a machine run down. The two men babbled at a forceless thing. The soldiers who had heart to go slowly were continually shaken in their resolves by a knowledge that comrades were slipping with speed back to the lines. It was difficult to think of reputation when others were thinking of skins. Wounded men were left crying on this black journey.

The smoke fringes and flames blustered always. The youth, peering once through a sudden rift in a cloud, saw a brown mass of troops, interwoven and magnified until they appeared to be thousands. A fierce-hued flag flashed before his vision.

Immediately, as if the uplifting of the smoke had been prearranged, the discovered troops burst into a rasping yell, and a hundred flames jetted toward the retreating band. A rolling gray cloud again interposed as the regiment doggedly replied. The youth had to depend again upon his misused ears, which were trembling and buzzing from the *mêlée* of musketry and yells.

The way seemed eternal. In the clouded haze men became panic-stricken with the thought that the regiment had lost its path, and was proceeding in a perilous direction. Once the men who headed the wild procession turned and came pushing back against their comrades, screaming that they were being fired upon from points which they had considered to be toward their own lines. At this cry a hysterical fear and dismay beset the troops. A soldier, who heretofore had been ambitious to make the regiment into a wise little band that would proceed calmly amid the huge-appearing difficulties, suddenly sank down and buried his face in his arms with an air of bowing to a doom. From another a shrill lamentation rang out filled with profane illusions to a general. Men ran hither and thither, seeking with their eyes roads of escape. With serene regularity, as if controlled by a schedule, bullets buffed into men.

The youth walked stolidly into the midst of the mob, and with his flag in his hands took a stand as if he expected an attempt to push him to the ground. He unconsciously assumed the attitude of the color bearer in the fight of the preceding day. He passed over his brow a hand that trembled. His breath did not come freely. He was choking during this small wait for the crisis.

His friend came to him. "Well, Henry, I guess this is good-by—John."

"Oh, shut up, you damned fool!" replied the youth, and he would not look at the other.

The officers labored like politicians to beat the mass into a proper circle to face the menaces. The ground was uneven and torn. The men curled into depressions and fitted themselves snugly behind whatever would frustrate a bullet.

The youth noted with vague surprise that the lieutenant was standing mutely with his legs far apart and his sword held in the manner of a cane. The youth wondered what had happened to his vocal organs that he no more cursed.

There was something curious in this little intent pause of the lieutenant. He was like a babe which, having wept its fill, raises its eyes and fixes them upon a distant toy. He was engrossed in this contemplation, and the soft under lip quivered from self-whispered words.

Some lazy and ignorant smoke curled slowly. The men, hiding from the bullets, waited anxiously for it to lift and disclose the plight of the regiment.

The silent ranks were suddenly thrilled by the eager voice of the youthful lieutenant bawling out: "Here they come! Right on to us, b'Gawd!" His further words were lost in a roar of wicked thunder from the men's rifles.

The youth's eyes had instantly turned in the direction indicated by the awakened and agitated lieutenant, and he had seen the haze of treachery disclosing a body of soldiers of the enemy. They were so near that he could see their features. There was a recognition as he looked at the types of faces. Also he perceived with dim amazement that their uniforms were rather gay in effect, being light gray, accented with a brilliant-hued facing. Moreover, the clothes seemed new.

These troops had apparently been going forward

with caution, their rifles held in readiness, when the youthful lieutenant had discovered them and their movement had been interrupted by the volley from the blue regiment. From the moment's glimpse, it was derived that they had been unaware of the proximity of their dark-suited foes or had mistaken the direction. Almost instantly they were shut utterly from the youth's sight by the smoke from the energetic rifles of his companions. He strained his vision to learn the accomplishment of the volley, but the smoke hung before him.

The two bodies of troops exchanged blows in the manner of a pair of boxers. The fast angry firings went back and forth. The men in blue were intent with the despair of their circumstances and they seized upon the revenge to be had at close range. Their thunder swelled loud and valiant. Their curving front bristled with flashes and the place resounded with the clangor of their ramrods. The youth ducked and dodged for a time and achieved a few unsatisfactory views of the enemy. There appeared to be many of them and they were replying swiftly. They seemed moving toward the blue regiment, step by step. He seated himself gloomily on the ground with his flag between his knees.

As he noted the vicious, wolflike temper of his comrades he had a sweet thought that if the enemy was about to swallow the regimental broom as a large prisoner, it could at least have the consolation of going down with bristles forward.

But the blows of the antagonist began to grow more weak. Fewer bullets ripped the air, and finally, when the men slackened to learn of the fight, they could see only dark, floating smoke. The regiment lay still and gazed. Presently some chance whim came to the pestering blur, and it began to coil heavily away. The men saw a ground vacant of fighters. It would have been an empty stage if it were not for a few corpses that lay thrown and twisted into fantastic shapes upon the sward.

At sight of this tableau, many of the men in blue sprang from behind their covers and made an ungainly dance of joy. Their eyes burned and a hoarse cheer of elation broke from their dry lips.

It had begun to seem to them that events were trying to prove that they were impotent. These little battles had evidently endeavored to demonstrate that the men could not fight well. When on the verge of submission to these opinions, the small duel had showed them that the proportions were not impossible, and by it they had revenged themselves upon their misgivings and upon the foe.

The impetus of enthusiasm was theirs again. They gazed about them with looks of uplifted pride, feeling new trust in the grim, always confident weapons in their hands. And they were men.

Presently they knew that no fighting threatened them. All ways seemed once more opened to them. The dusty blue lines of their friends were disclosed a short distance away. In the distance there were many colossal noises, but in all this part of the field there was a sudden stillness.

They perceived that they were free. The depleted band drew a long breath of relief and gathered itself into a bunch to complete its trip.

In this last length of journey the men began to show strange emotions. They hurried with nervous fear. Some who had been dark and unfaltering in the grimmest moments now could not conceal an anxiety that made them frantic. It was perhaps that they dreaded to be killed in insignificant ways after the times for proper military deaths had passed. Or, perhaps, they thought it would be too ironical to get killed at the portals of safety. With backward looks of perturbation, they hastened.

As they approached their own lines there was some sarcasm exhibited on the part of a gaunt and bronzed regiment that lay resting in the shade of trees. Questions were wafted to them.

"Where th' hell yeh been?"

"What yeh comin' back fer?"

"Why didn't yeh stay there?"

"Was it warm out there, sonny?"

"Goin' home now, boys?"

One shouted in taunting mimicry: "Oh, mother, come quick an' look at th' sojers!"

There was no reply from the bruised and battered regiment, save that one man made broadcast challenges to fist fights and the red-bearded officer walked rather near and glared in great swashbuckler style at a tall captain in the other regiment. But the lieutenant suppressed the man who wished to fist fight, and the tall captain, flushing at the little fanfare of the red-bearded one, was obliged to look intently at some trees.

The youth's tender flesh was deeply stung by these remarks. From under his creased brows he glowered with hate at the mockers. He meditated upon a few revenges. Still, many in the regiment hung their heads in criminal fashion, so that it came to pass that the men trudged with sudden heaviness, as if they bore upon their bended shoulders the coffin of their honor. And the youthful lieutenant, recollecting himself, began to mutter softly in black curses.

They turned when they arrived at their old position to regard the ground over which they had charged.

The youth in this contemplation was smitten with a large astonishment. He discovered that the distances, as compared with the brilliant measurings of his mind, were trivial and ridiculous. The stolid trees, where much had taken place, seemed incredibly near. The time, too, now that he reflected, he saw to have been short. He wondered at the number of emotions and events that had been crowded into such little spaces. Elfin thoughts must have exaggerated and enlarged everything, he said.

It seemed, then, that there was bitter justice in the speeches of the gaunt and bronzed veterans. He veiled a glance of disdain at his fellows who strewed the ground, choking with dust, red from perspiration, misty-eyed, disheveled.

They were gulping at their canteens, fierce to wring every mite of water from them, and they polished at their swollen and watery features with coat sleeves and bunches of grass. For a time the men were bewildered by it. "Good thunder!" they ejaculated, staring at the vanishing form of the general. They conceived it to be a huge mistake.

Presently, however, they began to believe that in truth their efforts had been called light. The youth could see this convention weigh upon the entire regiment until the men were like cuffed and cursed animals, but withal rebellious.

The friend, with a grievance in his eye, went to the youth. "I wonder what he does want," he said. "He must think we went out there an' played marbles! I never see sech a man!"

The youth developed a tranquil philosophy for

these moments of irritation. "Oh, well," he rejoined, "he probably didn't see nothing of it at all and got mad as blazes, and concluded we were a lot of sheep, just because we didn't do what he wanted done. It's a pity old Grandpa Henderson got killed yesterday—he'd have known that we did our best and fought good. It's just our awful luck, that's what."

"I should say so," replied the friend. He seemed to be deeply wounded at an injustice. "I should say we did have awful luck! There's no fun in fightin' fer people when everything yeh do—no matter what— ain't done right. I have a notion t' stay behind next time an' let 'em take their ol' charge an' go t' th' devil with it."

The youth spoke soothingly to his comrade. "Well, we both did good. I'd like to see the fool what'd say we both didn't do as good as we could!"

"Of course we did," declared the friend stoutly. "An' I'd break th' feller's neck if he was as big as a church. But we're all right, anyhow, for I heard one feller say that we two fit th' best in th' reg'ment, an' they had a great argument 'bout it. Another feller, 'a course, he had t' up an' say it was a lie—he seen all what was goin' on an' he never seen us from th' beginnin' t' th' end. An' a lot more struck in an' ses it wasn't a lie—we did fight like thunder, an' they give us quite a send-off. But this is what I can't stand—these everlastin' ol' soldiers, titterin' an' laughin', an' then that general, he's crazy."

The youth exclaimed with sudden exasperation: "He's a lunkhead! He makes me mad. I wish he'd come along next time. We'd show 'im what—"

He ceased because several men had come hurrying up. Their faces expressed a bringing of great news.

"O Flem, yeh jest oughta heard!" cried one, eagerly.

"Heard what?" said the youth.

"Yeh jest oughta heard!" repeated the other, and he arranged himself to tell his tidings. The others made an excited circle. "Well, sir, th' colonel met your lieutenant right by us—it was damnedest thing I everheard—an' he ses: 'Ahem! ahem!' he ses. 'Mr. Hasbrouck!' he ses, 'by th' way, who was that lad what carried th' flag?' he ses. There, Flemin', what d' yeh think 'a that? 'Who was th' lad what carried th' flag?' he ses, an' th' lieutenant, he speaks up right away: 'That's Flemin', an' he's a jimhickey,' he ses, right away. What? I say he did. 'A jimhickey,' he ses—those parently, finding it too prodigious, the brigade, after a little time, came marching airily out again with its fine formation in nowise disturbed. There were no traces of speed in its movements. The brigade was jaunty and seemed to point a proud thumb at the yelling wood.

On a slope to the left there was a long row of

guns, gruff and maddened, denouncing the enemy, who, down through the woods, were forming for another attack in the pitiless monotony of conflicts. The round red discharges from the guns made a crimson flare and a high, thick smoke. Occasional glimpses could be caught of groups of the toiling artillerymen. In the rear of this row of guns stood a house, calm and white, amid bursting shells. A congregation of horses, tied to a long railing, were tugging frenziedly at their bridles. Men were running hither and thither.

The detached battle between the four regiments lasted for some time. There chanced to be no interference, and they settled their dispute by themselves. They struck savagely and powerfully at each other for a period of minutes, and then the lighter-hued regiments faltered and drew back, leaving the dark-blue lines shouting. The youth could see the two flags shaking with laughter amid the smoke remnants.

Presently there was a stillness, pregnant with meaning. The blue lines shifted and changed a trifle and stared expectantly at the silent woods and fields before them. The hush was solemn and churchlike, save for a distant battery that, evidently unable to remain quiet, sent a faint rolling thunder over the ground. It irritated, like the noises of unimpressed boys. The men imagined that it would prevent their perched ears from hearing the first words of the new battle.

Of a sudden the guns on the slope roared out a message of warning. A spluttering sound had begun in the woods. It swelled with amazing speed to a profound clamor that involved the earth in noises. The splitting crashes swept along the lines until an interminable roar was developed. To those in the midst of it it became a din fitted to the universe. It was the whirring and thumping of gigantic machinery, complications among the smaller stars. The youth's ears were filled up. They were incapable of hearing more.

On an incline over which a road wound he saw wild and desperate rushes of men perpetually backward and forward in riotous surges. These parts of the opposing armies were two long waves that pitched upon each other madly at dictated points. To and fro they swelled. Sometimes, one side by its yells and cheers would proclaim decisive blows, but a moment later the other side would be all yells and cheers. Once the youth saw a spray of light forms go in houndlike leaps toward the waving blue lines. There was much howling, and presently it went away with a vast mouthful of prisoners. Again, he saw a blue wave dash with such thunderous force against a gray obstruction that it seemed to clear the earth of it and leave nothing but trampled sod. And always in their swift and deadly rushes to and fro the men screamed and yelled like maniacs.

Particular pieces of fence or secure positions behind collections of trees were wrangled over, as gold thrones or pearl bedsteads. There were desperate lunges at these chosen spots seemingly every instant, and most of them were bandied like light toys between the contending forces. The youth could not tell from the battle flags flying like crimson foam in many directions which color of cloth was winning.

His emaciated regiment bustled forth with undiminished fierceness when its time came. When assaulted again by bullets, the men burst out in a barbaric cry of rage and pain. They bent their heads in aims of intent hatred behind the projected hammers of their guns. Their ramrods clanged loud with fury as their eager arms pounded the cartridges into the rifle barrels. The front of the regiment was a smoke-wall penetrated by the flashing points of yellow and red.

Wallowing in the fight, they were in an astonishingly short time resmudged. They surpassed in stain and dirt all their previous appearances. Moving to and fro with strained exertion, jabbering the while, they were, with their swaying bodies, black faces, and glowing eyes, like strange and ugly fiends jigging heavily in the smoke.

The lieutenant, returning from a tour after a bandage, produced from a hidden receptacle of his mind new and portentous oaths suited to the emergency. Strings of expletives he swung lashlike over the backs of his men, and it was evident that his previous efforts had in nowise impaired his resources.

The youth, still the bearer of the colors, did not feel his idleness. He was deeply absorbed as a spectator. The crash and swing of the great drama made him lean forward, intent-eyed, his face working in small contortions. Sometimes he prattled, words coming unconsciously from him in grotesque exclamations. He did not know that he breathed; that the flag hung silently over him, so absorbed was he.

A formidable line of the enemy came within dangerous range. They could be seen plainly—tall, gaunt men with excited faces running with long strides toward a wandering fence.

At sight of this danger the men suddenly ceased their cursing monotone. There was an instant of strained silence before they threw up their rifles and fired a plumping volley at the foes. There had been no order given; the men, upon recognizing the menace, had immediately let drive their flock of bullets without waiting for word of command.

But the enemy were quick to gain the protection of the wandering line of fence. They slid down

behind it with remarkable celerity, and from this
position they began briskly to slice up the blue men.

These latter braced their energies for a great struggle. Often, white clinched teeth shone from the
dusky faces. Many heads surged to and fro, floating
upon a pale sea of smoke. Those behind the fence
frequently shouted and yelped in taunts and gibelike
cries, but the regiment maintained a stressed silence.
Perhaps, at this new assault the men recalled the fact
that they had been named mud diggers, and it made
their situation thrice bitter. They were breathlessly
intent upon keeping the ground and thrusting away
the rejoicing body of the enemy. They fought
swiftly and with a despairing savageness denoted in
their expressions.

The youth had resolved not to budge whatever
should happen. Some arrows of scorn that had
buried themselves in his heart had generated strange
and unspeakable hatred. It was clear to him that his
final and absolute revenge was to be achieved by his
dead body lying, torn and gluttering, upon the field.
This was to be a poignant retaliation upon the officer who had said "mule drivers," and later "mud
diggers," for in all the wild graspings of his mind for
a unit responsible for his sufferings and commotions
he always seized upon the man who had dubbed
him wrongly. And it was his idea, vaguely formu-

lated, that his corpse would be for those eyes a great and salt reproach.

The regiment bled extravagantly. Grunting bundles of blue began to drop. The orderly sergeant of the youth's company was shot through the cheeks. Its supports being injured, his jaw hung afar down, disclosing in the wide cavern of his mouth a pulsing mass of blood and teeth. And with it all he made attempts to cry out. In his endeavor there was a dreadful earnestness, as if he conceived that one great shriek would make him well.

The youth saw him presently go rearward. His strength seemed in nowise impaired. He ran swiftly, casting wild glances for succor.

Others fell down about the feet of their companions. Some of the wounded crawled out and away, but many lay still, their bodies twisted into impossible shapes.

The youth looked once for his friend. He saw a vehement young man, powder-smeared and frowzled, whom he knew to be him. The lieutenant, also, was unscathed in his position at the rear. He had continued to curse, but it was now with the air of a man who was using his last box of oaths.

For the fire of the regiment had begun to wane and drip. The robust voice, that had come strangely from the thin ranks, was growing rapidly weak.

The colonel came running along back of the line. There were other officers following him. "We must charge'm!" they shouted. "We must charge'm!" they cried with resentful voices, as if anticipating a rebellion against this plan by the men.

The youth, upon hearing the shout, began to study the distance between him and the enemy. He made vague calculations. He saw that to be firm soldiers they must go forward. It would be death to stay in the present place, and with all the circumstances to go backward would exalt too many others. Their hope was to push the galling foes away from the fence.

He expected that his companions, weary and stiffened, would have to be driven to this assault, but as he turned toward them he perceived with a certain surprise that they were giving quick and unqualified expressions of assent. There was an ominous, clanging overture to the charge when the shafts of the bayonets rattled upon the rifle barrels. At the yelled words of command the soldiers sprang forward in eager leaps. There was new and unexpected force in the movement of the regiment. A knowledge of its faded and jaded condition made the charge appear like a paroxysm, a display of the strength that comes before a final feebleness. The men scampered in insane fever of haste, racing as if to achieve a sudden success before an exhilarating fluid should leave them. It was a blind and despairing rush by the collection of men in dusty and tattered blue, over a green sward and under a sapphire sky, toward a fence, dimly outlined in smoke, from behind which spluttered the fierce rifles of enemies.

The youth kept the bright colors to the front. He was waving his free arm in furious circles, the while shrieking mad calls and appeals, urging on those that did not need to be urged, for it seemed that the mob of blue men hurling themselves on the dangerous group of rifles were again grown suddenly wild with an enthusiasm of unselfishness. From the many firings starting toward them, it looked as if they would merely succeed in making a great sprinkling of corpses on the grass between their former position and the fence. But they were in a state of frenzy, perhaps because of forgotten vanities, and it made an exhibition of sublime recklessness. There was no obvious questioning, nor figurings, nor diagrams. There was, apparently, no considered loopholes. It appeared that the swift wings of their desires would have shattered against the iron gates of the impossible.

He himself felt the daring spirit of a savage religion-mad. He was capable of profound sacrifices, a tremendous death. He had no time for dissections, but he knew that he thought of the bullets only as things that could prevent him from reaching the place of his endeavor. There were subtle flashings of joy within him that thus should be his mind.

He strained all his strength. His eyesight was shaken and dazzled by the tension of thought and muscle. He did not see anything excepting the mist of smoke gashed by the little knives of fire, but he knew that in it lay the aged fence of a vanished farmer protecting the snuggled bodies of the gray men.

As he ran a thought of the shock of contact gleamed in his mind. He expected a great concussion when the two bodies of troops crashed together. This became a part of his wild battle madness. He could feel the onward swing of the regiment about him and he conceived of a thunderous, crushing blow that would prostrate the resistance and spread consternation and amazement for miles. The flying regiment was going to have a catapultian effect. This dream made him run faster among his comrades, who were giving vent to hoarse and frantic cheers.

But presently he could see that many of the men in gray did intend to abide the blow. The smoke, rolling, disclosed men who ran, faces still turned. These grew to a crowd, who retired stubbornly. Individuals wheeled frequently to send a bullet at the blue wave.

But at one part of the line there was a grim and

obdurate group that made no movement. They were settled firmly down behind posts and rails. A flag, ruffled and fierce, waved over them and their rifles dinned fiercely.

The blue whirl of men got very near, until it seemed that in truth there would be a close and frightful scuffle. There was an expressed disdain in the opposition of the little group, that changed the meaning of the cheers of the men in blue. They became yells of wrath, directed, personal. The cries of the two parties were now in sound an interchange of scathing insults.

They in blue showed their teeth; their eyes shone all white. They launched themselves as at the throats of those who stood resisting. The space between dwindled to an insignificant distance.

The youth had centered the gaze of his soul upon that other flag. Its possession would be high pride. It would express bloody minglings, near blows. He had a gigantic hatred for those who made great difficulties and complications. They caused it to be as a craved treasure of mythology, hung amid tasks and contrivances of danger.

He plunged like a mad horse at it. He was resolved it should not escape if wild blows and darings of blows could seize it. His own emblem, quivering and aflare, was winging toward the other. It seemed there would shortly be an encounter of strange beaks and claws, as of eagles.

The swirling body of blue men came to a sudden halt at close and disastrous range and roared a swift volley. The group in gray was split and broken by this fire, but its riddled body still fought. The men in blue yelled again and rushed in upon it.

The youth, in his leapings, saw, as through a mist, a picture of four or five men stretched upon the ground or writhing upon their knees with bowed heads as if they had been stricken by bolts from the sky. Tottering among them was the rival color bearer, whom the youth saw had been bitten vitally by the bullets of the last formidable volley. He perceived this man fighting a last struggle, the struggle of one whose legs are grasped by demons. It was a ghastly battle. Over his face was the bleach of death, but set upon it were the dark and hard lines of desperate purpose. With this terrible grin of resolution he hugged his precious flag to him and was stumbling and staggering in his design to go the way that led to safety for it.

But his wounds always made it seem that his feet were retarded, held, and he fought a grim fight, as with invisible ghouls fastened greedily upon his limbs. Those in advance of the scampering blue men, howling cheers, leaped at the fence. The despair of the lost was in his eyes as he glanced back at them.

The youth's friend went over the obstruction in a tumbling heap and sprang at the flag as a panther at prey. He pulled at it and, wrenching it free, swung up its red brilliancy with a mad cry of exultation even as the color bearer, gasping, lurched over in a final throe and, stiffening convulsively, turned his dead face to the ground. There was much blood upon the grass blades.

At the place of success there began more wild clamorings of cheers. The men gesticulated and bellowed in an ecstasy. When they spoke it was as if they considered their listener to be a mile away. What hats and caps were left to them they often slung high in the air.

At one part of the line four men had been swooped upon, and they now sat as prisoners. Some blue men were about them in an eager and curious circle. The soldiers had trapped strange birds, and there was an examination. A flurry of fast questions was in the air.

One of the prisoners was nursing a superficial wound in the foot. He cuddled it, baby-wise, but he looked up from it often to curse with an astonishing utter abandon straight at the noses of his captors. He consigned them to red regions; he called upon the pestilential wrath of strange gods. And with it all he was singularly free from recognition of the finer points of the conduct of prisoners of war. It was as if a clumsy clod had trod upon his toe and he conceived it to be his privilege, his duty, to use deep, resentful oaths.

Another, who was a boy in years, took his plight with great calmness and apparent good nature. He conversed with the men in blue, studying their faces with his bright and keen eyes. They spoke of battles and conditions. There was an acute interest in all their faces during this exchange of viewpoints. It seemed a great satisfaction to hear voices from where all had been darkness and speculation.

The third captive sat with a morose countenance. He preserved a stoical and cold attitude. To all advances he made one reply without variation, "Ah, go t' hell!"

The last of the four was always silent and, for the most part, kept his face turned in unmolested directions. From the views the youth received he seemed to be in a state of absolute dejection. Shame was upon him, and with it profound regret that he was, perhaps, no more to be counted in the ranks of his fellows. The youth could detect no expression that would allow him to believe that the other was giving a thought to his narrowed future, the pictured dungeons, perhaps, and starvations and brutalities, liable to the imagination. All to be seen was shame for captivity and regret for the right to antagonize.

After the men had celebrated sufficiently they settled down behind the old rail fence, on the opposite side to the one from which their foes had been driven. A few shot perfunctorily at distant marks.

There was some long grass. The youth nestled in it and rested, making a convenient rail support the flag. His friend, jubilant and glorified, holding his treasure with vanity, came to him there. They sat side by side and congratulated each other.

The roarings that had stretched in a long line of sound across the face of the forest began to grow intermittent and weaker. The stentorian speeches of the artillery continued in some distant encounter, but the crashes of the musketry had almost ceased. The youth and his friend of a sudden looked up, feeling a deadened form of distress at the waning of these noises, which had become a part of life. They could see changes going on among the troops. There were marchings this way and that way. A battery wheeled leisurely. On the crest of a small hill was the thick gleam of many departing muskets.

The youth arose. "Well, what now, I wonder?" he said. By his tone he seemed to be preparing to resent some new monstrosity in the way of dins and smashes. He shaded his eyes with his grimy hand and gazed over the field.

His friend also arose and stared. "I bet we're goin' t' git along out of this an' back over th' river," said he.

"Well, I swan!" said the youth.

They waited, watching. Within a little while the regiment received orders to retrace its way. The men got up grunting from the grass, regretting the soft repose. They jerked their stiffened legs, and stretched their arms over their heads. One man swore as he rubbed his eyes. They all groaned "O Lord!" They had as many objections to this change as they would have had to a proposal for a new battle.

They trampled slowly back over the field across which they had run in a mad scamper.

The regiment marched until it had joined its fellows. The reformed brigade, in column, aimed through a wood at the road. Directly they were in a mass of dust-covered troops, and were trudging along in a way parallel to the enemy's lines as these had been defined by the previous turmoil.

They passed within view of a stolid white house, and saw in front of it groups of their comrades lying in wait behind a neat breastwork. A row of guns were booming at a distant enemy. Shells thrown in reply were raising clouds of dust and splinters. Horsemen dashed along the line of intrenchments.

At this point of its march the division curved from the field and went winding off in the direction of the river. When the significance of this movement had impressed itself upon the youth he turned his head and looked over his shoulder toward the trampled and *débris*-strewed ground. He breathed a breath of new satisfaction. He finally nudged his friend. "Well, it's all over," he said to him.

His friend gazed backward. "B'Gawd, it is," he assented. They mused.

For a time the youth was obliged to reflect in a puzzled and uncertain way. His mind was undergoing a subtle change. It took moments for it to cast off its battleful ways and resume its accustomed course of thought. Gradually his brain emerged from the clogged clouds, and at last he was enabled to more closely comprehend himself and circumstance.

He understood then that the existence of shot and counter-shot was in the past. He had dwelt in a land of strange, squalling upheavals and had come forth. He had been where there was red of blood and black of passion, and he was escaped. His first thoughts were given to rejoicings at this fact.

Later he began to study his deeds, his failures, and his achievements. Thus, fresh from scenes where many of his usual machines of reflection had been idle, from where he had proceeded sheeplike, he struggled to marshal all his acts.

At last they marched before him clearly. From this present viewpoint he was enabled to look upon them in spectator fashion and to criticize them with some correctness, for his new condition had already defeated certain sympathies.

Regarding his procession of memory he felt gleeful and unregretting, for in it his public deeds were paraded in great and shining prominence. Those performances which had been witnessed by his fellows marched now in wide purple and gold, having various deflections. They went gayly with music. It was pleasure to watch these things. He spent delightful minutes viewing the gilded images of memory.

He saw that he was good. He recalled with a thrill of joy the respectful comments of his fellows upon his conduct.

Nevertheless, the ghost of his flight from the first engagement appeared to him and danced. There were small shoutings in his brain about these matters. For a moment he blushed, and the light of his soul flickered with shame.

A specter of reproach came to him. There loomed the dogging memory of the tattered soldier—he who, gored by bullets and faint for blood, had fretted concerning an imagined wound in another; he who had loaned his last of strength and intellect for the tall soldier; he who, blind with weariness and pain, had been deserted in the field.

For an instant a wretched chill of sweat was upon him at the thought that he might be detected in the thing. As he stood persistently before his vision, he gave vent to a cry of sharp irritation and agony.

His friend turned. "What's the matter, Henry?" he demanded. The youth's reply was an outburst of crimson oaths.

As he marched along the little branch-hung roadway among his prattling companions this vision of cruelty brooded over him. It clung near him always and darkened his view of these deeds in purple and gold. Whichever way his thoughts turned they were followed by the somber phantom of the desertion in the fields. He looked stealthily at his companions, feeling sure that they must discern in his face evidences of this pursuit. But they were plodding in ragged array, discussing with quick tongues the accomplishments of the late battle.

"Oh, if a man should come up an' ask me, I'd say we got a dum good lickin'."

"Lickin'—in yer eye! We ain't licked, sonny. We're going down here aways, swing aroun', an' come in behint 'em."

"Oh, hush, with your comin' in behint 'em. I've seen all 'a that I wanta. Don't tell me about comin' in behint——"

"Bill Smithers, he ses he'd rather been in ten hundred battles than been in that heluva hospital. He ses they got shootin' in th' nighttime, an' shells dropped plum among 'em in th' hospital. He ses sech hollerin' he never see."

"Hasbrouck? He's th' best off'cer in this here reg'-ment. He's a whale."

"Didn't I tell yeh we'd come aroun' in behint 'em? Didn't I tell yeh so? We——"

"Oh, shet yer mouth!"

For a time this pursuing recollection of the tattered man took all elation from the youth's veins. He saw his vivid error, and he was afraid that it would stand before him all his life. He took no share in the chatter of his comrades, nor did he look at them or know them, save when he felt sudden suspicion that they were seeing his thoughts and scrutinizing each detail of the scene with the tattered soldier.

Yet gradually he mustered force to put the sin at a distance. And at last his eyes seemed to open to some new ways. He found that he could look back upon the brass and bombast of his earlier gospels and see them truly. He was gleeful when he discovered that he now despised them.

With the conviction came a store of assurance. He felt a quiet manhood, non-assertive but of sturdy and strong blood. He knew that he would no more quail before his guides wherever they should point. He had been to touch the great death, and found that, after all, it was but the great death. He was a man.

So it came to pass that as he trudged from the place of blood and wrath his soul changed. He came from hot plowshares to prospects of clover tranquilly, and it was as if hot plowshares were not. Scars faded as flowers.

It rained. The procession of weary soldiers became a bedraggled train, despondent and muttering, marching with churning effort in a trough of liquid brown mud under a low, wretched sky. Yet the youth smiled, for he saw that the world was a world for him, though many discovered it to be made of oaths and walking sticks. He had rid himself of the red sickness of battle. The sultry nightmare was in the past. He had been an animal blistered and sweating in the heat and pain of war. He turned now with a lover's thirst to images of tranquil skies, fresh meadows, cool brooks—an existence of soft and eternal peace.

Over the river a golden ray of sun came through the hosts of leaden rain clouds.

# Waterloo

[ **VICTOR HUGO** ]

L et us go back,—that is one of the story-teller's privileges,—and put ourselves once more in the year 1815, and even a little prior to the period when the action narrated in the first part of this book took place.

If it had not rained in the night between the 17th and the 18th of June, 1815, the fate of Europe would have been different. A few drops of water, more or less, made Napoleon waver. All that Providence required in order to make Waterloo the end of Austerlitz was a little more rain, and a cloud crossing the sky out of season sufficed to overthrow the world.

The battle of Waterloo could not be begun until half-past eleven o'clock, and that gave Blücher time to come up. Why? Because the ground was moist.

The artillery had to wait until it became a little firmer before they could manœuvre.

Napoleon was an artillery officer, and felt the effects of one. All his plans of battle were arranged for projectiles. The key to his victory was to make the artillery converge on one point. He treated the strategy of the hostile general like a citadel, and made a breach in it. He crushed the weak point with grape-shot; he joined and dissolved battles with artillery. There was something of the sharpshooter in his genius. To beat in squares, to pulverize regiments, to break lines, to destroy and disperse masses,—for him everything lay in this, to strike, strike, strike incessantly,—and he entrusted this task to the cannon-ball. It was a formidable method, and one which, united with genius, rendered this gloomy athlete of the pugilism of war invincible for the space of fifteen years.

On the 18th of June, 1815, he relied all the more on his artillery, because he had numbers on his side. Wellington had only one hundred and fifty-nine guns; Napoleon had two hundred and forty.

Suppose the soil dry, and the artillery capable of moving, the action would have begun at six o'clock in the morning. The battle would have been won and ended at two o'clock, three hours before the change of fortune in favour of the Prussians. How much blame attaches to Napoleon for the loss of this battle? Is the shipwreck due to the pilot?

Was it the evident physical decline of Napoleon that complicated this epoch by an inward diminution of force? Had the twenty years of war worn out the blade as it had worn the scabbard, the soul as well as the body? Did the veteran make himself disastrously felt in the leader? In a word, was this genius, as many historians of note have thought, eclipsed? Did he go into a frenzy in order to disguise his weakened powers from himself? Did he begin to waver under the delusion of a breath of adventure? Had he become—a grave matter in a general—unconscious of peril? Is there an age, in this class of material great men, who may be called the giants of action, when genius becomes short-sighted? Old age has no hold on ideal genius; for the Dantes and Michael Angelos to grow old is to grow in greatness; is it declension for the Hannibals and the Bonapartes? Had Napoleon lost the direct sense of victory? Had he reached the point where he could no longer recognize the rock, could no longer divine the snare, no longer discern the crumbling edge of the abyss? Had he lost his power of scenting out catastrophes? He who had in former days known all the roads to victory, and who, from the summit of his chariot of lightning, pointed them out with a sovereign finger, had he now reached that state of sinister amazement when he could lead his tumultuous legions harnessed to it, to the precipice? Was he seized at the age of forty-six with a supreme madness? Was that titanic charioteer of destiny now only a Phaëton?

We do not believe it.

His plan of battle was, by the confession of all, a masterpiece. To go straight to the centre of the Allies' lines, to make a breach in the enemy, to cut them in two, to drive the British half back on Halle, and the Prussian half on Tingres, to make two shattered fragments of Wellington and Blücher, to carry Mont-Saint-Jean, to seize Brussels, to hurl the German into the Rhine, and the Englishman into the sea. All this was contained in that battle, for Napoleon. Afterwards people would see.

Of course, we do not here pretend to furnish a history of the battle of Waterloo; one of the scenes of the foundation of the drama which we are relating is connected with this battle, but this history is not our subject; this history, moreover, has been finished, and finished in a masterly manner, from one point of view by Napoleon, from another by Charras.

For our part, we leave the historians to contend; we are but a distant witness, a passer-by along the plain, a seeker bending over that soil all made of human flesh, perhaps taking appearances for realities;

we have no right to oppose, in the name of science, a collection of facts which contain illusions, no doubt; we possess neither military practice nor strategic ability which authorize a system; in our opinion, a chain of accidents dominated the two captains at Waterloo; and when it becomes a question of destiny, that mysterious culprit, we judge like the people.

Those who wish to gain a clear idea of the battle of Waterloo have only to place, mentally, on the ground, a capital A. The left leg of the A is the road to Nivelles, the right one is the road to Genappe, the tie of the A is the hollow road to Ohain from Braine-l'Alleud. The top of the A is Mont-Saint-Jean, where Wellington is; the lower left tip is Hougomont, where Reille is stationed with Jérôme Bonaparte; the right tip is the Belle-Alliance, where Napoleon is. At the centre of this point is the precise point where the final word of the battle was pronounced. It was there that the lion has been placed, the involuntary symbol of the supreme heroism of the Imperial Guard.

The triangle comprised in the top of the A, between the two limbs and the tie, is the plateau of Mont-Saint-Jean. The dispute over this plateau was the whole battle. The wings of the two armies extended to the right and left of the two roads to

Genappe and Nivelles; d'Erlon facing Picton, Reille facing Hill.

Behind the point of the A, behind the plateau of Mont-Saint-Jean, is the forest of Soignes.

As for the plain itself, imagine a vast undulating sweep of ground; each ascent commands the next rise, and all the undulations mount towards Mont-Saint-Jean, and there end in the forest.

Two hostile troops on a field of battle are two wrestlers. It is a question of seizing the opponent round the waist. The one tries to throw the other. They cling at everything; a bush is a point of support; an angle of the wall offers them a rest to the shoulder; for the lack of a hovel under whose cover they can draw up, a regiment yields its ground; an unevenness in the ground, a chance turn in the landscape, a cross-path encountered at the right moment, a grove, a ravine, can stay the heel of that colossus which is called an army, and prevent its retreat. He who leaves the field is beaten; hence the necessity devolving on the responsible leader of examining the smallest clump of trees and of studying deeply the slightest rise in the ground.

The two generals had attentively studied the plain of Mont-Saint-Jean, which is known as the plain of Waterloo. In the preceding year, Wellington, with the sagacity of foresight, had examined it as the future seat of a great battle. Upon this spot, and for this duel, on the 18th of June, Wellington had the good post, Napoleon the bad post. The English army was above, the French army below.

It is almost superfluous here to sketch the appearance of Napoleon on horseback, telescope in hand, upon the heights of Rossomme, at daybreak, on June 18, 1815. All the world has seen him before we can show him. The calm profile under the little three-cornered hat of the school of Brienne, the green uniform, the white facings concealing the star of the Legion of Honour, his great coat hiding his epaulets, the corner of red ribbon peeping from beneath his vest, his leather breeches, the white horse with the saddle-cloth of purple velvet bearing on the corners crowned N's and eagles, Hessian boots over silk stockings, silver spurs, the sword of Marengo,—that whole appearance of the last of the Cæsars is present to all imagination, saluted with acclamations by some, severely regarded by others.

That figure stood for a long time wholly in the light; this arose from a certain legendary dimness evolved by the majority of heroes, and which always veils the truth of a longer or shorter time; but to-day history and daylight have arrived.

That illumination called history is pitiless; it possesses this peculiar and divine quality, that, pure light as it is, and precisely because it is wholly light, it often casts a shadow in places that had been luminous; from the same man it constructs two different phantoms, and the one attacks the other and executes justice on it, and the shadows of the despot contend with the brilliancy of the leader. Hence arises a truer measure in the definitive judgments of nations. Babylon violated diminishes Alexander, Rome enchained diminishes Cæsar, Jerusalem murdered diminishes Titus. Tyranny follows the tyrant. It is a misfortune for a man to leave behind him the night which bears his form.

All the world knows the first phase of this battle; an opening which was troubled, uncertain, hesitating, menacing to both armies, but still more so for the English than for the French.

It had rained all night, the ground was saturated, the water had accumulated here and there in the hollows of the plain as if in tubs; at some points the gear of the artillery carriages was buried up to the axles, the circingles of the horses were dripping with liquid mud. If the wheat and rye trampled down by this cohort of transports on the march had not filled in the ruts and strewn a litter beneath the wheels, all movement, particularly in the valleys, in the direction of Papelotte would have been impossible.

The battle began late. Napoleon, as we have already explained, was in the habit of keeping all his artillery well in hand, like a pistol, aiming it now at one point, now at another, of the battle; and it had been his wish to wait until the horse batteries could move and gallop freely. In order to do that it was necessary that the sun should come out and dry the soil. But the sun did not make its appearance. It was no longer the rendezvous of Austerlitz. When the first cannon was fired, the English general, Colville, looked at his watch, and saw that it was twenty-five minutes to twelve.

The action was begun furiously, with more fury, perhaps, than the Emperor would have wished, by the left wing of the French resting on Hougomont. At the same time Napoleon attacked the centre by hurling Quiot's brigade on La Haie-Sainte, and Ney pushed forward the right wing of the French against the left wing of the English, which leaned on Papelotte.

The attack on Hougomont was something of a feint; the plan was to attract Wellington thither, and to make him swerve to the left. This plan would have succeeded if the four companies of the English Guards and the brave Belgians of Perponcher's division had not held the position firmly, and Wellington, instead of massing his troops there, could confine himself to despatching thither, as reinforcements, only four more companies of Guards and one battalion of Brunswickers.

The attack of the right wing of the French on

Papelotte was calculated, in fact, to overthrow the English left, to cut off the road to Brussels, to bar the passage against possible Prussians, to force Mont-Saint-Jean, to turn Wellington back on Hougomont; thence on Braine-l'Alleud, thence on Halle; nothing easier. With the exception of a few incidents this attack succeeded. Papelotte was taken; La Haie-Sainte was carried.

A detail is to be noted. There were in the English infantry, particularly in Kempt's brigade, a great many young soldiers. These recruits were valiant in the presence of our redoubtable infantry; their inexperience extricated them intrepidly from the dilemma; they performed particularly excellent service as skirmishers: the soldier skirmisher, left somewhat to himself, becomes, so to speak, his own general. These recruits displayed some of the French ingenuity and fury. These novices had dash. This displeased Wellington.

After the taking of La Haie-Sainte the battle wavered.

There is in this day an obscure interval, from midday to four o'clock; the middle portion of this battle is almost indistinct, and participates in the sombreness of the hand-to-hand conflict. Twilight reigns over it. We perceive vast fluctuations in the midst, a dizzy mirage, paraphernalia of war almost unknown to-day, flaming colbacks, floating sabretaches, cross-belts, cartridge-boxes for grenades, hussar dolmans, red boots with a thousand wrinkles, heavy shakos garlanded with gold lace, the almost black infantry of Brunswick mingled with the scarlet infantry of England, the English soldiers with great, white circular pads on the slopes of their shoulders for epaulets, the Hanoverian light-horse with their oblong casques of leather, with brass hands and red horse-tails, the Highlanders with their bare knees and plaids, the great white gaiters of our grenadiers; pictures, not strategic lines—what a canvas for a Salvator Rosa requires, but Gribeauval would not have liked it.

A certain amount of tempest is always mingled with a battle. *Quid obscurum, quid divinum.* Each historian traces, to some extent, the particular feature which pleases him amid this pell-mell. Whatever may be the combinations of the generals, the shock of armed masses has an incalculable ebb and flow. During the action the plans of the two leaders enter into each other and become mutually thrown out of shape. Such a point of the field of battle devours more combatants than such another, just as more or less spongy soils soak up more or less quickly the water which is poured on them. It becomes necessary to pour out more soldiers than one would like; a series of expenditures which are the unforeseen. The line of battle floats and undulates like a thread, the trails of blood gush illogically, the fronts of the armies waver, the regiments form capes and gulfs as they enter and withdraw; all these reefs are continually moving in front of each other. Where the infantry stood the artillery arrives, the cavalry rushes in where the artillery was, the battalions are like smoke. There was something there; search for it. It has disappeared; the open spots change place, the sombre folds advance and retreat, a sort of wind from the sepulchre pushes forward, hurls back, distends, and disperses these tragic multitudes. What is a battle? an oscillation? The immobility of a mathematical plan expresses a minute, not a day. To depict a battle, there is required one of those powerful painters who have chaos in their brushes. Rembrandt is better than Vandermeulen; Vandermeulen, exact at noon, lies at three o'clock. Geometry is deceptive; the hurricane alone is true. That is what confers on Folard the right to contradict Polybius. Let us add, that there is a certain moment when the battle degenerates into a combat, becomes specialized, and disperses into innumerable detailed feats, which, to borrow the expression of Napoleon himself, "belong rather to the biography of the regiments than to the history of the army." The historian has, in this case, the evident right to sum up the whole. He cannot do more than catch the principal outlines of the struggle, and it is not given to any one narrator, however conscientious he may be, to fix, absolutely, the form of that horrible cloud which is called a battle.

This, which is true of all great armed encounters, is particularly applicable to Waterloo.

Nevertheless, at a certain moment in the afternoon the battle came to a decided point.

About four o'clock the condition of the English army was serious. The Prince of Orange was in command of the centre, Hill of the right wing, Picton of the left wing. The Prince of Orange, wild and intrepid, shouted to the Dutch Belgians: "Nassau! Brunswick! Don't yield an inch!" Hill, having been weakened, had come up to the support of Wellington; Picton was dead. At the very moment when the English had captured from the French the flag of the 105th of the line, the French had killed the English general, Picton, with a bullet through the head. The battle had, for Wellington, two bases of action, Hougomont and La Haie-Sainte; Hougomont still held out, but was on fire; La Haie-Sainte was taken. Of the German battalion which defended it, only forty-two men survived; all the officers, except five, were either dead or taken prisoners. Three thousand combatants had been massacred in that barn. A sergeant of the English Guards, the foremost boxer in England, reputed invulnerable by his companions, had been killed there by a little French drummer-boy. Barny had been dislodged. Alten sabred. Many flags had been lost, one from Alten's division, and one from the battalion of Lunenburg, carried by a prince of the house of Deux-Ponts. The Scots Greys no longer existed; Ponsonby's great dragoons had been cut to pieces. That valiant cavalry had bent beneath the lancers of Bro and beneath the cuirassiers of Travers; out of twelve hundred horses, six hundred remained; out of three lieutenant-colonels, two lay on the earth,—Hamilton wounded, Mater slain. Ponsonby had fallen, pierced by seven lance-thrusts. Gordon was dead. Marsh was dead. Two divisions, the fifth and the sixth, had been annihilated.

Hougomont attacked, La Haie-Sainte taken, there now existed but one rallying-point, the centre. That point still held firm. Wellington reinforced it. He summoned thither Hill, who was at Merle-Braine; he summoned Chassé, who was at Braine-l'Alleud.

The centre of the English army, rather concave, very dense, and very compact, was strongly posted. It occupied the plateau of Mont-Saint-Jean, having behind it the village, and in front of it the slope, which was tolerably steep then. It rested on that stout stone dwelling which at that time belonged to the domain of Nivelles, standing at the crossroads—a pile of the sixteenth century, and so robust that the cannonballs rebounded from it without injuring it. All about the plateau the English had cut the hedges here and there, formed embrasures in the hawthorn-trees, thrust the throat of a cannon between two branches, embattled the shrubs. There artillery was ambushed in the brushwood. This Punic task, incontestably authorized by war, which permits traps, was so well done, that Haxo, who had been despatched by the Emperor at nine o'clock in the morning to reconnoitre the enemy's batteries, had discovered nothing of it, and had returned and reported to Napoleon that there were no obstacles except the two barricades which barred the road to Nivelles and to Genappe. It was at the season when the grain is tall: on the edge of the plateau a battalion of Kempt's brigade, the 95th, armed with carbines, was concealed in the tall wheat.

Thus assured and buttressed, the centre of the Anglo-Dutch army was in a good position. The peril of this position lay in the forest of Soignes, then adjoining the field of battle, and intersected by the ponds of Groenendael and Boitsfort. An army could not retreat thither without dissolving; the regiments would have broken up immediately there. The artillery would have been lost among the marshes. The retreat, according to many a man versed in the art of war,—though it is disputed by others,—would have been a disorganized flight.

To this centre, Wellington added one of Chassé's brigades taken from the right wing, and one of Wincke's brigades taken from the left wing, plus Clinton's division. To his English, to the regiments of Halkett, to the brigades of Mitchell, to the guards of Maitland, he gave as reinforcements and aids, the infantry of Brunswick, Nassau's contingent, Kielmansegg's Hanoverians, and Ompteda's Germans. He had thus twenty-six battalions under his hand. The right wing, as Charras says, was thrown back on the centre. An enormous battery was masked by sacks of earth at the spot where there now stands what is called the "Museum of Waterloo." Besides this, Wellington had, behind a rise in the ground, Somerset's Dragoon Guards, fourteen hundred horse strong. It was the remaining half of the justly celebrated English cavalry. Ponsonby destroyed, Somerset remained.

The battery, which, if completed, would have been almost a redoubt, was ranged behind a very low wall, backed up with a coating of bags of sand and a wide slope of earth. This work was not finished; there had been no time to make a palisade for it.

Wellington, restless but impassive, was on horseback, and there remained the whole day in the same attitude, a little in front of the old mill of Mont-Saint-Jean, which is still in existence, beneath an elm, which an Englishman, an enthusiastic vandal, purchased later on for two hundred francs, cut down, and carried off. Wellington was coldly heroic. The bullets rained about him. His aide-de-camp, Gordon, fell at his side. Lord Hill, pointing to a shell which had burst, said to him: "My lord, what are your orders in case you are killed?" "Do as I am doing," replied Wellington. To Clinton he said laconically, "To hold this spot to the last man." The day was evidently turning out ill. Wellington shouted to his old companions of Talavera, of Vittoria, of Salamanca: "Boys, can retreat be thought of? Think of old England!"

About four o'clock, the English line drew back. Suddenly nothing was visible on the crest of the plateau except the artillery and the sharp-shooters; the rest had disappeared; the regiments, dislodged by the shells and the French bullets, retreated into the hollow, now intersected by the back road of the farm of Mont-Saint-Jean; a retrograde movement took place, the English front hid itself, Wellington recoiled. "The beginning of the retreat!" cried Napoleon.

The Emperor, though ill and discommoded on horseback by a local trouble, had never been so good tempered as on that day. His impenetrability had been smiling ever since the morning. On the 18th of June, that profound soul masked by marble was radiant. The man who had been gloomy at Austerlitz was gay at Waterloo. The greatest favourites of destiny make mistakes. Our joys are composed of shadow. The supreme smile is God's alone.

*Ridet Cæsar, Pompeius flebit,* said the legionaires of the Fulminatrix Legion. Pompey was not destined to weep on that occasion, but it is certain that Caesar laughed. While exploring on horseback at one o'clock on the preceding night, in storm and rain, in company with Bertrand, the hills in the neighbourhood of Rossomme, satisfied at the sight of the long line of the English camp-fires illuminating the whole horizon from Frischemont to Braine-l'Alleud, it had seemed to him that fate, to whom he had assigned a day on the field of Waterloo, was exact to the appointment; he stopped his horse, and remained for some time motionless, gazing at the lightning and listening to the thunder; and this fatalist was heard to cast into the darkness this mysterious saying, "We are in accord." Napoleon was mistaken. They were no longer in accord.

He had not slept a moment; every instant of that night was marked by a joy for him. He rode through the line of the principal outposts, halting here and there to talk to the sentinels. At half-past two, near the wood of Hougomont, he heard the tread of a column on the march; he thought at the moment that it was a retreat on the part of Wellington. He said: "It is the rear-guard of the English getting under way for the purpose of decamping. I will take prisoners the six thousand English who have just landed at Ostend." He talked expansively; he regained the animation which he had shown at his landing on the 1st of March, when he pointed out to the Grand-Marshal the enthusiastic peasant of the Gulf Juan, and cried, "Well, Bertrand, here is a reinforcement already!" On the night of the 17th to the 18th of June he made fun of Wellington. "That little Englishman needs a lesson," said Napoleon. The rain redoubled in violence; it thundered while the Emperor was speaking.

At half-past three o'clock in the morning, he lost one illusion; officers who had been despatched to reconnoitre announced to him that the enemy was not making any movement. Nothing was stirring; not a bivouac-fire had been extinguished; the English army was asleep. The silence on earth was profound; the only noise was in the heavens. At four o'clock, a peasant was brought in to him by the scouts; this peasant had served as guide to a brigade of English cavalry, probably Vivian's brigade, which was on its way to take up a position in the village of Ohain, at the extreme left. At five o'clock, two Belgian deserters reported to him that they had just quitted their regiment, and that the English army meant to fight. "All the better!" exclaimed Napoleon.

"I prefer to overthrow them rather than to drive them back."

At daybreak he dismounted in the mud on the slope which forms an angle with the Plancenoit road, had a kitchen table and a peasant's chair brought to him from the farm of Rossomme, seated himself, with a truss of straw for a carpet, and spread out on the table the chart of the battle-field, saying to Soult as he did so, "A pretty chess-board."

In consequence of the rains during the night, the transports of provisions, embedded in the soft roads, had not been able to arrive by morning; the soldiers had had no sleep; they were wet and famished. This did not prevent Napoleon from exclaiming cheerfully to Ney, "We have ninety chances out of a hundred." At eight o'clock the Emperor's breakfast was brought to him. He invited several generals to it. During breakfast, it was said that Wellington had been to a ball two nights before, in Brussels, at the Duchess of Richmond's; and Soult, a rough man of war, with the face of an archbishop said, "The ball will be to-day." The Emperor jested with Ney, who had said, "Wellington will not be so simple as to wait for Your Majesty." That was his way, however. "He was fond of a joke," says Fleury de Chaboulon. "A merry humour was at the foundation of his character," says Gourgaud. "He abounded in pleasantries, which were more peculiar than witty," says

Benjamin Constant. These gaieties of a giant are worthy of comment. It was he who called his grenadiers "his growlers"; he pinched their ears; he pulled their moustaches. "The Emperor did nothing but play pranks on us," is the remark of one of them. During the mysterious trip from the island of Elba to France, on the 27th of February, on the open sea, the French brig of war, *Le Zéphyr*, having encountered the brig *L'Inconstant*, on which Napoleon was concealed, and having asked the news of Napoleon from *L'Inconstant*, the Emperor, who still wore in his hat the white and violet cockade sown with bees, which he had adopted at the isle of Elba, laughingly seized the speaking-trumpet, and answered for himself, "The Emperor is quite well." A man who laughs like that is on familiar terms with events. Napoleon indulged in many fits of this laughter during the breakfast at Waterloo. After breakfast he meditated for a quarter of an hour; then two generals seated themselves on the truss of straw, pen in hand and their paper on their knees, and the Emperor dictated to them the order of battle.

At nine o'clock, at the instant when the French army ranged in echelons and moving in five columns, had deployed—the divisions in two lines, the artillery between the brigades, the music at their head; as they beat the march, with rolls on the drums and the blasts of trumpets, mighty, vast, joyous, a sea of casques, of sabres, and of bayonets on the horizon, the Emperor was touched, and twice exclaimed, "Magnificent! Magnificent!"

Between nine o'clock and half-past ten the whole army, incredible as it may appear, had taken up its position and was drawn up in six lines, forming, to repeat the Emperor's expression, "the figure of six V's." A few moments after the formation of the line, in the midst of that profound silence, like that which heralds the beginning of a storm, which precedes battle, the Emperor tapped Haxo on the shoulder, as he beheld the three batteries of twelve-pounders, detached by his orders from the corps of Erlon, Reille, and Lobau, and destined to begin the action by taking Mont-Saint-Jean, which was situated at the intersection of the Nivelles and the Genappe roads, and said to him, "There are four and twenty pretty girls, General."

Sure of the result, he encouraged with a smile, as they passed before him, the company of sappers of the first corps, which he had appointed to barricade Mont-Saint-Jean as soon as the village should be carried. All this serenity had been traversed by but a single word of human pity; perceiving on his left, at a spot where there now stands a large tomb, those admirable Scots Greys, with their superb horses, massing themselves, he said, "It is a pity."

Then he mounted his horse, advanced beyond

Rossomme, and selected for his coign of vantage a contracted elevation of turf to the right of the road from Genappe to Brussels, which was his second station during the battle. The third station, the one adopted at seven o'clock in the evening, between La Belle-Alliance and La Haie-Sainte, is formidable; it is a rather lofty mound, which still exists, and behind which the guard was massed in a hollow. Around this knoll the balls rebounded from the pavements of the road, up to Napoleon himself. As at Brienne, he had over his head the whistle of the bullets and canister. Mouldy cannon-balls, old sword-blades, and shapeless projectiles, eaten up with rust, have been picked up at the spot where his horse's feet stood. *Scabra rubigine*. A few years ago, a shell of sixty pounds, still charged, and with its fuse broken off level with the bomb, was unearthed. It was at this station that the Emperor said to his guide, Lacoste, a hostile and timid peasant, who was attached to the saddle of a hussar, and who turned round at every discharge of canister and tried to hide behind Napoleon: "You ass, it is shameful! You'll get yourself killed with a ball in the back." He who writes these lines has himself found, in the friable soil of this knoll, on turning over the sand, the remains of the neck of a bomb, rotted by the oxide of six and forty years, and old fragments of iron which parted like sticks of barley sugar between the fingers.

Every one is aware that the variously inclined undulations of the plains, where the encounter between Napoleon and Wellington took place, are no longer what they were on June 18, 1815. On taking from this mournful field the wherewithal to make a monument to it, its real relief has been taken away, and history, disconcerted, no longer finds her bearings there. It has been disfigured for the sake of glorifying it. Wellington, when he beheld Waterloo once more, two years later, exclaimed, "They have altered my field of battle!" Where the huge pyramid of earth, surmounted by the lion, rises to-day, there was a crest which descended in an easy slope towards the Nivelles road, but which was almost an escarpment on the side of the highway to Genappe. The elevation of this escarpment can still be imagined by the height of the two knolls of the two great sepulchres which enclose the road from Genappe to Brussels: one, the English tomb, is on the left; the other, the German tomb, is on the right. There is no French tomb. The whole of that plain is a sepulchre for France. Thanks to the thousands of cartloads of earth employed in erecting the mound one hundred and fifty feet in height and half a mile in circumference, the plateau of Mont-Saint-Jean is now accessible by an easy slope. On the day of battle, particularly on the side of La Haie-Sainte, it was abrupt and difficult of approach. The incline there is so steep that the English cannon could not see the farm, situated in the bottom of the valley, which was the centre of the combat. On the 18th of June, 1815, the rains had still further increased this acclivity, the mud complicated the problem of the ascent, and the men not only slipped back, but stuck fast in the mire. Along the crest of the plateau ran a sort of trench whose presence it was impossible for the distant observer to guess.

What was this trench? Let us explain. Braine-l'Alleud is a Belgian village; Ohain is another. These villages, both of them hidden in hollows of the landscape, are connected by a road about a league and a half in length, which traverses the plain along its undulating level, and often enters and buries itself in the hills like a furrow, which makes a ravine of this road in certain parts. In 1815, as to-day, this road cut the crest of the plateau of Mont-Saint-Jean between the two highways from Genappe and Niv-elles; only, it is now on a level with the plain; it was then a hollow way. Its two slopes have been appropriated for the monumental mound. This road was, and still is, a trench for the greater portion of its course; a hollow trench, sometimes a dozen feet in depth, and whose banks, being too steep, crumbled away here and there, particularly in winter, under driving rains. Accidents happened here. The road was so narrow at the Braine-l'Alleud entrance that a passer-by was crushed by a cart, as is proved by a stone cross which stands near the cemetery, and which gives the name of the dead, *Monsieur Bernard Debrye, Merchant of Brussels*, and the date of the accident, *February*, 1637. It was so deep on the plateau of Mont-Saint-Jean that a peasant, Mathieu Nicaise, was crushed there, in 1783, by a slide from the slope, as is stated on another stone cross, the top of which has disappeared in the excavations, but whose overturned pedestal is still visible on the grassy slope to the left of the highway between La Haie-Sainte and the farm of Mont-Saint-Jean.

On the day of battle, this hollow road whose existence was in no way indicated, bordering the crest of Mont-Saint-Jean, a trench at the top of the escarpment, a rut concealed in the soil, was invisible; that is to say, terrible.

On the morning of Waterloo, then, Napoleon was content.

He was right; the plan of battle drawn up by him was, as we have seen, really admirable.

The battle once begun, its various incidents,—the resistance of Hougomont; the tenacity of La Haie-Sainte; the killing of Dauduin; the disabling of Foy; the unexpected wall against which Soye's brigade was broken; Guilleminot's fatal heedlessness when he had neither petard nor powder sacks; the sticking of the batteries in the mud; the fifteen unescorted pieces overwhelmed in a hollow way by Uxbridge; the small effect of the shells falling in the English lines, and there embedding themselves in the rain soaked soil, and only succeeding in producing volcanoes of mud, so that the canister was turned into a splash; the inutility of Piré's demonstration on Braine-l'Alleud; all that cavalry, fifteen squadrons almost annihilated; the right wing of the English badly alarmed, the left wing poorly attacked; Ney's strange mistake in massing, instead of echelonning the four divisions of the first corps; men delivered over to grape-shot, arranged in ranks twenty-seven deep and with a frontage of two hundred; the terrible gaps made in these masses by the cannon-balls; attacking columns disorganized; the side-battery suddenly unmasked on their flank; Bourgeois, Donzelot, and Durutte compromised; Quiot repulsed; Lieutenant Vieux, that Hercules graduated at the Polytechnic School, wounded at the moment when he was beating in with an axe the door of La Haie-Sainte under the downright fire of the English barricade which barred the angle on the Genappe road; Marcognet's division caught between the infantry and the cavalry, shot down at the very muzzle of the guns amid the grain by Best and Pack, put to the sword by Ponsonby; his battery of seven pieces spiked; the Prince of Saxe-Weimar holding and guarding, in spite of the Comte d'Erlon, both Frischemont and Smohain; the flags of the 105th taken, the flags of the 45th captured; that black Prussian hussar stopped by the flying column of three hundred light cavalry on the scout between Wavre and Plancenoit; the alarming things that had been said by prisoners; Grouchy's delay; fifteen hundred men killed in the orchard of Hougomont in less than an hour; eighteen hundred men overthrown in a still shorter time about La Haie-Sainte,—all these stormy incidents passing like the clouds of battle before Napoleon, had hardly troubled his gaze and had not overshadowed his imperial face. Napoleon was accustomed to gaze steadily at war; he never added up the poignant details. He cared little for figures, provided that they furnished the total, victory; he was not alarmed if the beginnings did go astray, since he thought himself the master and the possessor at the end; he knew how to wait, supposing himself to be out of the question, and he treated destiny as his equal: he seemed to say to fate, You would not dare.

Composed half of light and half of shadow, Napoleon felt himself protected in good and tolerated in evil. He had, or thought that he had, a connivance, one might almost say a complicity, of events in his favour, which was equivalent to the invulnerability of antiquity.

Nevertheless, when one has Bérésina, Leipzig, and Fontainebleau behind one, it seems as though one might defy Waterloo. A mysterious frown becomes perceptible on the face of the heavens.

At the moment when Wellington retreated, Napoleon quivered. He suddenly beheld the plateau of Mont-Saint-Jean deserted, and the van of the English army disappear. It was rallying, but hiding itself. The Emperor half rose in his stirrups. Victory flashed from his eyes.

Wellington, driven into a corner at the forest of Soignes and destroyed—that was the definite conquest of England by France; it would be Crécy, Poitiers, Malplaquet, and Ramillies avenged. The man of Marengo was wiping out Agincourt.

So the Emperor, meditating on this terrible turn of fortune, swept his glass for the last time over all the points of the field of battle. His guard, standing behind him with grounded arms, watched him from below with a sort of religious awe. He pondered; he examined the slopes, noted the declivities, scrutinized the clumps of trees, the patches of rye, the path; he seemed to be counting each bush. He gazed with some intentness at the English barricades of the two highways,—two large masses of felled trees, the one on the road to Genappe above La Haie-Sainte, defended with two cannon, the only ones out of all the English artillery which commanded the extrem-

ity of the field of battle, and that on the road to Nivelles where gleamed the Dutch bayonets of Chassé's
brigade. Near this barricade he observed the old
chapel of Saint Nicholas, which stands at the angle
of the cross-road near Braine-l'Alleud; he bent down
and spoke in a low voice to the guide Lacoste. The
guide made a negative sign with his head, which was
probably perfidious.

The Emperor straightened himself up and reflected.

Wellington had withdrawn.

All that remained to do was to complete this
retreat by crushing him.

Napoleon turning round abruptly, despatched an
express at full speed to Paris to announce that the
battle was won.

Napoleon was one of those geniuses from whom
thunder issues.

He had just found his thunder-stroke.

He gave orders to Milhaud's cuirassiers to carry
the plateau of Mont-Saint-Jean.

There were three thousand five hundred of them.
They formed a front a quarter of a league in length.
They were giants, on colossal horses. There were six
and twenty squadrons of them; and they had behind
them to support them Lefebvre-Desnouettes's division,—the one hundred and six picked gendarmes,
the light cavalry of the Guard, eleven hundred and
ninety-seven men, and the lancers of the guard of

eight hundred and eighty lances. They wore casques without plumes, and cuirasses of beaten iron, with horse-pistols in their holsters, and long sabre-swords. That morning the whole army had admired them, when, at nine o'clock, with blare of trumpets and all the music playing "Let us watch o'er the Safety of the Empire," they had come in a solid column, with one of their batteries on their flank, another in their centre, and deployed in two ranks between the roads to Genappe and Frischemont, and taken up their position for battle in that powerful second line, so cleverly arranged by Napoleon, which, having on its extreme left Kellermann's cuirassiers and on its extreme right Milhaud's cuirassiers, had, so to speak, two wings of iron.

The aide-de-camp Bernard carried them the Emperor's orders. Ney drew his sword and placed himself at their head. The enormous squadrons were set in motion.

Then a formidable spectacle was seen.

The whole of the cavalry, with upraised swords, standards and trumpets flung to the breeze, formed in columns by divisions, descended, by a simultaneous movement and like one man, with the precision of a brazen battering-ram which is affecting a breach, the hill of La Belle-Alliance. They plunged into the terrible depths in which so many men had already fallen, disappeared there in the smoke, then emerging from that shadow, reappeared on the other side of the valley, still compact and in close ranks, mounting at a full trot, through a storm of grape-shot which burst upon them, the terrible muddy slope of the plateau of Mont-Saint-Jean. They ascended, grave, threatening, imperturbable; in the intervals between the musketry and the artillery, their colossal trampling was audible. Being two divisions, there were two columns of them; Wathier's division held the right, Delort's division was on the left. It seemed as though two immense steel lizards were to be seen crawling towards the crest of the plateau. They traversed the battle like a flash.

Nothing like it had been seen since the taking of the great redoubt of the Moskowa by the heavy cavalry; Murat was missing, but Ney was again present. It seemed as though that mass had become a monster and had but one soul. Each column undulated and swelled like the rings of a polyp. They could be seen through a vast cloud of smoke which was rent at intervals. A confusion of helmets, of cries, of sabres, a stormy heaving of horses amid the cannons and the flourish of trumpets, a terrible and disciplined tumult; over all, the cuirasses like the scales on the dragon.

These narrations seemed to belong to another age. Something parallel to this vision appeared, no doubt, in the ancient Orphic epics, which told of the centaurs, the old hippanthropes, those Titans with human heads and equestrian chests who scaled Olympus at a gallop, horrible, invulnerable, sublime—gods and brutes.

It was a curious numerical coincidence that twenty-six battalions rode to meet twenty-six battalions. Behind the crest of the plateau, in the shadow of the masked battery, the English infantry, formed into thirteen squares, two battalions to the square, in two lines, with seven in the first line, six in the second, the stocks of their guns to their shoulders, taking aim at that which was on the point of appearing, waited, calm, mute, motionless. They did not see the cuirassiers, and the cuirassiers did not see them. They listened to the rise of this tide of men. They heard the swelling sound of three thousand horse, the alternate and symmetrical tramp of their hoofs at full trot, the jingling of the cuirasses, the clang of the sabres, and a sort of grand and formidable breathing. There was a long and terrible silence; then, all at once, a long file of uplifted arms, brandishing sabres, appeared above the crest, and casques, trumpets, and standards, and three thousand heads with grey moustaches, shouting, "Vive l'Empereur!" All this cavalry debouched on the plateau, and it was like the beginning of an earthquake.

All at once, a tragic incident happened; on the English left, on our right, the head of the column of cuirassiers reared up with a frightful clamour. On arriving at the culminating point of the crest, ungovernable, utterly given over to fury and their course of extermination of the squares and cannon, the cuirassiers had just caught sight of a trench or grave,—a trench between them and the English. It was the sunken road of Ohain.

It was a frightful moment. The ravine was there, unexpected, yawning, directly under the horses' feet, two fathoms deep between its double slopes; the second file pushed the first into it, and the third pushed on the second; the horses reared and fell backward, landed on their haunches, slid down, all four feet in the air, crushing and overwhelming the riders; and there being no means of retreat,—the whole column being no longer anything more than a projectile,—the force which had been acquiring to crush the English crushed the French; the inexorable ravine could only yield when filled; horses and riders rolled there pell-mell, grinding each other, forming but one mass of flesh in this gulf: when this trench was full of living men, the rest marched over them and passed on. Nearly a third of Dubois's brigade fell into that abyss.

This began the loss of the battle.

A local tradition, which evidently exaggerates matters, says that two thousand horses and fifteen hundred men were buried in the sunken road of

Ohain. This figure probably comprises all the other corpses which were flung into this ravine the day after the combat.

Let us note in passing that it was Dubois's sorely tried brigade which, an hour previously, making a charge to one side, had captured the flag of the Lunenburg battalion.

Napoleon, before giving the order for this charge of Milhaud's cuirassiers, had scrutinized the ground, but had not been able to see that hollow road, which did not even form a wrinkle on the crest of the plateau. Warned, nevertheless, and put on his guard by the little white chapel which marks its angle of juncture with the Nivelles highway, he had put a question as to the possibility of an obstacle, to the guide Lacoste. The guide had answered No. We might almost say that Napoleon's catastrophe originated in the shake of a peasant's head.

Other fatalities were yet to arise.

Was it possible for Napoleon to win that battle? We answer No. Why? Because of Wellington? Because of Blücher? No. Because of God.

Bonaparte victor at Waterloo does not harmonise with the law of the nineteenth century. Another series of facts was in preparation, in which there was no longer any room for Napoleon. The ill will of events had declared itself long before.

It was time that this vast man should fall.

The excessive weight of this man in human destiny disturbed the balance. This individual alone counted for more than the universal group. These plethoras of all human vitality concentrated in a single head; the world mounting to the brain of one man,—this would be mortal to civilization were it to last. The moment had arrived for the incorruptible and supreme equity to alter its plan. Probably the principles and the elements, on which the regular gravitations of the moral, as of the material, world depend, had complained. Smoking blood, overcrowded cemeteries, mothers in tears,—these are formidable pleaders. When the earth is suffering from too heavy a burden, there are mysterious groanings of the shades, to which the abyss lends an ear.

Napoleon had been denounced in the infinite, and his fall had been decided on. He embarrassed God.

Waterloo is not a battle; it is a transformation on the part of the Universe.


The battery was unmasked simultaneously with the ravine.

Sixty cannons and the thirteen squares darted lightning point-blank on the cuirassiers. The intrepid General Delort made the military salute to the English battery.

The whole of the flying artillery of the English had re-entered the squares at a gallop. The cuirassiers had not had even the time for reflection. The disaster of the hollow road had decimated, but not discouraged them. They belonged to that class of men who, when diminished in number, increase in courage.

Wathier's column alone had suffered in the disaster; Delort's column, which had been deflected to the left, as though he had a presentiment of an ambush had arrived whole.

The cuirassiers hurled themselves on the English squares.

At full speed, with bridles loose, swords in their teeth, pistols in their hand,—such was the attack.

There are moments in battles in which the soul hardens the man until the soldier is changed into a statue, and when all flesh becomes granite. The English battalions, desperately assaulted, did not stir.

Then it was terrible.

All the faces of the English squares were attacked at once. A frenzied whirl enveloped them. That cold infantry remained impassive. The first rank knelt and received the cuirassiers on their bayonets, the second rank shot them down; behind the second rank the cannoneers charged their guns, the front of the square parted, permitted the passage of an eruption of grape-shot, and closed again. The cuirassiers replied by crushing them. Their great horses reared, strode across the ranks, leaped over the bayonets and fell, gigantic, in the midst of these four living walls. The cannon-balls ploughed furrows in these cuirassiers; the cuirassiers made breaches in the squares. Files of men disappeared, ground to dust under the horses. The bayonets plunged into the bellies of these centaurs; hence a hideousness of wounds which has probably never been seen any-where else. The squares, wasted by this mad cavalry, closed up their ranks without flinching. Inex-haustible in the matter of grape-shot, they created explosions in their assailants' midst. The form of this combat was monstrous. These squares were no longer battalions, they were craters; those cuirassiers were no longer cavalry, they were a tempest. Each square was a volcano attacked by a cloud; lava com-bated with lightning.

The extreme right square, the most exposed of all, being in the air, was almost annihilated at the very first attack. It was formed of the 75th regiment of Highlanders. The piper in the centre dropped his melancholy eyes, filled with the reflections of the forests and the lakes in profound inattention, while men were being exterminated around him, and seated on a drum, with his pibroch under his arm, played the Highland airs. These Scotchmen died thinking of Ben Lothian, as did the Greeks remem-bering Argos. The sword of a cuirassier, which hewed down the bagpipes and the arm which bore it, put an end to the song by killing the singer.

The cuirassiers, relatively few in number, and still further diminished by the catastrophe of the ravine, had almost the whole English army against them, but they multiplied themselves so that each man of them was equal to ten. Nevertheless, some Hanoverian battalions yielded. Wellington saw it, and thought of his cavalry. Had Napoleon at that same moment thought of his infantry, he would have won the battle. This forgetfulness was his great and fatal mistake.

All at once, the cuirassiers, who had been the assailants, found themselves assailed. The English cavalry was at their back. Before them two squares, behind them Somerset; Somerset meant fourteen hundred dragoons of the guard. On the right, Somerset had Dornberg with the German light-horse, and on his left, Trip with the Belgian carbineers; the cuirassiers attacked on the flank and in front, before and in the rear, by infantry and cavalry, had to face all sides. What did they care? They were a whirlwind. Their valour was indescribable.

In addition to this, they had behind them the battery, which was still thundering. It was necessary that it should be so, or they could never have been wounded in the back. One of their cuirasses, pierced on the shoulder by a ball, is in the Waterloo Museum.

For such Frenchmen nothing less than such En-
glishmen was needed. It was no longer a hand-to-
hand *mêlée*; it was a shadow, a fury, a dizzy transport
of souls and courage, a hurricane of lightning
swords. In an instant the fourteen hundred dragoon
guards numbered only eight hundred. Fuller, their
lieutenant-colonel, fell dead. Ney rushed up with
the lancers and Lefebvre-Desnouettes's light-horse.
The plateau of Mont-Saint-Jean was captured,
recaptured, captured again. The cuirassiers left the
cavalry to return to the infantry; or, to put it more
exactly, the whole of that formidable rout collared
each other without releasing the other. The squares
still held firm after a dozen assaults. Ney had four
horses killed under him. Half the cuirassiers
remained on the plateau. This struggle lasted two
hours.

The English army was profoundly shaken. There
is no doubt that, had they not been enfeebled in
their first shock by the disaster of the hollow road,
the cuirassiers would have overwhelmed the centre
and decided the victory. This extraordinary cavalry
petrified Clinton, who had seen Talavera and Bada-
joz. Wellington, three-quarters vanquished, admired
heroically. He said in an undertone, "Splendid!"

The cuirassiers annihilated seven squares out of
thirteen, took or spiked sixty guns, and captured

from the English regiments six flags, which three
cuirassiers and three chasseurs of the Guard bore to
the Emperor in front of the farm of La Belle-
Alliance.

Wellington's situation had grown worse. This
strange battle was like a duel between two savage,
wounded men, each of whom, still fighting and still
resisting, is expending all his blood.

Which will be the first to fall?

The conflict on the plateau continued.

What had become of the cuirassiers? No one
could have told. One thing is certain, that on the day
after the battle, a cuirassier and his horse were found
dead among the woodwork of the scales for vehicles
at Mont-Saint-Jean, at the very point where the four
roads from Nivelles, Genappe, La Hulpe, and Brussels
meet and intersect each other. This horseman had
pierced the English lines. One of the men who
picked up the body still lives at Mont-Saint-Jean.
His name is Dehaye. He was eighteen years old at
that time.

Wellington felt that he was yielding. The crisis
was at hand.

The cuirassiers had not succeeded, since the centre
was not broken through. As every one was in possession of the plateau, no one held it, and in fact it
remained, to a great extent, in the hands of the En-

glish. Wellington held the village and the plain; Ney had only the crest and the slope. They seemed rooted in that fatal soil on both sides.

But the weakening of the English seemed irremediable. The hæmorrhage of that army was horrible. Kempt, on the left wing, demanded reinforcements. "There are none," replied Wellington. Almost at that same moment, a singular coincidence which depicts the exhaustion of the two armies, Ney demanded infantry from Napoleon, and Napoleon exclaimed, "Infantry! Where does he expect me to get it? Does he think I can make it?"

Nevertheless, the English army was in the worse plight of the two. The furious onsets of those great squadrons with cuirasses of iron and breasts of steel had crushed the infantry. A few men clustered round a flag marked the post of a regiment; some battalions were commanded only by a captain or a lieutenant; Alten's division, already so roughly handled at La Haie-Sainte, was almost destroyed; the intrepid Belgians of Van Kluze's brigade strewed the rye-fields all along the Nivelles road; hardly anything was left of those Dutch grenadiers, who, intermingled with Spaniards in our ranks in 1811, fought against Wellington; and who, in 1815, rallied to the English standard, fought against Napoleon. The loss in officers was considerable. Lord Uxbridge, who had his leg buried on the following day, had a fractured knee. If, on the French side, in that tussle of the cuirassiers, Delort, l'Héritier, Colbert, Dnop, Travers, and Blancard were disabled, on the side of the English there was Alten wounded, Barne wounded, Delancey killed, Van Meeren killed, Ompteda killed, the whole of Wellington's staff decimated, and England had the heaviest loss of it in that balance of blood. The second regiment of foot-guards had lost five lieutenant-colonels, four captains, and three ensigns; the first battalion of the 30th infantry had lost 24 officers and 1200 soldiers; the 79th Highlanders had lost 24 officers wounded, 18 officers killed, 450 soldiers killed. Cumberland's Hanoverian hussars, a whole regiment, with Colonel Hacke at its head, who was destined to be tried later on and cashiered, had turned bridle in the presence of the fray, and had fled to the forest of Soignes, spreading the rout as far as Brussels. The transports, ammunition-wagons, the baggage-wagons, the wagons filled with wounded, on seeing that the French were gaining ground and approaching the forest, rushed into it. The Dutch, mowed down by the French cavalry, cried, "Alarm!" From Vert-Coucou to Groentendael, a distance of nearly two leagues in the direction of Brussels, according to the testimony of eye-witnesses who are still alive, the roads were dense with fugitives. This panic was such that it attacked the Prince de Condé at Mechlin, and Louis

XVIII at Ghent. With the exception of the feeble reserve echelonned behind the ambulance established at the farm of Mont-Saint-Jean, and of Vivian's and Vandeleur's brigades, which flanked the left wing, Wellington had no cavalry left. A number of batteries lay dismounted. These facts are attested by Siborne; and Pringle, exaggerating the disaster, goes so far as to say that the Anglo-Dutch army was reduced to thirty-four thousand men. The Iron Duke remained calm, but his lips blanched. Vincent, the Austrian commissioner, Alava, the Spanish commissioner, who were present at the battle in the English staff, thought the Duke lost. At five o'clock Wellington drew out his watch, and he was heard to murmur these sinister words, "Blücher, or night!"

It was about that moment that a distant line of bayonets gleamed on the heights in the direction of Frischemont.

This was the culminating point in this stupendous drama.

The awful mistake of Napoleon is well known. Grouchy expected, Blücher arriving. Death instead of life.

Fate has these turns; the throne of the world was expected; it was Saint Helena that was seen.

If the little shepherd who served as guide to

Bülow, Blücher's lieutenant, had advised him to debouch from the forest above Frischemont, instead of below Plancenoit, the form of the nineteenth century might, perhaps, have been different. Napoleon would have won the battle of Waterloo. By any other route than that below Plancenoit, the Prussian army would have come out upon a ravine impassable for artillery, and Bülow would not have arrived.

Now the Prussian general, Muffling, declares that one hour's delay, and Blücher would not have found Wellington on his feet. "The battle was lost."

It was time that Bülow should arrive, as we shall see. He had, moreover, been very much delayed. He had bivouacked at Dieu-le-Mont, and had set out at daybreak; but the roads were impassable, and his divisions stuck fast in the mud. The ruts were up to the axles of the cannons. Moreover, he had been obliged to pass the Dyle on the narrow bridge of Wavre; the street leading to the bridge had been fired by the French, so the caissons and ammunition-wagons could not pass between two rows of burning houses, and had been obliged to wait until the conflagration was extinguished. It was mid-day before Bülow's vanguard had been able to reach Chapelle-Saint-Lambert.

Had the action begun two hours earlier, it would have been over at four o'clock, and Blücher would have fallen on the battle won by Napoleon. Such are these immense risks proportioned to an infinite which we cannot comprehend.

The Emperor had been the first, as early as midday, to descry with his field-glass, on the extreme horizon, something which had attracted his attention. He had said, "I see over there a cloud, which seems to me to be troops." Then he asked the Duc de Dalmatie, "Soult, what do you see in the direction of Chapelle-Saint-Lambert?" The marshal, looking through his glass, answered, "Four or five thousand men, Sire." It was evidently Grouchy. But it remained motionless in the mist. All the glasses of the staff had studied "the cloud" pointed out by the Emperor. Some said: "They are columns halting." The truth is, that the cloud did not move. The Emperor detached Domon's division of light cavalry to reconnoitre in that direction.

Bülow had not moved in fact. His vanguard was very feeble, and could accomplish nothing. He was obliged to wait for the main body of the army corps, and he had received orders to concentrate his forces, before entering into line; but at five o'clock, perceiving Wellington's peril, Blücher ordered Bülow to attack, and uttered these remarkable words: "We must let the English army breathe."

A little later, the divisions of Losthin, Hiller, Hacke, and Ryssel deployed before Lobau's corps, the cavalry of Prince William of Russia debouched from the Bois de Paris, Plancenoit was in flames, and the Prussian cannon-balls began to rain even upon the ranks of the guard in reserve behind Napoleon.

The rest is known,—the irruption of a third army; the battle broken to pieces; eighty-six cannon thundering simultaneously; Pirch the first coming up with Bülow; Zieten's cavalry led by Blücher in person, the French driven back; Marcognet swept from the plateau of Ohain; Durutte dislodged from Papelotte; Donzelot and Quiot retreating; Lobau attacked on the flank; a fresh battle precipitating itself on our dismantled regiments at nightfall; the whole English line resuming the offensive and thrust forward; the gigantic breach made in the French army; the English grape-shot and the Prussian grape-shot aiding each other; the extermination; disaster in front; disaster on the flank; the Guard entering the line in the midst of this terrible crumbling of all things.

Conscious that they were about to die, they shouted, "Long live the Emperor!" History records nothing more touching than that death rattle bursting forth in acclamations.

The sky had been overcast all day. All of a sudden, at that very moment,—it was eight o'clock in the evening,—the clouds on the horizon parted, and allowed the sinister red glow of the setting sun to pass through, athwart the elms on the Nivelles road. They had seen it rise at Austerlitz.

Each battalion of the Guard was commanded by a general for this final *dénouement*. Friant, Michel, Roguet, Harlet, Mallet, Poret de Morvan, were there. When the tall bearskins of the grenadiers of the Guard, with their large plaques bearing the eagle, appeared, symmetrical, in line, tranquil, in the midst of that combat, the enemy felt a respect for France; they thought they beheld twenty victories entering the field of battle, with wings outspread, and those who were the conquerors, believing themselves to be vanquished, retreated; but Wellington shouted, "Up, Guards, and at them!" The red regiment of English Guards, lying flat behind the hedges, sprang up, a cloud of grape-shot riddled the tricoloured flag and whistled round our eagles; all hurled themselves forwards, and the supreme carnage began. In the darkness, the Imperial Guard felt the army losing ground around it, and in the vast shock of the rout it heard the desperate flight which had taken the place of the "Long live the Emperor!" and, with flight behind it, it continued to advance, more crushed, losing more men at every step it took. There were none who hesitated, no timid men in its ranks. The soldier in that troop was as much of a hero as the general. Not a man was missing in that heroic suicide.

Ney, bewildered, great with all the grandeur of accepted death, offered himself to all blows in that tempest. He had his fifth horse killed under him there. Perspiring, his eyes aflame, foam on his lips, with uniform unbuttoned, one of his epaulets half cut off by a sword-stroke from the horse-guard, his plaque with the great eagle dented by a bullet; bleeding, bemired, magnificent, a broken sword in his hand, he said, "Come and see how a Marshal of France dies on the field of battle!" But in vain; he did not die. He was haggard and angry. At Drouet d'Erlon he hurled this question, "Are you not going to get yourself killed?" In the midst of all that artillery engaged in crushing a handful of men, he shouted: "So there is nothing for me! Oh! I should like to have all these English bullets enter my chest!" Unhappy man, thou wert reserved for French bullets!

The rout in the rear of the Guard was melancholy.

The army yielded suddenly on all sides simultaneously—Hougomont, La Haie-Sainte, Papelotte, Plancenoit. The cry, "Treachery!" was followed by a cry of "Save yourselves who can!" An army which is disbanding is like a thaw. All yields, splits, cracks, floats, rolls, falls, collides, is precipitated. The disintegration is unprecedented. Ney borrows a horse, leaps upon it, and without hat, cravat, or sword, dashes across the Brussels road, stopping both English and French. He strives to detain the army, he recalls it to its duty, he insults it, he clings to the route. He is overwhelmed. The soldiers fly from him, shouting, "Long live Marshal Ney!" Two of Durutte's regiments go and come in affright as though tossed back and forth between the swords of the Uhlans and the fusillade of the brigades of Kempt, Best, Pack, and Ryland; the worst of hand-to-hand conflicts is the defeat; friends kill each other in order to escape; squadrons and battalions break and disperse against each other, like the tremendous foam of battle. Lobau at one extremity, and Reille at the other, are drawn into the tide. In vain does Napoleon erect walls from what is left to him of his Guard; in vain does he expend in a last effort his last serviceable squadrons. Quiot retreats before Vivian, Kellermann before Vandeleur, Lobau before Bülow, Morand before Pirch, Domon and Subervic before Prince William of Prussia; Guyot, who led the Emperor's squadrons to the charge, falls beneath the feet of the English dragoons. Napoleon gallops past the line of fugitives, harangues, urges, threatens, entreats them. All the mouths which in the morning had shouted, "Long live the Emperor!" remain gaping; they hardly recognize him. The Prussian cavalry, newly arrived, dashes forward, flies, hews, slashes, kills, exterminates. Horses lash out, the cannons flee; the soldiers of the artillery-train unharnass the caissons and use the horses to make their escape; wagons overturned, with all four wheels in the air, block the road and occasion massacres. Men are crushed, trampled down, others walk over the dead and the living. Arms are lost. A dizzy multitude fills the roads, the paths, the bridges, the plains, the hills, the valleys, the woods, encumbered by this invasion of forty thousand men. Shouts, despair, knapsacks and guns flung among the wheat, passages forced at the point of the sword, no more comrades, no more officers, no more generals, an indescribable terror. Zieten putting France to the sword at his leisure. Lions converted into goats. Such was the flight.

At Genappe, an effort was made to wheel about, to present a battle front, to draw up in line. Lobau rallied three hundred men. The entrance to the village was barricaded, but at the first volley of Prussian canister, all took to flight again, and Lobau was made prisoner. That volley of grape-shot can be seen today imprinted on the ancient gable of a brick building on the right of the road at a few minutes' distance before you reach Genappe. The Prussians threw themselves into Genappe, furious, no doubt, that they were not more entirely the conquerors. The pursuit was stupendous. Blücher ordered extermination. Roguet had set the lugubrious example of threatening with death any French grenadier who should bring him a Prussian prisoner. Blücher surpassed Roguet. Duchesme, the general of the Young Guard, hemmed in at the doorway of an inn at Genappe, surrendered his sword to a huzzar of death, who took the sword and slew the prisoner. The victory was completed by the assassination of the vanquished. Let us inflict punishment, since we are writing history; old Blücher disgraced himself. This ferocity put the finishing touch to the disaster. The desperate rout traversed Genappe, traversed Quatre-Bras, traversed Gosselies, traversed Frasnes, traversed Charleroi, traversed Thuin, and only halted at the frontier. Alas! and who, then, was fleeing in that manner? The Grand Army.

This vertigo, this terror, this downfall into ruin of the highest bravery which ever astounded history,—is that causeless? No. The shadow of an enormous right is projected across Waterloo. It is the day of destiny. The force which is mightier than man produced that day. Hence the terrified wrinkle of those brows; hence all those great souls surrendering their swords. Those who had conquered Europe have fallen prone on the earth, with nothing left to say nor to do, feeling the present shadow of a terrible presence. *Hoc erat in fatis.* That day the perspective of the human race was changed. Waterloo is the hinge of the nineteenth century. The disappearance of the great man was necessary for the advent of the great age, and he, who cannot be answered, took the responsibility on himself. The panic of heroes can be explained. In the battle of Waterloo there is something more than a cloud, there is something of the meteor.

At nightfall, in a meadow near Genappe, Bernard and Bertrand seized by the skirt of his coat and detained a man, haggard, pensive, sinister, gloomy, who, dragged to that point by the current of the rout, had just dismounted, had passed the bridle of his horse over his arm, and with wild eye was returning alone to Waterloo. It was Napoleon, the immense somnambulist of this dream which had crumbled, trying once more to advance.

# Fort William Henry
# 1757

[ FRANCIS PARKMAN ]

"I am going on the ninth to sing the war-song at the Lake of Two Mountains, and on the next day at Saut St. Louis,—a long, tiresome ceremony. On the twelfth I am off; and I count on having news to tell you by the end of this month or the beginning of next." Thus Montcalm wrote to his wife from Montreal early in July. All doubts had been solved. Prisoners taken on the Hudson and despatches from Versailles had made it certain that Loudon was bound to Louisbourg, carrying with him the best of the troops that had guarded the New York frontier. The time was come, not only to strike the English on Lake George, but perhaps to seize Fort Edward and carry terror to Albany itself. Only one difficulty remained, the want of provisions. Agents were sent to collect corn and bacon among the inhabitants; the curés and militia captains were ordered to aid in the work; and enough was presently found to feed twelve thousand men for a month.

The emissaries of the Governor had been busy all winter among the tribes of the West and North; and more than a thousand savages, lured by the prospect of gifts, scalps, and plunder, were now encamped at Montreal. Many of them had never visited a French settlement before. All were eager to see Montcalm, whose exploit in taking Oswego had inflamed their imagination; and one day, on a visit of ceremony, an orator from Michillimackinac addressed the General thus: "We wanted to see this famous man who tramples the English under his feet. We thought we should find him so tall that his head would be lost in the clouds. But you are a little man, my Father. It is when we look into your eyes that we see the greatness of the pine-tree and the fire of the eagle."

It remained to muster the Mission Indians settled in or near the limits of the colony; and it was to this end that Montcalm went to sing the war-song with the converts of the Two Mountains. Rigaud, Bougainville, young Longueuil, and others were of the party; and when they landed, the Indians came down to the shore, their priests at their head, and greeted the General with a volley of musketry; then received him after dark in their grand council-lodge, where the circle of wild and savage visages, half seen in the dim light of a few candles, suggested to Bougainville a midnight conclave of wizards. He acted vicariously the chief part in the ceremony. "I sang the war-song in the name of M. de Montcalm, and was much applauded. It was nothing but these words: 'Let us trample the English under our feet,' chanted over and over again, in cadence with the movements of the savages." Then came the war-feast, against which occasion Montcalm had caused three oxen to be roasted. On the next day the party went to Caughnawaga, or Saut St. Louis, where the ceremony was repeated; and Bougainville, who again sang the war-song in the name of his commander, was requited by adoption into the clan of the Turtle. Three more oxen were solemnly devoured, and with one voice the warriors took up the hatchet.

Meanwhile troops, Canadians and Indians, were moving by detachments up Lake Champlain. Fleets of bateaux and canoes followed each other day by day along the capricious lake, in calm or storm, sunshine or rain, till, towards the end of July, the whole force was gathered at Ticonderoga, the base of the intended movement. Bourlamaque had been there since May with the battalions of Béarn and Royal Roussillon, finishing the fort, sending out war-parties, and trying to discover the force and designs of the English at Fort William Henry.

Ticonderoga is a high rocky promontory between Lake Champlain on the north and the mouth of the outlet of Lake George on the south. Near its extremity and close to the fort were still encamped the two battalions under Bourlamaque, while bateaux and canoes were passing incessantly up the river of the outlet. There were scarcely two miles of navigable water, at the end of which the stream fell foaming over a high ledge of rock that barred the way. Here the French were building a saw-mill; and a wide space had been cleared to form an encampment defended on all sides by an abattis, within which stood the tents of the battalions of La Reine, La Sarre, Languedoc, and Guienne, all commanded by Lévis. Above the cascade the stream circled through the forest in a series of beautiful rapids, and from the camp of Lévis a road a mile and a half long had been cut to the navigable water above. At the end of this road there was another fortified camp, formed of colony regulars, Canadians, and Indians, under Rigaud. It was scarcely a mile farther to Lake George, where on the western side there was an outpost, chiefly of Canadians and Indians; while advanced parties were stationed at Bald Mountain, now called Rogers Rock, and elsewhere on the lake, to watch the movements of the English. The various encampments just mentioned were ranged along a valley extending four miles from Lake Champlain to

Lake George, and bordered by mountains wooded to
the top.

Here was gathered a martial population of eight
thousand men, including the brightest civilization
and the darkest barbarism: from the scholar-soldier
Montcalm and his no less accomplished aide-de-
camp; from Lévis, conspicuous for graces of person;
from a throng of courtly young officers, who would
have seemed out of place in that wilderness had
they not done their work so well in it; from these to
the foulest man-eating savage of the uttermost
northwest.

Of Indian allies there were nearly two thousand.
One of their tribes, the Iowas, spoke a language
which no interpreter understood; and they all
bivouacked where they saw fit: for no man could
control them. "I see no difference," says Bougainville,
"in the dress, ornaments, dances, and songs of the
various western nations. They go naked, excepting a
strip of cloth passed through a belt, and paint themselves black, red, blue, and other colors. Their heads
are shaved and adorned with bunches of feathers,
and they wear rings of brass wire in their ears. They
wear beaver-skin blankets, and carry lances, bows
and arrows, and quivers made of the skins of beasts.
For the rest they are straight, well made, and generally very tall. Their religion is brute paganism. I will
say it once for all, one must be the slave of these sav-

ages, listen to them day and night, in council and in private, whenever the fancy takes them, or whenever a dream, a fit of the vapors, or their perpetual craving for brandy, gets possession of them; besides which they are always wanting something for their equipment, arms, or toilet, and the general of the army must give written orders for the smallest trifle,—an eternal, wearisome detail, of which one has no idea in Europe."

It was not easy to keep them fed. Rations would be served to them for a week; they would consume them in three days, and come for more. On one occasion they took the matter into their own hands, and butchered and devoured eighteen head of cattle intended for the troops; nor did any officer dare oppose this "St. Bartholomew of the oxen," as Bougainville calls it. "Their paradise is to be drunk," says the young officer. Their paradise was rather a hell; for sometimes, when mad with brandy, they grappled and tore each other with their teeth like wolves. They were continually "making medicine," that is, consulting the Manitou, to whom they hung up offerings, sometimes a dead dog, and sometimes the belt-cloth which formed their only garment.

The Mission Indians were better allies than these heathen of the west; and their priests, who followed them to the war, had great influence over them. They were armed with guns, which they well knew

how to use. Their dress, though savage, was generally
decent, and they were not cannibals; though in other
respects they retained all their traditional ferocity
and most of their traditional habits. They held frequent war-feasts, one of which is described by
Roubaud, Jesuit missionary of the Abenakis of St.
Francis, whose flock formed a part of the company
present.

"Imagine," says the father, "a great assembly of
savages adorned with every ornament most suited to
disfigure them in European eyes, painted with vermilion, white, green, yellow, and black made of soot
and the scrapings of pots. A single savage face com-
bines all these different colors, methodically laid on
with the help of a little tallow, which serves for
pomatum. The head is shaved except at the top,
where there is a small tuft, to which are fastened
feathers, a few beads of wampum, or some such trin-
ket. Every part of the head has its ornament. Pendants hang from the nose and also from the ears,
which are split in infancy and drawn down by
weights till they flap at last against the shoulders.
The rest of the equipment answers to this fantastic
decoration: a shirt bedaubed with vermilion, wampum
collars, silver bracelets, a large knife hanging on the
breast, moose-skin moccasons, and a belt of various
colors always absurdly combined. The sachems and
war-chiefs are distinguished from the rest: the latter

by a gorget, and the former by a medal, with the King's portrait on one side, and on the other Mars and Bellona joining hands, with the device, *Virtus et Honor*."

Thus attired, the company sat in two lines facing each other, with kettles in the middle filled with meat chopped for distribution. To a dignified silence succeeded songs, sung by several chiefs in succession, and compared by the narrator to the howling of wolves. Then followed a speech from the chief orator, highly commended by Roubaud, who could not help admiring this effort of savage eloquence. "After the harangue," he continues, "they proceeded to nominate the chiefs who were to take command. As soon as one was named he rose and took the head of some animal that had been butchered for the feast. He raised it aloft so that all the company could see it, and cried: 'Behold the head of the enemy!' Applause and cries of joy rose from all parts of the assembly. The chief, with the head in his hand, passed down between the lines, singing his war-song, bragging of his exploits, taunting and defying the enemy, and glorifying himself beyond all measure. To hear his self-laudation in these moments of martial transport one would think him a conquering hero ready to sweep everything before him. As he passed in front of the other savages, they would respond by dull broken cries jerked up from the depths of their stomachs, and accompanied by movements of their bodies so odd that one must be well used to them to keep countenance. In the course of his song the chief would utter from time to time some grotesque witticism; then he would stop, as if pleased with himself, or rather to listen to the thousand confused cries of applause that greeted his ears. He kept up his martial promenade as long as he liked the sport; and when he had had enough, ended by flinging down the head of the animal with an air of contempt, to show that his warlike appetite craved meat of another sort." Others followed with similar songs and pantomime, and the festival was closed at last by ladling out the meat from the kettles, and devouring it.

Roubaud was one day near the fort, when he saw the shore lined with a thousand Indians, watching four or five English prisoners, who, with the war-party that had captured them, were approaching in a boat from the farther side of the water. Suddenly the whole savage crew broke away together and ran into the neighboring woods, whence they soon emerged, yelling diabolically, each armed with a club. The wretched prisoners were to be forced to "run the gauntlet," which would probably have killed them. They were saved by the chief who commanded the war-party, and who, on the persuasion of a French officer, claimed them as his own and forbade the game; upon which, according to rule in such cases, the rest abandoned it. On this same day the missionary met troops of Indians conducting several bands of English prisoners along the road that led through the forest from the camp of Lévis. Each of the captives was held by a cord made fast about the neck; and the sweat was starting from their brows in the extremity of their horror and distress. Roubaud's tent was at this time in the camp of the Ottawas. He presently saw a large number of them squatted about a fire, before which meat was roasting on sticks stuck in the ground; and, approaching, he saw that it was the flesh of an Englishman, other parts of which were boiling in a kettle, while near by sat eight or ten of the prisoners, forced to see their comrade devoured. The horror-stricken priest began to remonstrate; on which a young savage fiercely replied in broken French: "You have French taste; I have Indian. This is good meat for me;" and the feasters pressed him to share it.

Bougainville says that this abomination could not be prevented; which only means that if force had been used to stop it, the Ottawas would have gone home in a rage. They were therefore left to finish their meal undisturbed. Having eaten one of their prisoners, they began to treat the rest with the utmost kindness, bringing them white bread, and attending to all their wants,—a seeming change of heart due to the fact that they were a valuable commodity, for which the owners hoped to get a good price at Montreal. Montcalm wished to send them thither at once, to which after long debate the Indians consented, demanding, however, a receipt in full, and bargaining that the captives should be supplied with shoes and blankets.

These unfortunates belonged to a detachment of three hundred provincials, chiefly New Jersey men, sent from Fort William Henry under command of Colonel Parker to reconnoitre the French outposts. Montcalm's scouts discovered them; on which a band of Indians, considerably more numerous, went to meet them under a French partisan named Corbière, and ambushed themselves not far from Sabbath Day Point. Parker had rashly divided his force; and at daybreak of the twenty-sixth of July three of his boats fell into the snare, and were captured without a shot. Three others followed, in ignorance of what had happened, and shared the fate of the first. When the rest drew near, they were greeted by a deadly volley from the thickets, and a swarm of canoes darted out upon them. The men were seized with such a panic that some of them jumped into the water to escape, while the Indians leaped after them and speared them with their lances like fish. "Terrified," says Bougainville, "by the sight of these monsters, their agility, their firing, and their yells, they surrendered almost without resistance." About a hundred, however, made their escape. The rest were killed or captured, and three of the bodies were eaten on the spot. The journalist adds that the victory so elated the Indians that they became insupportable; "but here in the forests of America we can no more do without them than without cavalry on the plain."

Another success at about the same time did not tend to improve their manners. A hundred and fifty of them, along with a few Canadians under Marin, made a dash at Fort Edward, killed or drove in the pickets, and returned with thirty-two scalps and a prisoner. It was found, however, that the scalps were far from representing an equal number of heads, the Indians having learned the art of making two or three out of one by judicious division.

Preparations were urged on with the utmost energy. Provisions, camp equipage, ammunition, cannon, and bateaux were dragged by gangs of men up the road from the camp of Lévis to the head of the rapids. The work went on through heat and rain, by day and night, till, at the end of July, all was done. Now, on the eve of departure, Montcalm, anxious for harmony among his red allies, called them to a grand council near the camp of Rigaud. Forty-one tribes and sub-tribes, Christian and heathen, from the east and from the west, were represented in it.

Here were the mission savages,—Iroquois of
Caughnawaga, Two Mountains, and La Présentation;
Hurons of Lorette and Detroit; Nipissings of Lake
Nipissing; Abenakis of St. Francis, Becancour, Mis-
sisqui, and the Penobscot; Algonkins of Three Rivers
and Two Mountains; Micmacs and Malecites from
Acadia: in all eight hundred chiefs and warriors.
With these came the heathen of the west,—Ottawas
of seven distinct bands; Ojibwas from Lake Superior,
and Mississagas from the region of Lakes Erie and
Huron; Pottawattamies and Menomonies from Lake
Michigan; Sacs, Foxes, and Winnebagoes from Wis-
consin; Miamis from the prairies of Illinois, and
Iowas from the banks of the Des Moines: nine hundred and seventy-nine chiefs and warriors, men of
the forests and men of the plains, hunters of the
moose and hunters of the buffalo, bearers of steel
hatchets and stone war-clubs, of French guns and of
flint-headed arrows. All sat in silence, decked with
ceremonial paint, scalp-locks, eagle plumes, or horns
of buffalo; and the dark and wild assemblage was
edged with white uniforms of officers from France,
who came in numbers to the spectacle. Other officers were also here, all belonging to the colony. They
had been appointed to the command of the Indian
allies, over whom, however, they had little or no real
authority. First among them was the bold and hardy
Saint-Luc de la Corne, who was called general of

the Indians; and under him were others, each assigned to some tribe or group of tribes,—the intrepid Marin; Charles Langlade, who had left his squaw wife at Michillimackinac to join the war; Niverville, Langis, La Plante, Hertel, Longueuil, Herbin, Lorimier, Sabrevois, and Fleurimont; men familiar from childhood with forests and savages. Each tribe had its interpreter, often as lawless as those with whom he had spent his life; and for the converted tribes there were three missionaries,— Piquet for the Iroquois, Mathevet for the Nipissings, who were half heathen, and Roubaud for the Abenakis.

There was some complaint among the Indians because they were crowded upon by the officers who came as spectators. This difficulty being removed, the council opened, Montcalm having already explained his plans to the chiefs and told them the part he expected them to play.

Pennahouel, chief of the Ottawas, and senior of all the Assembly, rose and said: "My father, I, who have counted more moons than any here, thank you for the good words you have spoken. I approve them. Nobody ever spoke better. It is the Manitou of War who inspires you."

Kikensick, chief of the Nipissings, rose in behalf of the Christian Indians, and addressed the heathen of the west. "Brothers, we thank you for coming to help us defend our lands against the English. Our cause is good. The Master of Life is on our side. Can you doubt it, brothers, after the great blow you have just struck? It covers you with glory. The lake, red with the blood of Corlaer [*the English*] bears witness forever to your achievement. We too share your glory, and are proud of what you have done." Then, turning to Montcalm: "We are even more glad than you, my father, who have crossed the great water, not for your own sake, but to obey the great King and defend his children. He has bound us all together by the most solemn of ties. Let us take care that nothing shall separate us."

The various interpreters, each in turn, having explained this speech to the Assembly, it was received with ejaculations of applause; and when they had ceased, Montcalm spoke as follows: "Children, I am delighted to see you all joined in this good work. So long as you remain one, the English cannot resist you. The great King has sent me to protect and defend you; but above all he has charged me to make you happy and unconquerable, by establishing among you the union which ought to prevail among brothers, children of one father, the great Onontio." Then he held out a prodigious wampum belt of six thousand beads: "Take this sacred pledge of his word. The union of the beads of which it is made is the sign of your united strength. By it I bind you all together, so that none of you can separate from the rest till the English are defeated and their fort destroyed."

Pennahouel took up the belt and said: "Behold, brothers, a circle drawn around us by the great Onontio. Let none of us go out from it; for so long as we keep in it, the Master of Life will help all our undertakings." Other chiefs spoke to the same effect, and the council closed in perfect harmony. Its various members bivouacked together at the camp by the lake, and by their carelessness soon set it on fire; whence the place became known as the Burned Camp. Those from the missions confessed their sins all day; while their heathen brothers hung an old coat and a pair of leggings on a pole as tribute to the Manitou. This greatly embarrassed the three priests, who were about to say Mass, but doubted whether they ought to say it in presence of a sacrifice to the devil. Hereupon they took counsel of Montcalm. "Better say it so than not at all," replied the military casuist. Brandy being prudently denied them, the allies grew restless; and the greater part paddled up the lake to a spot near the place where Parker had been defeated. Here they encamped to wait the arrival of the army, and amused themselves meantime with killing rattlesnakes, there being a populous "den" of those reptiles among the neighboring rocks.

Montcalm sent a circular letter to the regular officers, urging them to dispense for a while with lux-
uries, and even comforts. "We have but few
bateaux, and these are so filled with stores that a
large division of the army must go by land;" and he
directed that everything not absolutely necessary
should be left behind, and that a canvas shelter to
every two officers should serve them for a tent, and
a bearskin for a bed. "Yet I do not forbid a mat-
tress," he adds. "Age and infirmities may make it
necessary to some; but I shall not have one myself,
and make no doubt that all who can will willingly
imitate me."

The bateaux lay ready by the shore, but could not
carry the whole force; and Lévis received orders to
march by the side of the lake with twenty-five hundred men, Canadians, regulars, and Iroquois. He set
out at daybreak of the thirtieth of July, his men
carrying nothing but their knapsacks, blankets, and
weapons. Guided by the unerring Indians, they
climbed the steep gorge at the side of Rogers Rock,
gained the valley beyond, and marched southward
along a Mohawk trail which threaded the forest in a
course parallel to the lake. The way was of the
roughest; many straggled from the line, and two officers completely broke down. The first destination of
the party was the mouth of Ganouskie Bay, now
called Northwest Bay, where they were to wait for

Montcalm, and kindle three fires as a signal that they had reached the rendezvous.

Montcalm left a detachment to hold Ticonderoga; and then, on the first of August, at two in the afternoon, he embarked at the Burned Camp with all his remaining force. Including those with Lévis, the expedition counted about seven thousand six hundred men, of whom more than sixteen hundred were Indians. At five in the afternoon they reached the place where the Indians, having finished their rattlesnake hunt, were smoking their pipes and waiting for the army. The red warriors embarked, and joined the French flotilla; and now, as evening drew near, was seen one of those wild pageantries of war which Lake George has often witnessed. A restless multitude of birch canoes, filled with painted savages, glided by shores and islands, like troops of swimming waterfowl. Two hundred and fifty bateaux came next, moved by sail and oar, some bearing the Canadian militia, and some the battalions of Old France in trim and gay attire: first, La Reine and Languedoc; then the colony regulars; then La Sarre and Guienne; then the Canadian brigade of Courtemanche; then the cannon and mortars, each on a platform sustained by two bateaux lashed side by side, and rowed by the militia of Saint-Ours; then the battalions of Béarn and Royal Roussillon; then the Canadians of Gaspé,

with the provision-bateaux and the field-hospital;
and, lastly, a rear guard of regulars closed the line. So,
under the flush of sunset, they held their course
along the romantic lake, to play their part in the his-
toric drama that lends a stern enchantment to its fascinating scenery. They passed the Narrows in mist
and darkness; and when, a little before dawn, they
rounded the high promontory of Tongue Mountain, they saw, far on the right, three fiery sparks
shining through the gloom. These were the signal-
fires of Lévis, to tell them that he had reached the
appointed spot.

Lévis had arrived the evening before, after his hard
march through the sultry midsummer forest. His
men had now rested for a night, and at ten in the
morning he marched again. Montcalm followed at
noon, and coasted the western shore, till, towards
evening, he found Lévis waiting for him by the mar-
gin of a small bay not far from the English fort,
though hidden from it by a projecting point of land.
Canoes and bateaux were drawn up on the beach,
and the united forces made their bivouac together.

The earthen mounds of Fort William Henry still
stand by the brink of Lake George; and seated at the
sunset of an August day under the pines that cover
them, one gazes on a scene of soft and soothing
beauty, where dreamy waters reflect the glories of
the mountains and the sky. As it is to-day, so it was

then; all breathed repose and peace. The splash of some leaping trout, or the dipping wing of a passing swallow, alone disturbed the summer calm of that unruffled mirror.

About ten o'clock at night two boats set out from the fort to reconnoitre. They were passing a point of land on their left, two miles or more down the lake, when the men on board descried through the gloom a strange object against the bank; and they rowed towards it to learn what it might be. It was an awning over the bateaux that carried Roubaud and his brother missionaries. As the rash oarsmen drew near, the bleating of a sheep in one of the French provision-boats warned them of danger; and turning, they pulled for their lives towards the eastern shore. Instantly more than a thousand Indians threw themselves into their canoes and dashed in hot pursuit, making the lake and the mountains ring with the din of their war-whoops. The fugitives had nearly reached land when their pursuers opened fire. They replied; shot one Indian dead, and wounded another; then snatched their oars again, and gained the beach. But the whole savage crew was upon them. Several were killed, three were taken, and the rest escaped in the dark woods. The prisoners were brought before Montcalm, and gave him valuable information of the strength and position of the English.

The Indian who was killed was a noted chief of the Nipissings; and his tribesmen howled in grief for their bereavement. They painted his face with vermilion, tied feathers in his hair, hung pendants in his ears and nose, clad him in a resplendent war-dress, put silver bracelets on his arms, hung a gorget on his breast with a flame colored ribbon, and seated him in state on the top of a hillock, with his lance in his hand, his gun in the hollow of his arm, his tomahawk in his belt, and his kettle by his side. Then they all crouched about him in lugubrious silence. A funeral harangue followed; and next a song and solemn dance to the booming of the Indian drum. In the gray of the morning they buried him as he sat, and placed food in the grave for his journey to the land of souls.

As the sun rose above the eastern mountains the French camp was all astir. The column of Lévis, with Indians to lead the way, moved through the forest towards the fort, and Montcalm followed with the main body; then the artillery boats rounded the point that had hid them from the sight of the English, saluting them as they did so with musketry and cannon; while a host of savages put out upon the lake, ranged their canoes abreast in a line from shore to shore, and advanced slowly, with measured paddle-strokes and yells of defiance.

The position of the enemy was full in sight before

them. At the head of the lake, towards the right, stood the fort, close to the edge of the water. On its left was a marsh; then the rough piece of ground where Johnson had encamped two years before; then a low, flat, rocky hill, crowned with an entrenched camp; and, lastly, on the extreme left, another marsh. Far around the fort and up the slopes of the western mountain the forest had been cut down and burned, and the ground was cumbered with blackened stumps and charred carcasses and limbs of fallen trees, strewn in savage disorder one upon another. This was the work of Winslow in the autumn before. Distant shouts and war-cries, the clatter of musketry, white puffs of smoke in the dismal clearing and along the scorched edge of the bordering forest, told that Lévis' Indians were skirmishing with parties of the English, who had gone out to save the cattle roaming in the neighborhood, and burn some outbuildings that would have favored the besiegers. Others were taking down the tents that stood on a plateau near the foot of the mountain on the right, and moving them to the entrenchment on the hill. The garrison sallied from the fort to support their comrades, and for a time the firing was hot.

Fort William Henry was an irregular bastioned square, formed by embankments of gravel surmounted by a rampart of heavy logs, laid in tiers crossed one upon another, the interstices filled with earth. The lake protected it on the north, the marsh on the east, and ditches with *chevaux-de-frise* on the south and west. Seventeen cannon, great and small, besides several mortars and swivels, were mounted upon it; and a brave Scotch veteran, Lieutenant-Colonel Monro, of the thirty-fifth regiment, was in command.

General Webb lay fourteen miles distant at Fort Edward, with twenty-six hundred men, chiefly provincials. On the twenty-fifth of July he had made a visit to Fort William Henry, examined the place, given some orders, and returned on the twenty-ninth. He then wrote to the Governor of New York, telling him that the French were certainly coming, begging him to send up the militia, and saying: "I am determined to march to Fort William Henry with the whole army under my command as soon as I shall hear of the farther approach of the enemy." Instead of doing so he waited three days, and then sent up a detachment of two hundred regulars under Lieutenant-Colonel Young, and eight hundred Massachusetts men under Colonel Frye. This raised the force at the lake to two thousand and two hundred, including sailors and mechanics, and reduced that of Webb to sixteen hundred, besides half as many more distributed at Albany and the intervening forts. If, according to his spirited intention, he should go to the rescue of Monro, he must leave some of his troops behind him to protect the lower posts from a possible French inroad by way of South Bay. Thus his power of aiding Monro was slight, so rashly had Loudon, intent on Louisbourg, left this frontier open to attack. The defect, however, was as much in Webb himself as in his resources. His conduct in the past year had raised doubts of his personal courage; and this was the moment for answering them. Great as was the disparity of numbers, the emergency would have justified an attempt to save Monro at any risk. That officer sent him a hasty note, written at nine o'clock on the morning of the third, telling him that the French were in sight on the lake; and, in the next night, three rangers came to Fort Edward, bringing another short note, dated at six in the evening, announcing that the firing had begun, and closing with the words: "I believe you will think it proper to send a reinforcement as soon as possible." Now, if ever, was the time to move, before the fort was invested and access cut off. But Webb lay quiet, sending expresses to New England for help which could not possibly arrive in time. On the next night another note came from Monro to say that the French were upon him in great numbers, well supplied with artillery, but that the garrison were all in good spirits. "I make no doubt," wrote the hard-pressed officer, "that you will soon send us a reinforcement;" and again on the same day: "We are very certain that a part of the enemy have got between you and us upon the high road, and would therefore be glad (if it meets with your approbation) the whole army was marched." But Webb gave no sign.

When the skirmishing around the fort was over, La Corne, with a body of Indians, occupied the road that led to Fort Edward, and Lévis encamped hard by to support him, while Montcalm proceeded to examine the ground and settle his plan of attack. He made his way to the rear of the entrenched camp and reconnoitred it, hoping to carry it by assault; but it had a breastwork of stones and logs, and he thought the attempt too hazardous. The ground where he stood was that where Dieskau had been defeated; and as the fate of his predecessor was not of flattering augury, he resolved to besiege the fort in form.

He chose for the site of his operations the ground now covered by the village of Caldwell. A little to the north of it was a ravine, beyond which he formed his main camp, while Lévis occupied a tract of dry ground beside the marsh, whence he could easily move to intercept succors from Fort Edward on the one hand, or repel a sortie from Fort William Henry on the other. A brook ran down the ravine and entered the lake at a small cove protected from the fire of the fort by a point of land; and at this place, still called Artillery Cove, Montcalm prepared to debark his cannon and mortars.

Having made his preparations, he sent Fontbrune, one of his aides-de-camp, with a letter to Monro. "I owe it to humanity," he wrote, "to summon you to surrender. At present I can restrain the savages, and make them observe the terms of a capitulation, as I might not have power to do under other circumstances; and an obstinate defence on your part could only retard the capture of the place a few days, and endanger an unfortunate garrison which cannot be relieved, in consequence of the dispositions I have made. I demand a decisive answer within an hour." Monro replied that he and his soldiers would defend themselves to the last. While the flags of truce were flying, the Indians swarmed over the fields before the fort; and when they learned the result, an Abenaki chief shouted in broken French: "You won't surrender, eh! Fire away then, and fight your best; for if I catch you, you shall get no quarter." Monro emphasized his refusal by a general discharge of his cannon.

The trenches were opened on the night of the fourth,—a task of extreme difficulty, as the ground was covered by a profusion of half-burned stumps, roots, branches, and fallen trunks. Eight hundred men toiled till daylight with pick, spade, and axe, while the cannon from the fort flashed through the darkness, and grape and round-shot whistled and screamed over their heads. Some of the English balls reached the camp beyond the ravine, and disturbed the slumbers of the officers off duty, as they lay wrapped in their blankets and bear-skins. Before daybreak the first parallel was made; a battery was nearly finished on the left, and another was begun on the right. The men now worked under cover, safe in their burrows; one gang relieved another, and the work went on all day.

The Indians were far from doing what was expected of them. Instead of scouting in the direction of Fort Edward to learn the movements of the enemy and prevent surprise, they loitered about the camp and in the trenches, or amused themselves by firing at the fort from behind stumps and logs. Some, in imitation of the French, dug little trenches for themselves, in which they wormed their way towards the rampart, and now and then picked off an artillery-man, not without loss on their own side. On the afternoon of the fifth, Montcalm invited them to a council, gave them belts of wampum, and mildly remonstrated with them. "Why expose yourselves without necessity? I grieve bitterly over the losses that you have met, for the least among you is precious to me. No doubt it is a good thing to annoy the English; but that is not the main point. You ought to inform me of everything the enemy is doing, and always keep parties on the road between the two forts." And he gently hinted that their place was not in his camp, but in that of Lévis, where missionaries were provided for such of them as were Christians, and food and ammunition for them all. They promised, with excellent docility, to do everything he wished, but added that there was something on their hearts. Being encouraged to relieve themselves of the burden, they complained that they had not been consulted as to the management of the siege, but were expected to obey orders like slaves. "We know more about fighting in the woods than you," said their orator; "ask our advice, and you will be the better for it."

Montcalm assured them that if they had been neglected, it was only through the hurry and confusion of the time; expressed high appreciation of their talents for bush-fighting, promised them ample satisfaction, and ended by telling them that in the morning they should hear the big guns. This greatly pleased them, for they were extremely impatient for the artillery to begin. About sunrise the battery of the left opened with eight heavy cannon and a mortar, joined, on the next morning, by the battery of the right, with eleven pieces more. The fort replied with spirit. The cannon thundered all day, and from a hundred peaks and crags the astonished wilderness roared back the sound. The Indians were delighted. They wanted to point the guns; and to humor them, they were now and then allowed to do so. Others lay behind logs and fallen trees, and yelled their satisfaction when they saw the splinters fly from the wooden rampart.

Day after day the weary roar of the distant cannonade fell on the ears of Webb in his camp at Fort Edward. "I have not yet received the least reinforcement," he writes to Loudon; "this is the disagreeable situation we are at present in. The fort, by the heavy firing we hear from the lake, is still in our possession; but I fear it cannot long hold out against so warm a cannonading if I am not reinforced by a sufficient number of militia to march to their relief." The militia were coming; but it was impossible that many could reach him in less than a week. Those from New York alone were within call, and two thousand of them arrived soon after he sent Loudon the above letter. Then, by stripping all the forts below, he could bring together forty-five hundred men; while several French deserters assured him that Montcalm had nearly twelve thousand. To advance to the relief of Monro with a force so inferior, through a defile of rocks, forests, and mountains, made by nature for ambuscades,—and this too with troops who had neither the steadiness of regulars nor the bush-fighting skill of Indians,—was an enterprise for firmer nerve than his.

He had already warned Monro to expect no help

from him. At midnight of the fourth, Captain Bart-
man, his aide-de-camp, wrote: "The General has
ordered me to acquaint you he does not think it
prudent to attempt a junction or to assist you till
reinforced by the militia of the colonies, for the
immediate march of which repeated expresses have
been sent." The letter then declared that the French
were in complete possession of the road between the
two forts, that a prisoner just brought in reported
their force in men and cannon to be very great, and
that, unless the militia came soon, Monro had better
make what terms he could with the enemy.

The chance was small that this letter would reach
its destination; and in fact the bearer was killed by La
Corne's Indians, who, in stripping the body, found
the hidden paper, and carried it to the General.
Montcalm kept it several days, till the English rampart was half battered down; and then, after saluting
his enemy with a volley from all his cannon, he sent
it with a graceful compliment to Monro. It was
Bougainville who carried it, preceded by a drummer
and a flag. He was met at the foot of the glacis,
blindfolded, and led through the fort and along the
edge of the lake to the entrenched camp, where
Monro was at the time. "He returned many thanks,"
writes the emissary in his Diary, "for the courtesy of
our nation, and protested his joy at having to do
with so generous an enemy. This was his answer to

the Marquis de Montcalm. Then they led me back, always with eyes blinded; and our batteries began to fire again as soon as we thought that the English grenadiers who escorted me had had time to re-enter the fort. I hope General Webb's letter may induce the English to surrender the sooner."

By this time the sappers had worked their way to the angle of the lake, where they were stopped by a marshy hollow, beyond which was a tract of high ground, reaching to the fort and serving as the garden of the garrison. Logs and fascines in large quantities were thrown into the hollow, and hurdles were laid over them to form a causeway for the cannon. Then the sap was continued up the acclivity beyond, a trench was opened in the garden, and a battery begun, not two hundred and fifty yards from the fort. The Indians, in great number, crawled forward among the beans, maize, and cabbages, and lay there ensconced. On the night of the seventh, two men came out of the fort, apparently to reconnoitre, with a view to a sortie, when they were greeted by a general volley and a burst of yells which echoed among the mountains; followed by responsive whoops pealing through the darkness from the various camps and lurking-places of the savage warriors far and near.

The position of the besieged was now deplorable. More than three hundred of them had been killed and wounded; small-pox was raging in the fort; the place was a focus of infection, and the casemates were crowded with the sick. A sortie from the entrenched camp and another from the fort had been repulsed with loss. All their large cannon and mortars had been burst, or disabled by shot; only seven small pieces were left fit for service; and the whole of Montcalm's thirty-one cannon and fifteen mortars and howitzers would soon open fire, while the walls were already breached, and an assault was imminent. Through the night of the eighth they fired briskly from all their remaining pieces. In the morning the officers held a council, and all agreed to surrender if honorable terms could be had. A white flag was raised, a drum was beat, and Lieutenant-Colonel Young, mounted on horseback, for a shot in the foot had disabled him from walking, went, followed by a few soldiers, to the tent of Montcalm.

It was agreed that the English troops should march out with the honors of war, and be escorted to Fort Edward by a detachment of French troops; that they should not serve for eighteen months; and that all French prisoners captured in America since the war began should be given up within three months. The stores, munitions, and artillery were to be the prize of the victors, except one field-piece, which the garrison were to retain in recognition of their brave defence.

Before signing the capitulation Montcalm called

the Indian chiefs to council, and asked them to con-
sent to the conditions, and promise to restrain their
young warriors from any disorder. They approved
everything and promised everything. The garrison
then evacuated the fort, and marched to join their
comrades in the entrenched camp, which was
included in the surrender. No sooner were they
gone than a crowd of Indians clambered through the
embrasures in search of rum and plunder. All the
sick men unable to leave their beds were instantly
butchered. "I was witness of this spectacle," says the
missionary Roubaud; "I saw one of these barbarians
come out of the casemates with a human head in his
hand, from which the blood ran in streams, and
which he paraded as if he had got the finest prize in
the world." There was little left to plunder; and the
Indians, joined by the more lawless of the Canadians, turned their attention to the entrenched camp,
where all the English were now collected.

The French guard stationed there could not or
would not keep out the rabble. By the advice of
Montcalm the English stove their rum-barrels; but
the Indians were drunk already with homicidal rage,
and the glitter of their vicious eyes told of the devil
within. They roamed among the tents, intrusive,
insolent, their visages besmirched with war-paint;
grinning like fiends as they handled, in anticipation
of the knife, the long hair of cowering women, of

whom, as well as of children, there were many in the camp, all crazed with fright. Since the last war the New England border population had regarded Indians with a mixture of detestation and horror. Their mysterious warfare of ambush and surprise, their midnight onslaughts, their butcheries, their burnings, and all their nameless atrocities, had been for years the theme of fire-side story; and the dread they excited was deepened by the distrust and dejection of the time. The confusion in the camp lasted through the afternoon. "The Indians," says Bougainville, "wanted to plunder the chests of the English; the latter resisted; and there was fear that serious disorder would ensue. The Marquis de Montcalm ran thither immediately, and used every means to restore tranquillity: prayers, threats, caresses, interposition of the officers and interpreters who have some influence over these savages." "We shall be but too happy if we can prevent a massacre. Detestable position! of which nobody who has not been in it can have any idea, and which makes victory itself a sorrow to the victors. The Marquis spared no efforts to prevent the rapacity of the savages and, I must say it, of certain persons associated with them, from resulting in something worse than plunder. At last, at nine o'clock in the evening, order seemed restored. The Marquis even induced the Indians to promise that, besides the escort agreed upon in the capitulation,

two chiefs for each tribe should accompany the English on their way to Fort Edward." He also ordered
La Corne and the other Canadian officers attached
to the Indians to see that no violence took place. He
might well have done more. In view of the disorders
of the afternoon, it would not have been too much
if he had ordered the whole body of regular troops,
whom alone he could trust for the purpose, to hold
themselves ready to move to the spot in case of out-
break, and shelter their defeated foes behind a hedge
of bayonets.

Bougainville was not to see what ensued; for
Montcalm now sent him to Montreal, as a special
messenger to carry news of the victory. He
embarked at ten o'clock. Returning daylight found
him far down the lake; and as he looked on its still
bosom flecked with mists, and its quiet mountains
sleeping under the flush of dawn, there was nothing
in the wild tranquillity of the scene to suggest the
tragedy which even then was beginning on the
shore he had left behind.

The English in their camp had passed a troubled
night, agitated by strange rumors. In the morning
something like a panic seized them; for they dis-
trusted not the Indians only, but the Canadians. In
their haste to be gone they got together at daybreak,
before the escort of three hundred regulars had
arrived. They had their muskets, but no ammuni-

tion; and few or none of the provincials had bayonets. Early as it was, the Indians were on the alert;
and, indeed, since midnight great numbers of them
had been prowling about the skirts of the camp,
showing, says Colonel Frye, "more than usual malice
in their looks." Seventeen wounded men of his regiment lay in huts, unable to join the march. In the
preceding afternoon Miles Whitworth, the regimental surgeon, had passed them over to the care of a
French surgeon, according to an agreement made at
the time of the surrender; but, the Frenchman being
absent, the other remained with them attending to
their wants. The French surgeon had caused special
sentinels to be posted for their protection. These
were now removed, at the moment when they were
needed most; upon which, about five o'clock in the
morning, the Indians entered the huts, dragged out
the inmates, and tomahawked and scalped them all,
before the eyes of Whitworth, and in presence of La
Corne and other Canadian officers, as well as of a
French guard stationed within forty feet of the spot;
and, declares the surgeon under oath, "none, either
officer or soldier, protected the said wounded men."
The opportune butchery relieved them of a trouble-
some burden.

A scene of plundering now began. The escort had
by this time arrived, and Monro complained to the
officers that the capitulation was broken; but got no

other answer than advice to give up the baggage to the Indians in order to appease them. To this the English at length agreed; but it only increased the excitement of the mob. They demanded rum; and some of the soldiers, afraid to refuse, gave it to them from their canteens, thus adding fuel to the flame. When, after much difficulty, the column at last got out of the camp and began to move along the road that crossed the rough plain between the entrenchment and the forest, the Indians crowded upon them, impeded their march, snatched caps, coats, and weapons from men and officers, tomahawked those that resisted, and, seizing upon shrieking women and children, dragged them off or murdered them on the spot. It is said that some of the interpreters secretly fomented the disorder. Suddenly there rose the screech of the war-whoop. At this signal of butchery, which was given by Abenaki Christians from the mission of the Penobscot, a mob of savages rushed upon the New Hampshire men at the rear of the column, and killed or dragged away eighty of them. A frightful tumult ensued, when Montcalm, Lévis, Bourlamaque, and many other French officers, who had hastened from their camp on the first news of disturbance, threw themselves among the Indians, and by promises and threats tried to allay their frenzy. "Kill me, but spare the English who are under my protection," exclaimed Montcalm. He took from one of them a young officer whom the savage had seized; upon which several other Indians immediately tomahawked their prisoners, lest they too should be taken from them. One writer says that a French grenadier was killed and two wounded in attempting to restore order; but the statement is doubtful. The English seemed paralyzed, and fortunately did not attempt a resistance, which, without ammunition as they were, would have ended in a general massacre. Their broken column straggled forward in wild disorder, amid the din of whoops and shrieks, till they reached the French advance-guard, which consisted of Canadians; and here they demanded protection from the officers, who refused to give it, telling them that they must take to the woods and shift for themselves. Frye was seized by a number of Indians, who, brandishing spears and tomahawks, threatened him with death and tore off his clothing, leaving nothing but breeches, shoes, and shirt. Repelled by the officers of the guard, he made for the woods. A Connecticut soldier who was present says of him that he leaped upon an Indian who stood in his way, disarmed and killed him, and then escaped; but Frye himself does not mention the incident. Captain Burke, also of the Massachusetts regiment, was stripped, after a violent struggle, of all his clothes; then broke loose, gained the woods, spent the night shivering in the thick grass of a marsh, and on the next day reached Fort Edward. Jonathan Carver, a provincial volunteer, declares that, when the tumult was at its height, he saw officers of the French army walking about at a little distance and talking with seeming unconcern. Three or four Indians seized him, brandished their tomahawks over his head, and tore off most of his clothes, while he vainly claimed protection from a sentinel, who called him an English dog, and violently pushed him back among his tormentors. Two of them were dragging him towards the neighboring swamp, when an English officer, stripped of everything but his scarlet breeches, ran by. One of Carver's captors sprang upon him, but was thrown to the ground; whereupon the other went to the aid of his comrade and drove his tomahawk into the back of the Englishman. As Carver turned to run, an English boy, about twelve years old, clung to him and begged for help. They ran on together for a moment, when the boy was seized, dragged from his protector, and, as Carver judged by his shrieks, was murdered. He himself escaped to the forest, and after three days of famine reached Fort Edward.

The bonds of discipline seem for the time to have been completely broken; for while Montcalm and his chief officers used every effort to restore order, even at the risk of their lives, many other officers, chiefly of the militia, failed atrociously to do their duty. How many English were killed it is impossible to tell with exactness. Roubaud says that he saw forty or fifty corpses scattered about the field. Lévis says fifty; which does not include the sick and wounded before murdered in the camp and fort. It is certain that six or seven hundred persons were carried off, stripped, and otherwise maltreated. Montcalm succeeded in recovering more than four hundred of them in the course of the day; and many of the French officers did what they could to relieve their wants by buying back from their captors the clothing that had been torn from them. Many of the fugitives had taken refuge in the fort, whither Monro himself had gone to demand protection for his followers; and here Roubaud presently found a crowd of half-frenzied women, crying in anguish for husbands and children. All the refugees and redeemed prisoners were afterwards conducted to the entrenched camp, where food and shelter were provided for them and a strong guard set for their protection until the fifteenth, when they were sent under an escort to Fort Edward. Here cannon had been fired at intervals to guide those who had fled to the woods, whence they came dropping in from day to day, half dead with famine.

On the morning after the massacre the Indians decamped in a body and set out for Montreal, carrying with them their plunder and some two hundred prisoners, who, it is said, could not be got out of their hands. The soldiers were set to the work of demolishing the English fort; and the task occupied several days. The barracks were torn down, and the huge pine-logs of the rampart thrown into a heap. The dead bodies that filled the casemates were added to the mass, and fire was set to the whole. The mighty funeral pyre blazed all night. Then, on the sixteenth, the army reimbarked. The din of ten thousand combatants, the rage, the terror, the agony, were gone; and no living thing was left but the wolves that gathered from the mountains to feast upon the dead.

# Trenches

[ ALDEN BROOKS ]

I t was a terribly dark night, wet and piercing
cold. The pavements were slippery with a
muddy slush. They tramped along in silence; not
a word; each man his own thoughts, yet each man's
thoughts the same. Slowly, however, their blood
warmed a little, and their shoulderstraps settled into
place. The trenches were five kilometres away to the
north. By the time they reached the field kitchens,
the night was a little less dark; dawn was coming.
There was a wee light burning. They halted beside it
and wondered what was going to happen next. One
or two went and knocked on the rough huts where
the cooks slept. Perhaps there might be some chance
of getting a little coffee.

"Coffee for us? You're crazy. Do you think they'd
waste coffee on us?"

But it so happened that they had halted for just that reason. From the wee light there came a man with great buckets of hot coffee. They gathered about him and held out their tin cups. The man told them not to crowd around so, he could not see what he was doing, and there was plenty for everybody. Standing up, they gulped it down. It was hot. It warmed. Shortly afterward they were filing along the channels through the earth—the third trenches, the second trenches, then slowly into the first trenches. The watchers there rose stiffly and made room for them. A blue rocket shot up from the Germans opposite. It lit up the landscape with a weird light. The earth seemed to grow colder. Then the artillery began intermittently. Then it got to work in earnest, and for half an hour or more it tore the sky above into shreds. They became impatient. They wanted to know what they were waiting for. It was the captain.

"What in the hell is he fussing about now?"

"Oh, he's fussing about the machine-guns!"

"Oh, he's always fussing about something or other!"

"Hell, that's his business!"

Presently the captain came creeping along. He spoke in a low whisper to the young lieutenant in charge of De Barsac's section.

"Are your men ready?"

"Yes, all ready."

"You've placed your machine-guns the way I told you?"

"Yes."

"Good. Then, you understand, you attack right after us. Give me a few minutes, then come out and dash right up."

There was silence again. The captain moved off. Presently George snickered.

"That's all. Dash right up. Well, I'll promise you one thing, old whiskers," he murmured to a watcher by his side, "if I've got to rot and stink out here for the next month, I'll try and carry my carcass as near as I can to their nostrils rather than to yours."

"Shut up," growled Jules.

George looked around.

"God! you're not funking it, are you?"

"Oh, what do you lose? Nothing. Eh! What do you leave behind?"

"Old man, I leave behind more wives than you."

"Yes, I guess you do—yes, I guess you do—yes, I guess that's about it."

"Stop that noise," whispered the lieutenant.

The artillery fire ceased. A minute later they heard the shouts of the other company over to the left, and above the shouting, the rapid, deadly, pank-pank-pank of the German machine-guns. They stood up instinctively; they swung on their knapsacks; they drew out their bayonets and fixed them on their rifles, and while they did so, their breath steamed upon the cold, damp air. Then, standing there in a profound silence, they looked across at each other through that murky morning light and gave up now definitely everything life had brought them. It was a bitter task, much harder for some than for others; but when the lieutenant suddenly said, "At 'em, boys!" all were ready. A low, angry snarl shot from their lips. Like hunted beasts, ready to tear the first thing they met to pieces in a last death-struggle, they scrambled out of the trench. Creeping through the barbed wire, they advanced stealthily until a hail of bullets was turned upon them, then they leaped up with a mighty yell, ran some twenty paces, fell flat upon the ground, and leaped up once more. Head bent down, De Barsac plunged forward. Bullets sang and hissed about him. Every instant he expected death to strike him. He stumbled on, trying to offer it the brain and nothing else. He fell headlong over shell holes, but each time picked himself up and staggered on and on. Hours seemed to pass. He remembered George's words. Not rot here—nor here nor here—but carry one's carcass higher and higher. Finally, he heard the young lieutenant yelling: "Come on, boys, come on, we're almost there." He looked up. Clouds of smoke, bullets ripping up the earth, comrades falling about him, a few hurrying on, all huddled up like men in a terrible rain-storm. Of a sudden he found himself among barbed wire and pit holes. The white bleached face of a man, dead weeks ago, leered at him. He stepped over the putrid body and flung himself through the wire. It tore his clothes, but failed to hold him. Bullets whizzed around his head, but they all seemed to be too high. Then, of a sudden, he realized that he was actually going to reach the trench. He started up. He gripped his rifle in both hands and let out a terrible yell. He became livid with rage. Up out of the ground rose a wave of Germans. He saw George drive his bayonet into the foremost; and as the bayonet snapped off, heard him shout: "Keep it and give it to your sweetheart for a hatpin!" A tall, haggard German charged full at him. He stood his ground, parried the thrust. The German's rifle swung off to one side and exposed his body. With a savage snort he drove his bayonet into the muddy uniform. He felt it go in and in, and instinctively plunged it farther and twisted it around, then heard the wretch scream, and saw him drop his rifle and grasp at life with extended arms, and watched him fall off the bayonet and sink down, bloody hands clasped over his stomach, and a golden ring upon the fourth finger. He stood there weak and flabby. His head began to whirl. Only just in time did he ward off the vicious lunge of a sweating bearded monster. Both rifles rose up locked together into the air. Between their upstretched arms the two men glared at each other.

"Schwein!" hissed the German.

With an adroit twist, De Barsac threw the other off and brought the butt of his rifle down smack upon the moist red forehead. The fellow sank to his knees with a grunt and, eyes closed, vaguely lifted his hand toward his face. De Barsac half fell over him, turned about, and clubbed the exposed neck as hard as he could with his rifle. Bang! went the rifle almost in his sleeve. He swore angrily. But the bullet had only grazed his arm. He leaped on with a loud shout. Within a crater-like opening in the earth a wild, uproarious fight was going on. He caught one glimpse of George swinging the broken leg of a machine-gun and battering in heads right and left, then was engulfed in the melee.

A furious struggle took place—a score of Frenchmen against a score of Germans—in a cockpit of poisoned, shell-tossed earth. None thought of victory, honor. It was merely a wild, frenzied survival of the fittest, wherein each man strove to tear off, rid himself of this fiendish thing against him. Insane with fury, his senses steeped in gore, De Barsac stabbed and clubbed and stabbed; while close by his side a tall Breton, mouth ripped open with a bayonet point, lip flapping down, bellowed horribly: "Kill! Kill! Kill!"

They killed and they killed; then as the contest began to turn rapidly in their favor, their yells became short, swift exclamations of barbaric triumph; then, unexpectedly, it was all over, and the handful of them that remained understood that, by God and by Heaven, they ten, relic though they were of two hundred better men, had actually come through it all alive and on top. The lieutenant, covered with blood, his sword swinging idly from his wrist, staggered over and leaned upon De Barsac's shoulder. In his other hand he held the bespattered broken leg of the machine-gun. So George must be dead. De Barsac burst out laughing nervously. The lieutenant laughed until he had to double up with a fit of coughing. What a picnic! Others sat down, breathing heavily, and told the whole damned German army to come along and see what was waiting for them. But a bullet flew out of the heap of fallen. It burned the skin on De Barsac's forehead like a hot poker. In a twinkling all ten were on their feet again glaring like savages. The lieutenant reached the offender first. The broken leg of the machine-gun came down with an angry thud; then the rest of them turned about and swarmed over the sloping sides of the pit and exterminated, exterminated.

"He's only playing dead. Give him one just the same. Hell! Don't waste a bullet. Here let me. There, take that, sausage!"

The lieutenant climbed up and took a cautious peep over the top of the crater. There was nothing to see. A dull morning sky over a flat rising field. A bit of communicating trench blown in. Way over to the left, like something far off and unreal, the pank-pank-pank of machine-guns and the uproar of desperate fighting. Behind, on the other side, a field littered with fallen figures in light blue, many crawling slowly away.

"What's happening?" asked De Barsac, still out of breath.

"Can't see. The fighting's all over to the left. Everybody seems to have forgotten us. As far as I can judge, this was an outpost, not a real trench."

"Well, whatever it was, it's ours now," said someone.

"Well, why don't they follow us up?"

"Yes, by God, right away, or else—"

"Oh, they will soon!" said the lieutenant, "so get busy—no time to waste. Block up that opening, and fill your sand-bags, all the sand-bags you can find, and dig yourselves in."

But they stood there astonished, irritated. Yes, where were the reinforcements? If reinforcements did not come up, they were as good as rats trapped in a cage. The lieutenant had to repeat his command. Angrily they shoved the dead out of their way and dug themselves in and filled up the sand-bags and built a rampart with them along the top of the hollow. They swore darkly. No reinforcements! Not a man sent to help them! So it was death, after all. By chance they uncovered a cement trough covered with boards and earth, a sort of shelter; and down there were a great number of cartridge-bands for a machine-gun. The sight of them inspired the lieutenant. He went and busied himself over the captured machine-gun, still half buried in the dirt. Only one leg was broken off; that was all. Hurriedly he cleaned the gun and propped it up between the bags. Then he stood back and rubbed his hands together and laughed boyishly and seemed very pleased. The sun came up in the distance; it glittered upon the frost in the fields. But with it came the shells. Cursing furiously, the ten ducked down into the trough, and for an hour or more hooted at the marksmanship. Only one shell exploded in the crater. Though it shrivelled them all up, it merely tossed about a few dead bodies and left a nasty trail of gas. They became desperate savages again. Then the firing ceased, and the lieutenant scrambled out and peered through the sand-bags. He turned back quickly, eyes flashing.

"Here they come, boys!"

They jumped up like madmen and pushed their rifles through the sandbags. The lieutenant sat down at the machine-gun. De Barsac fed the bands. Over the field came a drove of gray-coated men. Their bayonets sparkled wonderfully in the new morning light; yet they ran along all doubled up like men doing some Swedish drill. They seemed to be a vast multitude until the machine-gun began to shoot. Then the ten saw that they were not so many after all.

"Take care she doesn't jam, old man," said the lieutenant to De Barsac.

"Oh, don't worry, she isn't going to jam!"

They were both very cool.

"Ah! now she's getting into them beautifully," said the lieutenant; "look at them fall. There we go. Spit, little lady, spit; that's the way—steady, old man."

As if by some miracle the gray line of a sudden began to break up. Many less came rushing on. They were singing some guttural song. The rifles between the sand-bags answered them like tongues aflame with hate; but the machine-gun answered them even faster still, a remorseless stream of fire. Finally, there were only some seven or eight left. The lieutenant did not seem to notice them.

"You see how idiotic it all is," he said nonchalantly. "These attacks with a company or two? Why, our little friend here could have taken care of a whole battalion!"

Only one man remained. He was yelling fiercely at the top of his lungs. He looked like some devil escaped from hell. He came tearing on. Bullets

[ 148 ]

would not hit him. Then he was right upon them. But he saw now he was alone and his whole expression changed. Across his eyes glistened the light film of fear. The man with the torn lip jumped up.

"Here you are," he spluttered hideously, "all yours!"

A loud report in De Barsac's ears, smoke and the muddy soles of a pair of hobnailed boots trembling against the nozzle of the machine-gun.

"Do you see what I mean?" continued the lieutenant. "What is the use of it? Did I say a battalion? Why we could have managed a whole regiment—now, then, somebody shove those pig feet out of the way, so that I can finish off the whole lot properly."

The sun came up now in earnest and warmed them; but though they sat back in their little caves and ate some of the food they had brought and then rolled cigarettes and smoked them, they were very nervous and impatient. Every so often one of them would go up the other side of the pit and look back. Always the same sight through the tangle of barbed wire—a foreground heaped with dead, a field sprinkled with fallen blue figures, and three or four hundred yards away the trenches they had come from; otherwise, not a soul. Once they waved a handkerchief on a bayonet. It only brought a shower of bullets. So that was it. After they had accomplished the impossible, they were going to be left here to die like this. A little later the shells once more began to explode about them. The aim once more was very poor, but they knew it was the prelude to another attack. Death was again angling for them—and this time—

"Here they come!" shouted the lieutenant.

They stood up and, pushing their rifles well out through the sand-bags, glanced along the barrels. They swore furiously at what they saw—twice as many of the pig-eaters as before. De Barsac anxiously fed the bands to the vibrating machine before him. The lieutenant's face was very stern and set. It had lost its boyish look. Suddenly there was a terrific explosion, clouds of smoke, and a strange new pungent odor of gas. A man left his post and, eyes closed, turned round and round and went staggering down the slope and stumbled over a dead man and lay where he fell. They stopped firing and huddled against their caves until the lieutenant shouted out something and the machine-gun trembled again. Then there were two more frightful explosions right over their heads. Great God! It was their own artillery!

Through the fog of smoke De Barsac could only see the lieutenant, cringed up over the machine. His face became purple with rage as he hissed into De Barsac's ear his whole opinion of the matter. If he had not said anything before, it was because it was not fit that he should; but before dying now he wanted to tell one man, one other Frenchman, what he thought of a general staff who could first send men out stupidly to their slaughter, then abandon them in positions won, and finally kill them off with their own artillery. But De Barsac, now that the smoke had rolled away a little, was hypnotized by the huge gray wave roaring toward them nearer and nearer. The machine-gun seemed to be helpless among them. However many fell, others came rushing on. Then, unexpectedly, a shell skimmed just over the heads of the nine and exploded full among the advancing throngs. It was the most beautiful sight any of the nine had ever seen. The gray figures were not simply knocked over, but blown into pieces. And in quick succession came explosion after explosion. Priceless vengeance! The field seemed to be a mass of volcanoes. The ranks faltered, broke, plunged about blindly in the smoke, turned, and fled. Only a few came charging wildly on. But the trembling little machine-gun lowered its head angrily. One by one the figures went sprawling, just as if each in turn had of a sudden walked on to slippery ice. So ended the second attack. The third attack, following right after, was a fiasco. The artillery now had their measure to a yard. The shells blew up among them before they were half started. The nine along the crater top did not fire a shot. Shortly afterward they heard the roar of an aeroplane overhead. It must have been there all the time, head in the wind. Under the wings were concentric circles of red and white about a blue dot. The mere sight of it intoxicated them like champagne. And when it was all over for the moment, and the distant figure, moving off, waved his hand, they gave him a cheer it was a great pity he could not hear.

"You see, boys," said the lieutenant gayly, "he's telling us that it's all right now. Reinforcements will be up after dark."

They sat back once more and scraped the blood and muck off their uniforms and smoked and found another meal, and for want of a suitable oath mumbled abstractedly to themselves. Long, tedious hours followed. Little by little it grew colder; then, at last, the sun began to go down. A dreary, desolate landscape stretched out all around. But the thought that reinforcements would soon be coming cheered them. They rose up and got ready to go, then stood about impatiently. The lieutenant had to tell them to never mind what was going on behind them, but stick to their posts. It grew darker, and darker still. Now help would be here any minute. They heard voices; but they were mistaken. It became quite dark, night, half an hour, an hour, two hours, and still no one came, only an ever-increasing cannon fire all around them, shells whistling and screaming to and fro over their heads, red and blue rockets, cataclysms of sound ceaselessly belched into the hollow. At last they threw their knapsacks off in disgust and sat down and cursed and swore as they had never cursed or sworn before.

The night air became painfully cold. They had to stand up again and stamp about to keep warm and not fall asleep. The lieutenant told them to fire off their rifles from time to time. Jules came nearer to De Barsac.

"Ah!" grumbled De Barsac, "they're making monkeys of us."

"Yes—or else they don't know we've taken this place."

"Oh, they know that well enough. Look at the artillery. No; they don't want this hole. They never wanted it. We were never meant to get here."

"Yes," said a voice in the darkness, "it's like this: They went to Joffre and said: 'General, some damned fools have gone and taken an outpost over there.' 'The hell they have!' says Joffre. 'Why, the damned fools! Well, give them all the military medal.' 'Very well, General,' says the Johnny who brought the message, 'but they are rather hard to reach,' 'Oh, in that case,' says Joffre, 'just finish the poor devils off with a couple of shells.'"

"Look here, boys," said the lieutenant, "cut that talk out. You know, as well as I do, that Joffre had nothing to do with this—"

"Well, why the devil then doesn't he send some one up to reinforce us?"

"Well," said the lieutenant after a pause, "look at all those fireworks. There's enough iron in the air to kill ten army corps. They don't dare come up."

"Don't dare? Christ! we dared, didn't we?"

"Well, they may come up by and by."

But no one came; just the furious interchange of shells all night long. So dawn appeared once more and found them stiff, weary, half frozen, and in their dull, hollow eyes no longer a ray of hope. And soon the shells began to fall again upon the hollow. Heedlessly the young lieutenant stood up and took a long look back at those trenches from which help should come. A shell broke just above him. He was still standing upright; but the top of his head was gone, only the lower jaw remained. Blood welled up for a second, then the figure slowly sank into a heap. De Barsac took the revolver out of the clinched hand and removed the cartridge-belt. He went back and sat down at the machine-gun.

"Feed the bands, will you, when the time comes?" he said to Jules.

"Look here," said a man, "it's sure death hanging on here any longer. I'm going to make a dash back for it before it is too light."

"Stay where you are," growled De Barsac.

"No, I'm going to take my chance."

"Do you hear what I say? Get back where you belong, or I'll blow your brains out."

More shells exploded over them. They were caught unawares. They had barely time to crawl into the trough. In fact, some of them had not. The man, who at last wanted to run away, doubled himself up grotesquely and coughed blood until he slowly rolled down toward the bottom of the pit. And there amidst the smoke was the man with the torn lip, lying on one elbow, and both legs smashed off above the knees. De Barsac and Jules tried to haul him under cover.

"Don't bother, boys; no, don't bother—I'm done for now—my mouth was nothing—but this finishes me—no, you can't stop it bleeding—so get back quick—and I'm not frightened of death—I like it—really, I do—I've been waiting for it for a long time."

The bombardment continued. It soon became a tremendous affair. It was the worst bombardment any of them had ever experienced. It was as if they were trying to hide in the mouth of a volcano. They never could have imagined such a thing possible. Then it grew even worse still. The very inside of hell was torn loose and hurled at them. Sheltered though they were in the cement trough, they were slowly buried under earth and stones and wood and dead flesh. And so, while they lay there thus, suffocated by gas and smoke, blind, deaf, senseless, the bombardment went on hour after hour. In fact, it was a great wonder that any of them lived on. But they were only six. And it is always difficult to kill the last six among a crowd of dead; the very dead themselves rise up and offer protection. At last the French artillery once more began to gain the master hand, and the bombardment gradually weakened, and finally it ceased altogether. Slowly, very slowly, the six unravelled themselves. They did not recognize their surroundings. Most of the dead had disappeared, just morsels of flesh and bone and uniform, here and there. They did not recognize themselves. As for rifles, knapsacks, machine-gun, ammunition, they had no idea where any of these were. Should an attack come now, they were defenseless. But that was just the point. They had not come out to live, but to die. The bottom of the pit was more or less empty now. One by one they went and sat down there and stared stupidly at the ground. If another shell came into the crater, they would all be killed outright. But no shell came—just a nice, warm midday sun ahead. So, presently, for want of something better to do, they gathered about a blood-soaked loaf of bread, a box of sardines, a canteen full of wine, and in this cockpit of poisonous, shell-tossed earth, with only a blue sky overhead and a few distant melodious shells singing past, they ate their last meal together.

As they ate they slowly decided several things.

First of all, they decided they were cursed; but that,
such being the case and since it was their fate to die
like this, forgotten in this bloodstained hole, they
would die like men, like Frenchmen. Then they
decided that this hole was their property. Back of
them lay France and her millions of acres and her
millions of men; but right here in the very forefront
of the fighting was this sanguinary pit; it belonged
to them, all six of them, and they would die defending it. Then, finally, as soldiers of experience, they
decided many things about modern warfare that all
the thousand and one generals and ministers did not
know. They decided that knapsacks were useless, and
rifles also. What one wanted was a knife, a long
knife—look, about as long as that, well, perhaps a little longer—a revolver, bombs, and endless machine-
guns, light and easy to carry. They agreed it was a
pity none of them would survive to give these valuable conclusions to the others back there.

But after the six had finished their meal and had
smoked up all the tobacco of the only man who had
any left, they decided that death was not so hard
upon them as they first thought. They could still
meet it as it should be met. They rose stiffly and
found here a spade, there a rifle, and eventually the
machine-gun. Under De Barsac's direction they
threw up once more a semblance of a bulwark along
the top of the hollow, and to show that there was still

some fight left in them, fired a few volleys at the Germans, that is to say, all the cartridges they had left, save a full magazine for that last minute when one goes under, killing as many as one can. But whether because the Germans had grown to be a trifle frightened of them, or for some other reason, they received no reply to their taunts beyond an occasional bullet—just a sweet little afternoon when people in cities flock about, straighten their shoulders, sniff the soft atmosphere, and inform each other that Spring is coming. After a time they slumped down where they were, all of them, and stretching out their wet, mud-soaked legs, fell asleep like tired children, and slept on and on until they were awakened in the dark by scores of mysterious figures who patted them on the back, told them they were all heroes, and explained how each time the German artillery had driven them back, and how all they had to do now was to take hold of the rope there and go home to Bray.

So they got up slowly and, hands upon the rope, wandered off. Once they stopped. They heard men digging away busily toward them. They said nothing. They wandered on.

But before the six could reach even the men digging toward them, the darkness was suddenly rent with stupefying explosions, and shell fragments slashed among them. They fell apart, tumbled into shell holes, rose up, fell down again, lost touch with each other, and what became of them all no one will ever know. One or two must have been killed outright; the others must have crawled about in the dark until Fate decided what she wished to do with them. It was rather a sad end; for they deserved better than this, and the Germans did not prevent reinforcements from coming up. But thus ended the six; who they were and what became of them the world will never know.

De Barsac fell flat upon his stomach and put his hands over his head. The ground shook under him. The darkness was a bedlam of endless explosions and death hisses. He rose up again and made a dash for it, a wild, frenzied dash for life and safety. But though he ran on some distance, it was blind work and the ground was littered with obstacles, and suddenly he was lying half buried under a pile of earth. He was in great pain; such that he moaned and moaned; yet he could not move, and now it was less cold and it was morning. Slowly he extricated his right arm, but his left he could not move, and he had to take the dirt away handful by handful, until the sun made his head ache. When his arm was at last uncovered, he could not move it. His whole sleeve was a mass of blood, and the sun had gone of a sudden and it was raining, and the wet ground was tossing him about again like a man in a blanket, and his leg was broken and blood was trickling into his eyes. He moaned upon his arm until the sun again made his head ache, and Jules and his father had disappeared. He asked them to stay there a little longer, but the man next him was so repulsive he could not die thus beside him. Leaning on his right elbow and pushing with his left foot, he moved away inch by inch; only the dead man followed him, or it was his brother, and he was repelled as before, so he took the canteen away from the dead man across his path and drank the stuff down. Then he began to shout at the top of his lungs. A race of bullets swished by over his head. He fell back again on his side and cried weakly into his arm. But presently he crawled on, inch by inch, until even the sun got tired watching him, and he fell down into a sort of trench. There were a lot of dead men there, but all their canteens were empty except one, and he had a great loaf of bread strapped on his knapsack. It was very good inside under the crust.

He sat up and looked around slowly. Just an empty trench, not a living soul, just the dead. How he had got here he could not remember, except that it had taken days, weeks. If his leg were not broken, he might get up now and walk away somewhere. Ah, what dirty luck! As if his arm were not enough! He judged it was late afternoon. He wondered what had happened to the others—well, he would get the machine-gun into place all by himself and kill, kill, right up to the end. Then he remembered that, of course, that was over. Yes, of course.

"I'm out of my head."

He took some more cognac out of the canteen. He found his knife and his emergency roll. Slowly he cut off his sleeve, and slowly over the great bloody hole in his arm he wound the bandage; then he emptied the iodine bottle over it, and yelled and moaned with pain. But by and by he felt better. Some one spoke to him. It was a white face among the black dead men. He gave the fellow cognac. They sat up together and ate bread and drank cognac. They talked together. All the friend had was a bullet through his chest, just a little hole, but he said it hurt him every time he tried to breathe. He belonged to the 45th. The trench here had been taken by the Germans, only the Germans had to abandon it because they had lost a trench over there to the left.

"Yes," said De Barsac. "That was us."

By and by De Barsac asked the friend if he could get up and walk. The friend said he thought he could now. So he got up and fell down, and got up and fell down, until the third time he did not fall.

"Wait," said De Barsac, "my leg's broken."

They helped each other. They went along scraping the sides of the channel. De Barsac moaned in constant agony. But they saw two men with a

stretcher in the fields above. De Barsac halloed feebly. The men turned around with a start; then one of
them said, with a scowl: "All right, wait a minute."
Then there was the ordinary explosion overhead.
They saw nothing more of the two men; just a bit of
broken stretcher and canvas sticking up out of the
ground and a large cloud of dark smoke rolling away
fainter and fainter. The trench was muddy. The
trench smelled. The whole land smelled. The earth
about was all burned yellow. The clay was red. There
were boards in the bottom of the trench, but the
boards wabbled and one could not hop along them.
They slopped and twisted about.

"Here," said the friend, "lean on me some more."

But he only fainted. So they both lay huddled up
in the mud of the channel, and death came down
very near them both. But De Barsac's face was lying
against a tin can in the mud, and he lifted himself up
and saw that it was nearly dark and he shivered with
cold. He remembered the cognac. He gulped it all
down. It hurt his arm, made it throb, throb, throb;
but it somehow also made him feel like laughing. So
he laughed; then he cried; then he laughed; all
because the friend at his side was dead and he loved
him. He had not known him very long, but he loved
him. He turned the head up and the friend's eyes
opened. He was not dead, after all. Quickly De

Barsac hunted for the cognac and at last he found it. He was horrified. He had drunk it all and not left the friend any. But there were just a few drops.

"Thanks, old camel," said the friend.

De Barsac slowly got up and, after he had got up, he helped the friend up.

"Come on."

"All right."

"Here, you get on my back."

"No, you get on mine."

But they both fell again. So they decided to crawl along. Only it was growing colder and colder, and the waits were awful. Finally, the white face said:

"I'm—I'm going to sleep a little—you go on— you see—then you call me—then I'll come along."

De Barsac wondered why they had not thought of doing it that way before. He crawled on and on. At last he stopped and called back. The friend did not come the way he said he would. He was asleep of course. De Barsac started back to fetch him, only some men came along and stepped on him until they suddenly stepped off.

"Yes, he's alive."

De Barsac pointed feebly up the channel.

"He's back there," he said.

"Who?"

"The friend."

"He's delirious," said a voice.

"Well, pass him back to the stretcher-bearers and look lively with those machine-guns."

The dressing-station was all under ground and lined with straw. It was very warm, only it was also very crowded. They gave him some hot soup with vegetables in it. He lay back on the stretcher and perspired; and though he was now in very great pain, he said nothing, because he had nothing to say. The surgeon, sleeves rolled up, bent over him. He set his leg and slapped plaster about. He swabbed his head and made him nearly scream. Then he unwound the bandage on his arm and swore and stood up and said: "Too late. Put on the tag, 'Operate at once.'" It was cold between the two wheels under the open stars amid the cigarette smoke, but the ambulances in Bray made a powerful noise, and through the darkness a sergeant looked at him under a lantern and said impatiently: "Well, I don't give a damn, there isn't an inch of space left. Fire him along to Villers-Bretonneux with that convoy that's starting." The ambulance rocked and bounced over the roads, and it was twice as cold as before. He had not enough blankets. The ambulance smelled so he knew the man to his left must be dead; yes, the man to his left, not the man above, for the man above from time to time dripped hot blood upon him, now upon his neck, now upon his face. In the big shed at Villers-Bretonneux it was warm again, and he lay there upon the straw with the others while crowds of peasant people stared at them. One woman came up and offered him half an orange. He did not take it. Another woman said: "He's out of his head, poor fellow." He said: "No, I'm not." After the man on the stretcher next him had told him he was wounded in the stomach, left shoulder, and both legs, the man on the stretcher next him asked him where he came from and how things were getting on there. He said: "All right." Then the man on the stretcher next him said weakly: "Well, you seem to have picked up all the mud there is up there." So he said: "Oh, there's plenty left!" and a neat little man in black, with a red ribbon in his buttonhole, shook his head and said to a large man staring with a heavy scowl: "They're all that way, you know; a joke on their lips up to the end."

They carried him out through the crowd, and when he was opposite the bloody table under the great arc-light, the men carrying him had to stop a second and the doctor said to the man holding the end of the leg: "Bend down, idiot, haven't you ever sawed wood?" And he saw that there were beads of perspiration upon the doctor's forehead, and he wondered why. In the train it was very, very warm, only it smelled dreadfully—that same smell. He knew now it was the man in the bunk next to him that was dead, and he wanted to tell the attendant so, only the shadows on the wooden ceiling danced about as the train rushed along over bridges and through tunnels. The shadows danced about, and sometimes they were horsemen on chargers and sometimes they were just great clouds flying out across the ocean, and all the time that the shadows danced about and the train rushed on and on a man in the other end of the compartment yelled and swore. But although he called the attendants all the names a man has ever called another, the attendants did not move. One said:

"Well, if they do shunt us over on to that other service, that'll mean we'll get down to Paris now and then."

And the first man answered:

"Oh, well, anything for a change—pass me the morphine again, will you, if you're through with it."

The train stopped, and every one wanted to know where they were. One of the attendants told them, "Amiens." He was taken out slowly and carried before a man with a glossy, black beard, smoking a pipe, who read the tag on his buttonhole and wrote something on a sheet of paper. They took him out into the cold, biting wind of a railway yard and carried him across railway tracks and set the stretcher down in pools of black mud, and argued whose turn it was, while a long freight-train rolled slowly by and a man blew a whistle. The ambulance bobbed lightly over cobbles amid the clang of street-cars and the thousand noises of a city. This ambulance also smelled that same smell; but it could not be the man next him, for he was all alone. Then the ambulance ran along a smooth drive and stopped, and the flaps were opened and he was lifted out and carried into a long hallway, where a small man in red slippers scampered about and told others to come, and a white-hooded woman bent over him.

"What's the matter with him?"

"Operation."

"Yes—his left arm—the smell is sufficient indication. George, tell the doctor not to go away."

The white-hooded woman again leaned over him. Her face was wrinkled and tired, but her eyes were very beautiful—they were so gentle and so sad.

"How do you feel?"

"Yes," he mumbled.

"Poor boy! What's your name?"

"Pierre De Barsac."

She took his hand gently and held it.

"Well, Pierre, don't worry. We are going to take care of you."

A little later she said:

"Poor fellow! Are you suffering?"

Tears came into his eyes and he nodded his head.

They carried him up-stairs. They went up slowly, very carefully, and as they turned the corners of the staircase the eyes of the little man with the red slippers glittered and strained over the end of the stretcher. They undressed him. They washed him. They put him to bed. They unwound his arm. Then they stood away and stopped talking. They left him alone with a great wad of damp cotton upon his arm until the doctor came and said:

"My boy, we've got to amputate your left arm at the shoulder."

"At the shoulder," he repeated mechanically.

"Yes, it's the only thing that will save you. What's your profession?"

"Lawyer."

The doctor smiled pleasantly.

"Oh, then you are all right! An arm the less will be a distinction."

They went away. He turned over a little and looked at his arm. He realized that this was the dead thing he had so often smelled. The arm was all brown. It crackled under his finger; then came the large cotton wad where there were strips of black flesh. The hand was crumpled up like a fallen leaf. He saw the scar on his forefinger where, as a little boy, he had cut through the orange too swiftly. What a scene that was, and his mother was dead now, and his father was very old, and the hand now was going to be taken away from him! He turned his head back and cried weakly, not on account of his hand, but because he was in such pain, his arm, his leg, his head, everything. They rolled him into another room. They fussed about him. They hurt him dreadfully; but he said nothing, because he had nothing to say. Then he was back there again, beside the lieutenant, only the machine-gun jammed and he had to break the leg off and use it against the hordes of pig-eaters, and smoke, more smoke, down one's nostrils, and then it was awful, awful, never like this, and he clutched the pig-eater by the throat and swore, swore, until now more smoke came rolling into his nostrils, and the white-hooded nurse was standing by his bed.

She went away; and when he woke up again, he was all alone. There was a bandage upon his left arm; no, his left shoulder. His arm hurt much less; he felt much better. By and by he moved his right hand over. The sleeve of the nightgown was empty.

He lay there quietly a long time and looked up into the sky through some pine boughs swaying in the wind. They reminded him of other trees he knew of—trees way back there in Brittany by the seaside where he was born. They swayed beautifully to and fro, and every so often they bent over and swished against the window-pane.

Presently he smiled, smiled quietly, happily. Life, when one can live it, is such a really wonderful thing.

# Gunga Din

### [ RUDYARD KIPLING ]

You may talk o' gin and beer
When you're quartered safe out 'ere,
An' you're sent to penny-fights an' Aldershot it;
But when it comes to slaughter
You will do your work on water,
An' you'll lick the bloomin' boots of 'im that's got it.
Now in Injia's sunny clime,
Where I used to spend my time
A-servin' of 'Er Majesty the Queen,
Of all them blackfaced crew
The finest man I knew
Was our regimental bhisti, Gunga Din.
    He was "Din! Din! Din!
  "You limpin' lump o' brick-dust, Gunga Din!
    "Hi! Slippy *hitherao!*

"Water, get it! *Panee lao*,[1]

"You squidgy-nosed old idol, Gunga Din."


The uniform 'e wore
Was nothin' much before,
An' rather less than 'arf o' that be'ind,
For a piece o' twisty rag
An' a goatskin water-bag
Was all the field-equipment 'e could find.
When the sweatin' troop-train lay
In a sidin' through the day,
Where the 'eat would make your bloomin' eyebrows
   crawl,
We shouted "Harry By!"[2]
Till our throats were bricky-dry,
Then we wopped 'im 'cause 'e couldn't serve us all.
    It was "Din! Din! Din!
  "You 'eathen, where the mischief 'ave you been?
    "You put some *juldee*[3] in it
    "Or I'll *marrow*[4] you this minute
    "If you don't fill up my helmet, Gunga Din!"


'E would dot an' carry one


[1]Bring water swiftly.
[2]O brother.
[3]Be quick.
[4]Hit you.

Till the longest day was done;

An' 'e didn't seem to know the use o' fear.

If we charged or broke or cut,

You could bet your bloomin' nut,

'E'd be waitin' fifty paces right flank rear.

With 'is mussick[5] on 'is back,

'E would skip with our attack,

An' watch us till the bugles made "Retire,"

An' for all 'is dirty 'ide

'E was white, clear white, inside

When 'e went to tend the wounded under fire!

    It was "Din! Din! Din!"

  With the bullets kickin' dust-spots on the green.

    When the cartridges ran out,

    You could hear the front-ranks shout,

  "Hi! ammunition-mules an' Gunga Din!"


I shan't forgit the night

When I dropped be'ind the fight

With a bullet where my belt-plate should 'a' been.

I was chokin' mad with thirst,

An' the man that spied me first

Was our good old grinnin', gruntin' Gunga Din.

'E lifted up my 'ead,

An' he plugged me where I bled,

An' 'e guv me 'arf-a-pint o' water green.

---

[5]Water-skin.

It was crawlin' and it stunk,

But of all the drinks I've drunk,

I'm gratefullest to one from Gunga Din.

      It was "Din! Din! Din!

   " 'Ere's a beggar with a bullet through 'is spleen;

     " 'E's chawin' up the ground,

      "An' 'e's kickin' all around:

    "For Gawd's sake git the water, Gunga Din!"


'E carried me away

To where a dooli lay,

An' a bullet come an' drilled the beggar clean.

'E put me safe inside,

An' just before 'e died,

"I 'ope you liked your drink," sez Gunga Din.

So I'll meet 'im later on

At the place where 'e is gone—

Where it's always double drill and no canteen.

'E'll be squattin' on the coals

Givin' drink to poor damned souls,

An' I'll get a swig in hell from Gunga Din!

      Yes, Din! Din! Din!

   You Lazarushian-leather Gunga Din!

     Though I've belted you and flayed you,

      By the livin' Gawd that made you,

    You're a better man than I am, Gunga Din!

# Andrey and Bagration: A Rearguard Action

[ LEO TOLSTOY ]

Prince Andrey mounted his horse but lingered at the battery, looking at the smoke of the cannon from which the ball had flown. His eyes moved rapidly over the wide plain. He only saw that the previously immobile masses of the French were heaving to and fro, and that it really was a battery on the left. The smoke still clung about it. Two Frenchmen on horseback, doubtless adjutants, were galloping on the hill. A small column of the enemy, distinctly visible, were moving downhill, probably to strengthen the line. The smoke of the first shot had not cleared away, when there was a fresh puff of smoke and another shot. The battle was beginning. Prince Andrey turned his horse and galloped back to Grunte to look for Prince Bagration. Behind him he heard the cannonade becoming louder and more frequent. Our men were evidently beginning to reply. Musket shots could be heard below at the spot where the lines were closest. Lemarrois had only just galloped to Murat with Napoleon's menacing letter, and Murat, abashed and anxious to efface his error, at once moved his forces to the centre and towards both flanks, hoping before evening and the arrival of the Emperor to destroy the insignificant detachment before him.

"It has begun! Here it comes!" thought Prince Andrey, feeling the blood rush to his heart. "But where? What form is my Toulon to take?" he wondered.

Passing between the companies that had been eating porridge and drinking vodka a quarter of an hour before, he saw everywhere nothing but the same rapid movements of soldiers forming in ranks and getting their guns, and on every face he saw the same eagerness that he felt in his heart. "It has begun! Here it comes! Terrible and delightful!" said the face of every private and officer. Before he reached the earthworks that were being thrown up, he saw in the evening light of the dull autumn day men on horseback crossing towards him. The foremost, wearing a cloak and an Astrachan cap, was riding on a white horse. It was Prince Bagration. Prince Andrey stopped and waited for him to come up. Prince Bagration stopped his horse, and recognising Prince

Andrey nodded to him. He still gazed on ahead
while Prince Andrey told him what he had been
seeing.

The expression: "It has begun! it is coming!" was
discernible even on Prince Bagration's strong, brown
face, with his half-closed, lustreless, sleepy-looking
eyes. Prince Andrey glanced with uneasy curiosity at
that impassive face, and he longed to know: Was that
man thinking and feeling, and what was he thinking
and feeling at that moment? "Is there anything at all
there behind that impassive face?" Prince Andrey
wondered, looking at him. Prince Bagration nodded
in token of his assent to Prince Andrey's words, and
said: "Very good," with an expression that seemed to
signify that all that happened, and all that was told
him, was exactly what he had foreseen. Prince
Andrey, panting from his rapid ride, spoke quickly.
Prince Bagration uttered his words in his Oriental
accent with peculiar deliberation, as though impress-
ing upon him that there was no need of hurry. He
did, however, spur his horse into a gallop in the
direction of Tushin's battery. Prince Andrey rode
after him with his suite. The party consisted of an
officer of the suite, Bagration's private adjutant,
Zherkov, an orderly officer, the staff-officer on duty,
riding a beautiful horse of English breed, and a civilian official, the auditor, who had asked to be present
from curiosity to see the battle. The auditor, a plump

man with a plump face, looked about him with a naïve smile of amusement, swaying about on his horse, and cutting a queer figure in his cloak on his saddle among the hussars, Cossacks, and adjutants.

"This gentleman wants to see a battle," said Zherkov to Bolkonsky, indicating the auditor, "but has begun to feel queer already."

"Come, leave off," said the auditor, with a beaming smile at once naïve and cunning, as though he were flattered at being the object of Zherkov's jests, and was purposely trying to seem stupider than he was in reality.

"It's very curious, *mon Monsieur Prince*," said the staff-officer on duty (He vaguely remembered that the title *prince* was translated in some peculiar way in French, but could not get it quite right.) By this time they were all riding up to Tushin's battery, and a ball struck the ground before them.

"What was that falling?" asked the auditor, smiling naïvely.

"A French pancake," said Zherkov.

"That's what they hit you with, then?" asked the auditor. "How awful!" And he seemed to expand all over with enjoyment. He had hardly uttered the words when again there was a sudden terrible whiz, which ended abruptly in a thud into something soft, and flop—a Cossack, riding a little behind and to the right of the auditor, dropped from his horse to the ground. Zherkov and the staff-officer bent forward over their saddles and turned their horses away. The auditor stopped facing the Cossack, and looking with curiosity at him. The Cossack was dead, the horse was still struggling.

Prince Bagration dropped his eyelids, looked round, and seeing the cause of the delay, turned away indifferently, seeming to ask, "Why notice these trivial details?" With the ease of a first-rate horseman he stopped his horse, bent over a little and disengaged his sabre, which had caught under his cloak. The sabre was an old-fashioned one, unlike what are worn now. Prince Andrey remembered the story that Suvorov had given his saber to Bagration in Italy, and the recollection was particularly pleasant to him at that moment. They had ridden up to the very battery from which Prince Andrey had surveyed the field of battle.

"Whose company?" Prince Bagration asked of the artilleryman standing at the ammunition boxes.

He asked in words: "Whose company?" but what he was really asking was, "You're not in a panic here?" And the artilleryman understood that.

"Captain Tushin's, your excellency," the red-haired, freckled artilleryman sang out in a cheerful voice, as he ducked forward.

"To be sure, to be sure," said Bagration, pondering something, and he rode by the platforms up to the end cannon. Just as he reached it, a shot boomed from the cannon, deafening him and his suite, and in the smoke that suddenly enveloped the cannon the artillerymen could be seen hauling at the cannon, dragging and rolling it back to its former position. A broad-shouldered, gigantic soldier, gunner number one, with a mop, darted up to the wheel and planted himself, his legs wide apart; while number two, with a shaking hand, put the charge into the cannon's mouth; a small man with stooping shoulders, the officer Tushin, stumbling against the cannon, dashed forward, not noticing the general, and looked out, shading his eyes with his little hand.

"Another two points higher, and it will be just right," he shouted in a shrill voice, to which he tried to give a swaggering note utterly out of keeping with his figure. "Two!" he piped. "Smash away, Medvyedev!"

Bagration called to the officer, and Tushin went up to the general, putting three fingers to the peak of his cap with a timid and awkward gesture, more like a priest blessing some one than a soldier saluting. Though Tushin's guns had been intended to cannonade the valley, he was throwing shells over the village of Schöngraben, in part of which immense masses of French soldiers were moving out.

No one had given Tushin instructions at what or with what to fire, and after consulting his sergeant,

Zaharchenko, for whom he had a great respect, he had decided that it would be a good thing to set fire to the village. "Very good!" Bagration said, on the officer's submitting that he had done so, and he began scrutinizing the whole field of battle that lay unfolded before him. He seemed to be considering something. The French had advanced nearest on the right side. In the hollow where the stream flowed, below the eminence on which the Kiev regiment was stationed, could be heard a continual roll and crash of guns, the din of which was overwhelming. And much further to the right, behind the dragoons, the officer of the suite pointed out to Bagration a column of French outflanking our flank. On the left the horizon was bounded by the copse close by. Prince Bagration gave orders for two battalions from the center to go to the right to reinforce the flank. The officer of the suite ventured to observe to the prince that the removal of these battalions would leave the cannon unprotected. Prince Bagration turned to the officer of the suite and stared at him with his lustreless eyes in silence. Prince Andrey thought that the officer's observation was a very just one, and that really there was nothing to be said in reply. But at that instant an adjutant galloped up with a message from the colonel of the regiment in the hollow that immense masses of the French were coming down upon them, that his men were in disorder and retreating upon the Kiev grenadiers, Prince Bagration nodded to signify his assent and approval. He rode at a walking pace to the right, and sent an adjutant to the dragoons with orders to attack the French. But the adjutant returned half an hour later with the news that the colonel of the dragoons had already retired beyond the ravine, as a destructive fire had been opened upon him, and he was losing his men for nothing, and so he had concentrated his men in the wood.

"Very good!" said Bagration.

Just as he was leaving the battery, shots had been heard in the wood on the left too; and as it was too far to the left flank for him to go himself, Prince Bagration despatched Zherkov to tell the senior general—the general whose regiment had been inspected by Kutuzov at Braunau—to retreat as rapidly as possible beyond the ravine, as the right flank would probably not long be able to detain the enemy. Tushin, and the battalion that was to have defended his battery, was forgotten. Prince Andrey listened carefully to Prince Bagration's colloquies with the commanding officers, and to the orders he gave them, and noticed, to his astonishment, that no orders were really given by him at all, but that Prince Bagration confined himself to trying to appear as though everything that was being done of necessity, by chance, or at the will of individual officers, was all done, if not by his orders, at least in accordance with his intentions. Prince Andrey observed, however, that, thanks to the tact shown by Prince Bagration, notwithstanding that what was done was due to chance, and not dependent on the commander's will, his presence was of the greatest value. Commanding officers, who rode up to Bagration looking distraught, regained their composure; soldiers and officers greeted him cheerfully, recovered their spirits in his presence, and were unmistakably anxious to display their pluck before him.

After riding up to the highest point of our right flank, Prince Bagration began to go downhill, where a continuous roll of musketry was heard and nothing could be seen for the smoke. The nearer they got to the hollow the less they could see, and the more distinctly could be felt the nearness of the actual battlefield. They began to meet wounded men. Two soldiers were dragging one along, supporting him on each side. His head was covered with blood; he had no cap, and was coughing and spitting. The bullet had apparently entered his mouth or throat. Another one came towards them, walking pluckily alone without his gun, groaning aloud and wringing his hands from the pain of a wound from which the blood was flowing, as though from a bottle, over his greatcoat. His face looked more frightened than in pain. He had been wounded only a moment before. Crossing the road, they began going down a deep descent, and on the slope they saw several men lying on the ground. They were met by a crowd of soldiers, among them some who were not wounded. The soldiers were hurrying up the hill, gasping for breath, and in spite of the general's presence, they were talking loudly together and gesticulating with their arms. In the smoke ahead of them they could see now rows of grey coats, and the commanding officer, seeing Bagration, ran after the group of retreating soldiers, calling upon them to come back. Bagration rode up to the ranks, along which there was here and there a rapid snapping of shots drowning the talk of the soldiers and the shouts of the officers. The whole air was reeking with smoke. The soldiers' faces were all full of excitement and smudged with powder. Some were plugging with their ramrods, others were putting powder on the touch-pans, and getting charges out of their pouches, others were firing their guns. But it was impossible to see at whom they were firing from the smoke, which the wind did not lift. The pleasant hum and whiz of the bullets was repeated pretty rapidly. "What is it?" wondered Prince Andrey, as he rode up to the crowd of soldiers. "It can't be the line, for they are all crowded together; it can't be an attacking party, for they are not moving; it can't be a square, they are not standing like one."

A thin, weak-looking colonel, apparently an old man, with an amiable smile, and eyelids that half-covered his old-looking eyes and gave him a mild air, rode up to Prince Bagration and received him as though he were welcoming an honoured guest into his house. He announced to Prince Bagration that his regiment had had to face a cavalry attack of the French, that though the attack had been repulsed, the regiment had lost more than half of its men. The colonel said that the attack had been repulsed, sup-posing that to be the proper military term for what had happened; but he did not really know himself what had been taking place during that half hour in the troops under his command, and could not have said with any certainty whether the attack had been repelled or his regiment had been beaten by the attack. All he knew was that at the beginning of the action balls and grenades had begun flying all about his regiment, and killing men, that then some one had shouted "cavalry," and our men had begun fir-ing. And they were firing still, though not now at the cavalry, who had disappeared, but at the French infantry, who had made their appearance in the hol-low and were firing at our men. Prince Bagration nodded his head to betoken that all this was exactly what he had desired and expected. Turning to an adjutant, he commanded him to bring down from the hill the two battalions of the Sixth Chasseurs, by whom they had just come. Prince Andrey was struck at that instant by the change that had come over Prince Bagration's face. His face wore the look of concentrated and happy determination, which may be seen in a man who in a hot day takes the final run before a header into the water. The lustreless, sleepy look in the eyes, the affectation of profound thought had gone. The round, hard, eagle eyes looked ecstatically and rather disdainfully before him, obviously not resting on anything, though there was still the same deliberation in his measured movements.

The colonel addressed a protest to Prince Bagration, urging him to go back, as there it was too dangerous for him. "I beg of you, your excellency, for God's sake!" he kept on saying, looking for support to the officer of the suite, who only turned away from him.

"Only look, your excellency!" He called his attention to the bullets which were continually whizzing, singing, and hissing about them. He spoke in the tone of protest and entreaty with which a carpenter speaks to a gentleman who has picked up a hatchet. "We are used to it, but you may blister your fingers." He talked as though these bullets could not kill him, and his half-closed eyes gave a still more persuasive effect to his words. The staff-officer added his protests to the colonel, but Bagration made them no answer. He merely gave the order to cease firing, and to form so as to make room for the two battalions of reinforcements. Just as he was speaking the cloud of smoke covering the hollow was lifted as by an unseen hand and blown by the rising wind from right to left, and the opposite hill came into sight with the French moving across it. All eyes instinctively fastened on that French column moving down upon them and winding in and out over the ups and downs of the ground. Already they could see the fur caps of the soldiers, could distinguish officers from privates, could see their flag flapping against its staff.

"How well they're marching," said some one in Bagration's suite.

The front part of the column was already dipping down into the hollow. The engagement would take place then on the nearer side of the slope . . .

The remnants of the regiment that had already been in action, forming hurriedly, drew off to the right; the two battalions of the Sixth Chasseurs marched up in good order, driving the last stragglers before them. They had not yet reached Bagration, but the heavy, weighty tread could be heard of the whole mass keeping step. On the left flank, nearest of all to Bagration, marched the captain, a round-faced imposing-looking man, with a foolish and happy expression of face. It was the same infantry officer who had run out of the shanty after Tushin. He was obviously thinking of nothing at the moment, but that he was marching before his commander in fine style. With the complacency of a man on parade, he stepped springing on his muscular legs, drawing himself up without the slightest effort, as though he were swinging, and this easy elasticity was a striking contrast to the heavy tread of the soldiers keeping step with him. He wore hanging by his leg an unsheathed, slender, narrow sword (a small bent sabre, more like a toy than a weapon), and looking about him, now at the commander, now behind, he turned his whole powerful frame round without getting out of step. It looked as though all the force of his soul was directed to marching by his commander in the best style possible. And conscious that he was accomplishing this, he was happy. "Left . . . left . . . left . . ." he seemed to be inwardly repeating at each alternate step. And the wall of soldierly figures, weighed down by their knapsacks and guns, with their faces all grave in different ways, moved by in the same rhythm, as though each of the hundreds of soldiers were repeating mentally at each alternate step, "Left . . . left . . . left . . ." A stout major skirted a bush on the road, puffing and shifting his step. A soldier, who had dropped behind, trotted after the company, looking panic-stricken at his own defection. A cannon ball, whizzing through the air, flew over the heads of Prince Bagration and his suite, and in time to the same rhythm, "Left . . . left . . ." it fell into the column.

"Close the ranks!" rang out the jaunty voice of the captain. The soldiers marched in a half circle round something in the place where the ball had fallen, and an old cavalryman, an under officer, lingered behind near the dead, and overtaking his line, changed feet with a hop, got into step, and looked angrily about him. "Left . . . left . . . left . . ." seemed to echo out of the menacing silence and the monotonous sound of the simultaneous tread of the feet on the ground.

"Well done, lads!" said Prince Bagration.

"For your ex . . . slen, slen, slency!" rang out along the ranks. A surly-looking soldier, marching on the left, turned his eyes on Bagration as he shouted, with an expression that seemed to say, "We know that without telling." Another, opening his mouth wide, shouted without glancing round, and marched on, as though afraid of letting his attention stray. The order was given to halt and take off their knapsacks.

Bagration rode round the ranks of men who had marched by him, and then dismounted from his horse. He gave the reins to a Cossack, took off his cloak and handed it to him, stretched his legs and set his cap straight on his head. The French column with the officers in front came into sight under the hill.

"With God's help!" cried Bagration in a resolute, sonorous voice. He turned for one instant to the front line, and swinging his arms a little with the awkward, lumbering gait of a man always on horseback, he walked forward over the uneven ground. Prince Andrey felt that some unseen force was drawing him forward, and he had a sensation of great happiness.[1]

The French were near. Already Prince Andrey, walking beside Bagration, could distinguish clearly the sashes, the red epaulettes, even the faces of the French. (He saw distinctly one bandy-legged old French officer, wearing Hessian boots, who was getting up the hill with difficulty, taking hold of the bushes.) Prince Bagration gave no new command, and still marched in front of the ranks in the same silence. Suddenly there was the snap of a shot among the French, another and a third . . . and smoke rose and firing rang out in all the broken-up ranks of the enemy. Several of our men fell, among them the

---

[1]This was the attack of which Thiers says: "The Russians behaved valiantly and, which is rare in warfare, two bodies of infantry marched resolutely upon each other, neither giving way before the other came up." And Napoleon on St. Helena said: "Some Russian battalions showed intrepidity."

round-faced officer, who had been marching so carefully and complacently. But at the very instant of the first shot, Bagration looked round and shouted, "Hurrah!" "Hura . . . a . . . a . . . ah!" rang out along our lines in a prolonged roar, and outstripping Prince Bagration and one another, in no order, but in an eager and joyous crowd, our men ran downhill after the routed French.

The attack of the Sixth Chasseurs covered the retreat of the right flank. In the centre Tushin's forgotten battery had succeeded in setting fire to Schöngraben and delaying the advance of the French. The French stayed to put out the fire, which was fanned by the wind, and this gave time for the Russians to retreat. The retreat of the centre beyond the ravine was hurried and noisy; but the different companies kept apart. But the left flank, which consisted of the Azovsky and Podolsky infantry and the Pavlograd hussars, was simultaneously attacked in front and surrounded by the cream of the French army under Lannes, and was thrown into disorder. Bagration had sent Zherkov to the general in command of the left flank with orders to retreat immediately.

Zherkov, keeping his hand still at his cap, had briskly started his horse and galloped off. But no sooner had he ridden out of Bagration's sight than his courage failed him. He was overtaken by a panic he could not contend against, and he could not bring himself to go where there was danger.

After galloping some distance towards the troops of the left flank, he rode not forward where he heard firing, but off to look for the general and the officers in a direction where they could not by any possibility be; and so it was that he did not deliver the message.

The command of the left flank belonged by right of seniority to the general of the regiment in which Dolohov was serving—the regiment which Kutuzov had inspected before Braunau. But the command of the extreme left flank had been entrusted to the colonel of the Pavlograd hussars, in which Rostov was serving. Hence arose a misunderstanding. Both commanding officers were intensely exasperated with one another, and at a time when fighting had been going on a long while on the right flank, and the French had already begun their advance on the left, these two officers were engaged in negotiations, the sole aim of which was the mortification of one another. The regiments—cavalry and infantry alike were by no means in readiness for the engagement. No one from the common soldier to the general expected a battle; and they were all calmly engaged in peaceful occupations—feeding their horses in the cavalry, gathering wood in the infantry.

"He is my senior in rank, however," said the German colonel of the hussars, growing very red and addressing an adjutant, who had ridden up. "So let him do as he likes. I can't sacrifice my hussars. Bugler! Sound the retreat!"

But things were becoming urgent. The fire of cannon and musketry thundered in unison on the right and in the centre, and the French tunics of Lannes's sharpshooters had already passed over the milldam, and were forming on this side of it hardly out of musket-shot range.

The infantry general walked up to his horse with his quivering strut, and mounting it and drawing himself up very erect and tall, he rode up to the Pavlograd colonel. The two officers met with affable bows and concealed fury in their hearts.

"Again, colonel," the general said, "I cannot leave half my men in the wood. I *beg* you, I *beg* you," he repeated, "to occupy the *position*, and prepare for an attack."

"And I beg you not to meddle in what's not your business," answered the colonel, getting hot. "If you were a cavalry officer . . ."

"I am not a cavalry officer, colonel, but I am a Russian general, and if you are unaware of the fact . . ."

"I am fully aware of it, your excellency," the colonel screamed suddenly, setting his horse in motion and becoming purple in the face. "If you care to come to the front, you will see that this position cannot be held. I don't want to massacre my regiment for your satisfaction."

"You forget yourself, colonel. I am not considering my own satisfaction, and I do not allow such a thing to be said."

Taking the colonel's proposition as a challenge to his courage, the general squared his chest and rode scowling beside him to the front line, as though their whole difference would inevitably be settled there under the enemy's fire. They reached the line, several bullets flew by them, and they stood still without a word. To look at the front line was a useless proceeding, since from the spot where they had been standing before, it was clear that the cavalry could not act, owing to the bushes and the steep and broken character of the ground, and that the French were outflanking the left wing. The general and the colonel glared sternly and significantly at one another, like two cocks preparing for a fight, seeking in vain for a symptom of cowardice. Both stood the test without flinching. Since there was nothing to be said, and neither was willing to give the other grounds for asserting that he was the first to withdraw from under fire, they might have remained a long while standing there, mutually testing each other's pluck, if there had not at that moment been heard in the copse, almost behind them, the snap of musketry and a confused shout of voices. The French were attack-ing the soldiers gathering wood in the copse. The hussars could not now retreat, nor could the infantry. They were cut off from falling back on the left by the French line. Now, unfavourable as the ground was, they must attack to fight a way through for themselves.

The hussars of the squadron in which Rostov was an ensign had hardly time to mount their horses when they were confronted by the enemy. Again, as on the Enns bridge, there was no one between the squadron and the enemy, and between them lay that terrible border-line of uncertainty and dread, like the line dividing the living from the dead. All the soldiers were conscious of that line, and the question whether they would cross it or not, and how they would cross it, filled them with excitement.

The colonel rode up to the front, made some angry reply to the questions of the officers, and, like a man desperately insisting on his rights, gave some command. No one said anything distinctly, but through the whole squadron there ran a vague rumour of attack. The command to form in order rang out, then there was the clank of sabres being drawn out of their sheaths. But still no one moved. The troops of the left flank, both the infantry and the hussars, felt that their commanders themselves did not know what to do, and the uncertainty of the commanders infected the soldiers.

"Make haste, if only they'd make haste," thought Rostov, feeling that at last the moment had come to taste the joys of the attack, of which he had heard so much from his comrades.

"With God's help, lads," rang out Denisov's voice, "forward, quick, gallop!"

The horses' haunches began moving in the front line. Rook pulled at the reins and set off of himself.

On the right Rostov saw the foremost lines of his own hussars, and still further ahead he could see a dark streak, which he could not distinguish clearly, but assumed to be the enemy. Shots could be heard, but at a distance.

"Quicker!" rang out the word of command, and Rostov felt the drooping of Rook's hindquarters as he broke into a gallop. He felt the joy of the gallop coming, and was more and more lighthearted. He noticed a solitary tree ahead of him. The tree was at first in front of him, in the middle of that border-land that had seemed so terrible. But now they had crossed it and nothing terrible had happened, but he felt more lively and excited every moment. "Ah, won't I slash at him!" thought Rostov, grasping the hilt of his sabre tightly. "Hur . . . r . . . a . . . a!" roared voices.

"Now, let him come on, whoever it may be,"

thought Rostov, driving the spurs into Rook, and outstripping the rest, he let him go at full gallop. Already the enemy could be seen in front. Suddenly something swept over the squadron like a broad broom. Rostov lifted his sabre, making ready to deal a blow, but at that instant the soldier Nikitenko galloped ahead and left his side, and Rostov felt as though he were in a dream being carried forward with supernatural swiftness and yet remaining at the same spot. An hussar, Bandartchuk, galloped up from behind close upon him and looked angrily at him. Bandartchuk's horse started aside, and he galloped by.

"What's the matter? I'm not moving? I've fallen, I'm killed . . ." Rostov asked and answered himself all in one instant. He was alone in the middle of the field. Instead of the moving horses and the hussars' backs, he saw around him the motionless earth and stubblefield. There was warm blood under him.

"No, I'm wounded, and my horse is killed." Rook tried to get up on his forelegs, but he sank again, crushing his rider's leg under his leg. Blood was flowing from the horse's head. The horse struggled, but could not get up. Rostov tried to get up, and fell down too. His sabretache had caught in the saddle. Where our men were, where were the French, he did not know. All around him there was no one.

Getting his leg free, he stood up. "Which side,

where now was that line that had so sharply divided the two armies?" he asked himself, and could not answer. "Hasn't something gone wrong with me? Do such things happen, and what ought one to do in such cases?" he wondered as he was getting up. But at that instant he felt as though something superfluous was hanging on his benumbed left arm. The wrist seemed not to belong to it. He looked at his hand, carefully searching for blood on it. "Come, here are some men," he thought joyfully, seeing some men running towards him. "They will help me!" In front of these men ran a single figure in a strange shako and a blue coat, with a swarthy sunburnt face and a hooked nose. Then came two men, and many more were running up behind. One of them said some strange words, not Russian. Between some similar figures in similar shakoes behind stood a Russian hussar. He was being held by the arms; behind him they were holding his horse too.

"It must be one of ours taken prisoner. . . . Yes. Surely they couldn't take me too? What sort of men are they?" Rostov was still wondering, unable to believe his own eyes. "Can they be the French?" He gazed at the approaching French, and although only a few seconds before he had been longing to get at these Frenchmen and to cut them down, their being so near seemed to him now so awful that he could not believe his eyes. "Who are they? What are they running for? Can it be to me? Can they be running to me? And what for? To kill me? *Me*, whom every one's so fond of?" He recalled his mother's love, the love of his family and his friends, and the enemy's intention of killing him seemed impossible. "But they may even kill me." For more than ten seconds he stood, not moving from the spot, nor grasping his position. The foremost Frenchman with the hook nose was getting so near that he could see the expression of his face. And the excited, alien countenance of the man, who was running so lightly and breathlessly towards him, with his bayonet lowered, terrified Rostov. He snatched up his pistol, and instead of firing with it, flung it at the Frenchman and ran to the bushes with all his might. Not with the feeling of doubt and conflict with which he had moved at the Enns bridge, did he now run, but with the feeling of a hare fleeing from the dogs. One unmixed feeling of fear for his young, happy life took possession of his whole being. Leaping rapidly over the hedges with the same impetuosity with which he used to run when he played games, he flew over the field, now and then turning his pale, good-natured, youthful face, and a chill of horror ran down his spine. "No, better not to look," he thought, but as he got near to the bushes he looked round once more. The French had given it up, and just at the moment when he looked round the foremost man was just dropping from a run into a walk, and turning round to shout something loudly to a comrade behind. Rostov stopped. "There's some mistake," he thought; "it can't be that they meant to kill me." And meanwhile his left arm was as heavy as if a hundred pound weight were hanging on it. He could run no further. The Frenchman stopped too and took aim. Rostov frowned and ducked. One bullet and then another flew hissing by him; he took his left hand in his right, and with a last effort ran as far as the bushes. In the bushes there were Russian sharpshooters.

The infantry, who had been caught unawares in the copse, had run away, and the different companies all confused together had retreated in disorderly crowds. One soldier in a panic had uttered those words—terrible in war and meaningless: "Cut off!" and those words had infected the whole mass with panic.

"Out flanked! Cut off! Lost!" they shouted as they ran.

When their general heard the firing and the shouts in the rear he had grasped at the instant that something awful was happening to his regiment; and the thought that he, an exemplary officer, who had served so many years without ever having been guilty of the slightest shortcoming, might be held responsible by his superiors for negligence or lack of discipline, so affected him that, instantly oblivious of the insubordinate cavalry colonel and his dignity as a general, utterly oblivious even of danger and of the instinct of self-preservation, he clutched at the crupper of his saddle, and spurring his horse, galloped off to the regiment under a perfect hail of bullets that luckily missed him. He was possessed by the one desire to find out what was wrong, and to help and correct the mistake whatever it might be, if it were a mistake on his part, so that after twenty-two years of exemplary service, without incurring a reprimand for anything, he might avoid being responsible for this blunder.

Galloping successfully between the French forces, he reached the field behind the copse across which our men were running downhill, not heeding the word of command. That moment had come of moral vacillation which decides the fate of battles. Would these disorderly crowds of soldiers hear the voice of their commander, or, looking back at him, run on further? In spite of the despairing yell of the commander, who had once been so awe-inspiring to his soldiers, in spite of his infuriated, purple face, distorted out of all likeness to itself, in spite of his brandished sword, the soldiers still ran and talked together, shooting into the air and not listening to the word of command. The moral balance which decides the fate of battle was unmistakably falling on the side of panic.

The general was choked with screaming and gunpowder-smoke, and he stood still in despair. All seemed lost; but at that moment the French, who had been advancing against our men, suddenly, for no apparent reason, ran back, vanished from the edge of the copse, and Russian sharp-shooters appeared in the copse. This was Timohin's division, the only one that had retained its good order in the copse, and hiding in ambush in the ditch behind the copse, had suddenly attacked the French. Timohin had rushed with such a desperate yell upon the French, and with such desperate and drunken energy had he dashed at the enemy with only a sword in his hand, that the French flung down their weapons and fled without pausing to recover themselves. Dolohov, running beside Timohin, killed one French soldier at close quarters, and was the first to seize by the collar an officer who surrendered. The fleeing Russians came back; the battalions were brought together; and the French, who had been on the point of splitting the forces of the left flank into two parts, were for the moment held in check. The reserves had time to join the main forces, and the runaways were stopped. The general stood with Major Ekonomov at the bridge, watching the retreating companies go by, when a soldier ran up to him, caught hold of his stirrup and almost clung on to it. The soldier was wearing a coat of blue fine cloth, he had no knapsack nor shako, his head was bound up, and across his shoulders was slung a French cartridge case. In his hand he held an officer's sword. The soldier was pale, his blue eyes looked impudently into the general's face, but his mouth was smiling. Although the general was engaged in giving instructions to Major Ekonomov, he could not help noticing this soldier.

"Your excellency, here are two trophies," said Dolohov, pointing to the French sword and cartridge case. "An officer was taken prisoner by me. I stopped the company." Dolohov breathed hard from weariness; he spoke in jerks. "The whole company can bear me witness. I beg you to remember me, your excellency!"

"Very good, very good," said the general, and he turned to Major Ekonomov. But Dolohov did not leave him; he undid the bandage, and showed the blood congealed on his head.

"A bayonet wound; I kept my place in the front. Remember me, your excellency."

Tushin's battery had been forgotten, and it was only at the very end of the action that Prince Bagration, still hearing the cannonade in the centre, sent the staff-officer on duty and then Prince Andrey to command the battery to retire as quickly as possible.

The force which had been stationed near Tushin's cannons to protect them had by somebody's orders retreated in the middle of the battle. But the battery still kept up its fire, and was not taken by the French simply because the enemy could not conceive of the reckless daring of firing from four cannons that were quite unprotected. The French supposed, on the contrary, judging from the energetic action of the battery, that the chief forces of the Russians were concentrated here in the centre, and twice attempted to attack that point, and both times were driven back by the grapeshot fired on them from the four cannons which stood in solitude on the heights. Shortly after Prince Bagration's departure, Tushin had succeeded in setting fire to Schöngraben.

"Look, what a fuss they're in! It's flaming! What a smoke! Smartly done! First-rate! The smoke! the smoke!" cried the gunners, their spirits reviving.

All the guns were aimed without instructions in the direction of the conflagration. The soldiers, as though they were urging each other on, shouted at every volley: "Bravo! That's something like now! Go it! . . . First-rate!" The fire, fanned by the wind, soon spread. The French columns, who had marched out beyond the village, went back, but as though in revenge for this mischance, the enemy stationed ten cannons a little to the right of the village, and began firing from them on Tushin.

In their childlike glee at the conflagration of the village, and the excitement of their successful firing on the French, our artillerymen only noticed this battery when two cannon-balls and after them four more fell among their cannons, and one knocked over two horses and another tore off the foot of a gunner. Their spirits, however, once raised, did not flag; their excitement simply found another direction. The horses were replaced by others from the ammunition carriage; the wounded were removed, and the four cannons were turned facing the ten of the enemy's battery. The other officer, Tushin's comrade, was killed at the beginning of the action, and after an hour's time, of the forty gunners of the battery, seventeen were disabled, but they were still as merry and as eager as ever. Twice they noticed the French appearing below close to them, and they sent volleys of grapeshot at them.

The little man with his weak, clumsy movements, was continually asking his orderly *for just one more pipe for that stroke*, as he said, and scattering sparks from it, he kept running out in front and looking from under his little hand at the French.

"Smash away, lads!" he was continually saying, and he clutched at the cannon wheels himself and unscrewed the screws. In the smoke, deafened by the incessant booming of the cannons that made him shudder every time one was fired, Tushin ran from one cannon to the other, his short pipe never out of his mouth. At one moment he was taking aim, then reckoning the charges, then arranging for the changing and unharnessing of the killed and wounded horses, and all the time shouting in his weak, shrill, hesitating voice. His face grew more and more eager. Only when men were killed and wounded he knitted his brows, and turning away from the dead man, shouted angrily to the men, slow, as they always are, to pick up a wounded man or a dead body. The soldiers, for the most part fine, handsome fellows (a couple of heads taller than their officer and twice as broad in the chest, as they mostly are in the artillery), all looked to their commanding officer like children in a difficult position, and the expression they found on his face was invariably reflected at once on their own.

Owing to the fearful uproar and noise and the necessity of attention and activity, Tushin experienced not the slightest unpleasant sensation of fear; and the idea that he might be killed or badly wounded never entered his head. On the contrary, he felt more and more lively. It seemed to him that the moment in which he had first seen the enemy and had fired the first shot was long, long ago, yesterday perhaps, and that the spot of earth on which he stood was a place long familiar to him, in which he

was quite at home. Although he thought of everything, considered everything, did everything the
very best officer could have done in his position, he
was in a state of mind akin to the delirium of fever
or the intoxication of a drunken man.

The deafening sound of his own guns on all sides,
the hiss and thud of the enemy's shells, the sight of
the perspiring, flushed gunners hurrying about the
cannons, the sight of the blood of men and horses,
and of the puffs of smoke from the enemy on the
opposite side (always followed by a cannon-ball that
flew across and hit the earth, a man, a horse, or a cannon)—all these images made up for him a fantastic
world of his own, in which he found enjoyment at
the moment. The enemy's cannons in his fancy were
not cannons, but pipes from which an invisible
smoker blew puffs of smoke at intervals.

"There he's puffing away again," Tushin murmured to himself as a cloud of smoke rolled downhill, and was borne off by the wind in a wreath to
the left. "Now, your ball—throw it back."

"What is it, your honour?" asked a gunner who
stood near him, and heard him muttering something.

"Nothing, a grenade . . ." he answered. "Now for
it, our Matvyevna," he said to himself. Matvyevna
was the name his fancy gave to the big cannon, cast
in an old-fashioned mould, that stood at the end.

The French seemed to be ants swarming about their cannons. The handsome, drunken soldier, number one gunner of the second cannon, was in his dream-world "uncle"; Tushin looked at him more often than at any of the rest, and took delight in every gesture of the man. The sound—dying away, then quickening again—of the musketry fire below the hill seemed to him like the heaving of some creature's breathing. He listened to the ebb and flow of these sounds.

"Ah, she's taking another breath again," he was saying to himself. He himself figured in his imagination as a mighty man of immense stature, who was flinging cannon balls at the French with both hands.

"Come, Matvyevna, old lady, stick by us!" he was saying, moving back from the cannon, when a strange, unfamiliar voice called over his head. "Captain Tushin! Captain!"

Tushin looked round in dismay. It was the same staff-officer who had turned him out of the booth at Grunte. He was shouting to him in a breathless voice:

"I say, are you mad? You've been commanded twice to retreat, and you . . ."

"Now, what are they pitching into me for?" . . . Tushin wondered, looking in alarm at the superior officer.

"I . . . don't . . ." he began, putting two fingers to the peak of his cap. "I . . ."

But the staff-officer did not say all he had meant to. A cannon ball flying near him made him duck down on his horse. He paused, and was just going to say something more, when another ball stopped him. He turned his horse's head and galloped away.

"Retreat! All to retreat!" he shouted from a distance.

The soldiers laughed. A minute later an adjutant arrived with the same message. This was Prince Andrey. The first thing he saw, on reaching the place where Tushin's cannons were stationed, was an unharnessed horse with a broken leg, which was neighing beside the harnessed horses. The blood was flowing in a perfect stream from its leg. Among the platforms lay several dead men. One cannon ball after another flew over him as he rode up, and he felt a nervous shudder running down his spine. But the very idea that he was afraid was enough to rouse him again. "I can't be frightened," he thought, and he deliberately dismounted from his horse between the cannons. He gave his message, but he did not leave the battery. He decided to stay and assist in removing the cannons from the position and getting them away. Stepping over the corpses, under the fearful fire from the French, he helped Tushin in getting the cannons ready.

"The officer that came just now ran off quicker than he came," said a gunner to Prince Andrey, "not like your honour."

Prince Andrey had no conversation with Tushin. They were both so busy that they hardly seemed to see each other. When they had got the two out of the four cannons that were uninjured on to the platforms and were moving downhill (one cannon that had been smashed and a howitzer were left behind), Prince Andrey went up to Tushin.

"Well, good-bye till we meet again," said Prince Andrey, holding out his hand to Tushin.

"Good-bye, my dear fellow," said Tushin, "dear soul! good-bye, my dear fellow," he said with tears, which for some unknown reason started suddenly into his eyes.

The wind had sunk, black storm-clouds hung low over the battlefield, melting on the horizon into the clouds of smoke from the powder. Darkness had come, and the glow of conflagrations showed all the more distinctly in two places. The cannonade had grown feebler, but the snapping of musketry-fire in the rear and on the right was heard nearer and more often. As soon as Tushin with his cannons, continually driving round the wounded and coming upon them, had got out of fire and were descending the ravine, he was met by the staff, among whom was the staff-officer and Zherkov, who had twice been sent to Tushin's battery, but had not once reached it. They all vied with one another in giving him orders, telling him how and where to go, finding fault and making criticisms. Tushin gave no orders, and in silence, afraid to speak because at every word he felt, he could not have said why, ready to burst into tears, he rode behind on his artillery nag. Though orders were given to abandon the wounded, many of them dragged themselves after the troops and begged for a seat on the cannons. The jaunty infantry-officer—the one who had run out of Tushin's shanty just before the battle—was laid on Matvyevna's carriage with a bullet in his stomach. At the bottom of the hill a pale ensign of hussars, holding one arm in the other hand, came up to Tushin and begged for a seat.

"Captain, for God's sake. I've hurt my arm," he said timidly. "For God's sake. I can't walk. For God's sake!" It was evident that this was not the first time the ensign had asked for a lift, and that he had been everywhere refused. He asked in a hesitating and piteous voice. "Tell them to let me get on, for God's sake!"

"Let him get on, let him get on," said Tushin. "Put a coat under him, you, Uncle." He turned to his favourite soldier. "But where's the wounded officer?"

"We took him off; he was dead," answered some one.

"Help him on. Sit down, my dear fellow, sit down. Lay the coat there, Antonov."

The ensign was Rostov. He was holding one hand in the other. He was pale, and his lower jaw was trembling as though in a fever. They put him on Matvyevna, the cannon from which they had just removed the dead officer. There was blood on the coat that was laid under him, and Rostov's riding-breeches and arm were smeared with it.

"What, are you wounded, my dear?" said Tushin, going up to the cannon on which Rostov was sitting.

"No; it's a sprain."

"How is it there's blood on the frame?" asked Tushin.

"That was the officer, your honour, stained it," answered an artillery-man, wiping the blood off with the sleeve of his coat, and as it were apologising for the dirty state of the cannon.

With difficulty, aided by the infantry, they dragged the cannon uphill, and halted on reaching the village of Guntersdorf. It was by now so dark that one could not distinguish the soldiers' uniforms ten paces away, and the firing had begun to subside. All of a sudden there came the sound of firing and shouts again close by on the right side. The flash of the shots could be seen in the darkness. This was the

last attack of the French. It was met by the soldiers
in ambush in the houses of the village. All rushed
out of the village again, but Tushin's cannons could
not move, and the artillerymen, Tushin, and the
ensign looked at one another in anticipation of their
fate. The firing on both sides began to subside, and
some soldiers in lively conversation streamed out of
a side street.

"Not hurt, Petrov?" inquired one.

"We gave it them hot, lads. They won't meddle
with us now," another was saying.

"One couldn't see a thing. Didn't they give it to
their own men! No seeing for the darkness, mates.
Isn't there something to drink?"

The French had been repulsed for the last time.
And again, in the complete darkness, Tushin's cannons moved forward, surrounded by the infantry,
who kept up a hum of talk.

In the darkness they flowed on like an unseen,
gloomy river always in the same direction, with a
buzz of whisper and talk and the thud of hoofs and
rumble of wheels. Above all other sounds, in the
confused uproar, rose the moans and cries of the
wounded, more distinct than anything in the darkness of the night. Their moans seemed to fill all the
darkness surrounding the troops. Their moans and
the darkness seemed to melt into one. A little later a
thrill of emotion passed over the moving crowd.

Some one followed by a suite had ridden by on a white horse, and had said something as he passed.

"What did he say? Where we are going now? To halt, eh? Thanked us, what?" eager questions were heard on all sides, and the whole moving mass began to press back on itself (the foremost, it seemed, had halted), and a rumour passed through that the order had been given to halt. All halted in the muddy road, just where they were.

Fires were lighted and the talk became more audible. Captain Tushin, after giving instructions to his battery, sent some of his soldiers to look for an ambulance or a doctor for the ensign, and sat down by the fire his soldiers had lighted by the roadside. Rostov too dragged himself to the fire. His whole body was trembling with fever from the pain, the cold, and the damp. He was dreadfully sleepy, but he could not go to sleep for the agonising pain in his arm, which ached and would not be easy in any position. He closed his eyes, then opened them to stare at the fire, which seemed to him dazzling red, and then at the stooping, feeble figure of Tushin, squatting in Turkish fashion near him. The big, kindly, and shrewd eyes of Tushin were fixed upon him with sympathy and commiseration. He saw that Tushin wished with all his soul to help him, but could do nothing for him.

On all sides they heard the footsteps and the chatter of the infantry going and coming and settling themselves round them. The sound of voices, of steps, and of horses' hoofs tramping in the mud, the crackling firewood far and near, all melted into one fluctuating roar of sound.

It was not now as before an unseen river flowing in the darkness, but a gloomy sea subsiding and still agitated after a storm. Rostov gazed vacantly and listened to what was passing before him and around him. An infantry soldier came up to the fire, squatted on his heels, held his hands to the fire, and turned his face.

"You don't mind, your honour?" he said, looking inquiringly at Tushin. "Here I've got lost from my company, your honour; I don't know myself where I am. It's dreadful!"

With the soldier an infantry officer approached the fire with a bandaged face. He asked Tushin to have the cannon moved a very little, so as to let a store wagon pass by. After the officer two soldiers ran up to the fire. They were swearing desperately and fighting, trying to pull a boot from one another.

"No fear! you picked it up! that's smart!" one shouted in a husky voice. Then a thin, pale soldier approached, his neck bandaged with a blood-stained rag. With a voice of exasperation he asked the artillerymen for water.

"Why, is one to die like a dog?" he said.

Tushin told them to give him water. Next a good-humoured soldier ran up, to beg for some red-hot embers for the infantry.

"Some of your fire for the infantry! Glad to halt, lads. Thanks for the loan of the firing; we'll pay it back with interest," he said, carrying some glowing firebrands away into the darkness.

Next four soldiers passed by, carrying something heavy in an overcoat. One of them stumbled.

"Ay, the devils, they've left firewood in the road," grumbled one.

"He's dead; why carry him?" said one of them.

"Come on, you!" And they vanished into the darkness with their burden.

"Does it ache, eh?" Tushin asked Rostov in a whisper.

"Yes, it does ache."

"Your honour's sent for to the general. Here in a cottage he is," said a gunner, coming up to Tushin.

"In a minute, my dear." Tushin got up and walked away from the fire, buttoning up his coat and setting himself straight.

In a cottage that had been prepared for him not far from the artillery-men's fire, Prince Bagration was sitting at dinner, talking with several commanding officers, who had gathered about him. The little old colonel with the half-shut eyes was there, greedily gnawing at a mutton-bone, and the general of twenty-two years' irreproachable service, flushed with a glass of vodka and his dinner, and the staff-officer with the signet ring, and Zherkov, stealing uneasy glances at every one, and Prince Andrey, pale with set lips and feverishly glittering eyes.

In the corner of the cottage room stood a French flag, that had been captured, and the auditor with the naïve countenance was feeling the stuff of which the flag was made, and shaking his head with a puzzled air, possibly because looking at the flag really interested him, or possibly because he did not enjoy the sight of the dinner, as he was hungry and no place had been laid for him. In the next cottage there was the French colonel, who had been taken prisoner by the dragoons. Our officers were flocking in to look at him. Prince Bagration thanked the several commanding officers, and inquired into details of the battle and of the losses. The general, whose regiment had been inspected at Braunau, submitted to the prince that as soon as the engagement began, he had fallen back from the copse, mustered the men who were cutting wood, and letting them pass by him, had made a bayonet charge with two battalions and repulsed the French.

"As soon as I saw, your excellency, that the first

battalion was thrown into confusion, I stood in the road and thought, 'I'll let them get through and then open fire on them'; and that's what I did."

The general had so longed to do this, he had so regretted not having succeeded in doing it, that it seemed to him now that this was just what had happened. Indeed might it not actually have been so? Who could make out in such confusion what did and what did not happen?

"And by the way I ought to note, your excellency," he continued, recalling Dolohov's conversation with Kutuzov and his own late interview with the degraded officer, "that the private Dolohov, degraded to the ranks, took a French officer prisoner before my eyes and particularly distinguished himself."

"I saw here, your excellency, the attack of the Pavlograd hussars," Zherkov put in, looking uneasily about him. He had not seen the hussars at all that day, but had only heard about them from an infantry officer. "They broke up two squares, your excellency."

When Zherkov began to speak, several officers smiled, as they always did, expecting a joke from him. But as they perceived that what he was saying all redounded to the glory of our arms and of the day, they assumed a serious expression, although many were very well aware that what Zherkov was saying was a lie utterly without foundation. Prince Bagration turned to the old colonel.

"I thank you all, gentlemen; all branches of the service behaved heroically—infantry, cavalry, and artillery. How did two cannons come to be abandoned in the centre?" he inquired, looking about for some one. (Prince Bagration did not ask about the cannons of the left flank; he knew that all of them had been abandoned at the very beginning of the action.) "I think it was you I sent," he added, addressing the staff-officer.

"One had been disabled," answered the staff-officer, "but the other, I can't explain; I was there all the while myself, giving instructions, and I had scarcely left there. . . . It was pretty hot, it's true," he added modestly.

Some one said that Captain Tushin was close by here in the village, and that he had already been sent for.

"Oh, but you went there," said Prince Bagration, addressing Prince Andrey.

"To be sure, we rode there almost together," said the staff-officer, smiling affably to Bolkonsky.

"I had not the pleasure of seeing you," said Prince Andrey, coldly and abruptly. Every one was silent.

Tushin appeared in the doorway, timidly edging in behind the generals' backs. Making his way round the generals in the crowded hut, embarrassed as he always was before his superior officers, Tushin did not see the flag-staff and tumbled over it. Several of the officers laughed.

"How was it a cannon was abandoned?" asked Bagration, frowning, not so much at the captain as at the laughing officers, among whom Zherkov's laugh was the loudest. Only now in the presence of the angry-looking commander, Tushin conceived in all its awfulness the crime and disgrace of his being still alive when he had lost two cannons. He had been so excited that till that instant he had not had time to think of that. The officers' laughter had bewildered him still more. He stood before Bagration, his lower jaw quivering, and could scarcely articulate:

"I don't know . . . your excellency . . . I hadn't the men, your excellency."

"You could have got them from the battalions that were covering your position!" That there were no battalions there was what Tushin did not say, though it was the fact. He was afraid of getting another officer into trouble by saying that, and without uttering a word he gazed straight into Bagration's face, as a confused schoolboy gazes at the face of an examiner.

The silence was rather a lengthy one. Prince Bagration, though he had no wish to be severe, apparently found nothing to say; the others did not venture to intervene. Prince Andrey was looking from under his brows at Tushin and his fingers moved nervously.

"Your excellency," Prince Andrey broke the silence with his abrupt voice, "you sent me to Captain Tushin's battery. I went there and found two-thirds of the men and horses killed, two cannons disabled and no forces near to defend them."

Prince Bagration and Tushin looked now with equal intensity at Bolkonsky, as he went on speaking with suppressed emotion.

"And if your excellency will permit me to express my opinion," he went on, "we owe the success of the day more to the action of that battery and the heroic steadiness of Captain Tushin and his men than to anything else," said Prince Andrey, and he got up at once and walked away from the table, without waiting for a reply.

Prince Bagration looked at Tushin and, apparently loath to express his disbelief in Bolkonsky's off-handed judgment, yet unable to put complete faith in it, he bent his head and said to Tushin that he could go. Prince Andrey walked out after him.

"Thanks, my dear fellow, you got me out of a scrape," Tushin said to him.

Prince Andrey looked at Tushin, and walked away without uttering a word. Prince Andrey felt bitter and melancholy. It was all so strange, so unlike what he had been hoping for.

# The Trojan Horse

[ V I R G I L ]

The Grecian leaders, now disheartened by the war, and baffled by the Fates, after a revolution of so many years, build a horse to the size of a mountain, and interweave its ribs with planks of fir. This they pretend to be an offering, in order to procure a safe return; which report spread. Hither having secretly conveyed a select band, chosen by lot, they shut them up into the dark sides, and fill its capacious caverns and womb with armed soldiers. In sight of Troy lies Tenedos, an island well known by fame, and flourishing while Priam's kingdom stood: now only a bay, and a station unfaithful for ships. Having made this island, they conceal themselves in that desolate shore. We imagined they were gone, and that they had set sail for Mycenae. In consequence of this, all Troy is released from its long distress: the gates are thrown open; with joy we issue forth, and view the Grecian camp, the deserted plains, and the abandoned shore. Some view with amazement that baleful offering of the virgin Minerva, and wonder at the stupendous bulk of the horse; and Thymoetes first advises that it be dragged within the walls and lodged in the tower, whether with treacherous design, or that the destiny of Troy now would have it so. But Capys, and all whose minds had wiser sentiments, strenuously urge either to throw into the sea the treacherous snare and suspected oblation of the Greeks; or by applying flames consume it to ashes; or to lay open and ransack the recesses of the hollow womb. The fickle populace is split into opposite inclinations. Upon this, Laocoön, accompanied with numerous troop, first before all, with ardour hastens down from the top of the citadel; and while yet a great way off cries out, "O, wretched countrymen, what desperate infatuation is this? Do you believe the enemy gone? or think you any gifts of the Greeks can be free from deceit? Is Ulysses thus known to you? Either the Greeks lie concealed within this wood, or it is an engine framed against our walls, to overlook our houses, and to come down upon our city; or some mischievous design lurks beneath it. Trojans, put no faith in this horse. Whatever it be, I dread the Greeks, even when they bring gifts." Thus said, with valiant strength he hurled his massive spear against the sides and belly of the monster, where it swelled out with its jointed timbers; the weapon stood quivering, and the womb being shaken, the hollow caverns rang, and sent forth a groan. And had not the decrees of heaven been adverse, if our minds had not been infatuated, he had prevailed on us to mutilate with the sword this dark recess of the Greeks; and thou, Troy, should still have stood, and thou, lofty tower of Priam, now remained!

In the meantime, behold, Trojan shepherds, with loud acclamations, came dragging to the king a youth, whose hands were bound behind him; who, to them a mere stranger, had voluntarily thrown himself in the way, to promote this same design, and open Troy to the Greeks; a resolute soul, and prepared for either event, whether to execute his perfidious purpose, or submit to inevitable death. The Trojan youth pour tumultuously around from every quarter, from eagerness to see him, and they vie with one another in insulting the captive. Now learn the treachery of the Greeks, and from one crime take a specimen of the whole nation. For as he stood among the gazing crowds perplexed, defenceless, and threw his eyes around the Trojan bans, "Ah!" says he, "what land, what seas can now receive me? or to what further extremity can I, a forlorn wretch, be reduced, for whom there is no shelter anywhere among the Greeks? and to complete my misery the Trojans too, incensed against me, sue for satisfaction with my blood." By which mournful accents our affections at once were moved towards him, and all our resentment suppressed.

At these tears we grant him his life, and pity him from our hearts. Priam himself first gives orders that the manacles and strait bonds be loosened from the man, then thus addresses him in the language of a friend: "Whoever you are, now henceforth forget the Greeks you have lost; ours you shall be: and give me an ingenuous reply to these questions: To what purpose raised they this stupendous bulk of a horse? Who was the contriver? or what do they intend? what was the religious motive? or what warlike engine is it?" he said. The other, practised in fraud and Grecian artifice, lifted up to heaven his hands, loosed from the bonds: "Troy can never be razed by the Grecian sword, unless they repent the omens at Argos, and carry back the goddess whom they had conveyed in their curved ships. And now, that they have sailed for their native Mycenae with the wind, they are providing themselves with arms; and, they will come upon you unexpected. For he declared that "if your hands should violate this offering sacred to Minerva, then signal ruin awaited Priam's empire and the Trojans. But, if by your hands it mounted into the city, that Asia, without further provocation given, would advance with a formidable war to the very walls, and our posterity be doomed to the same fate." By such treachery and artifice of perjured Sinon, the story was believed: and we, whom neither Diomede, nor Achilles, nor a siege of ten years, nor a thousand ships, had subdued, were ensnared by guile and constrained tears.

Meanwhile they urge with general voice to convey the statue to its proper seat, and implore the favour of the goddess. We make a breach in the walls, and lay open the bulwarks of the city. All keenly ply the work; and under the feet apply smooth-rolling wheels; stretch hempen ropes from the neck. The fatal machine passes over our walls, pregnant with arms. It advances, and with menacing aspect slides into the heart of the city. O country, O Ilium, the habitation of gods, and ye walls of Troy by war renowned! Four times it stopped in the very threshold of the gate, and four times the arms resounded in its womb: yet we, heedless, and blind with frantic zeal, urge on, and plant the baneful monster in the sacred citadel. Unhappy we, to whom that day was to be the last, adorn the temples of the gods throughout the city with festive boughs. Meanwhile, the heavens change, and night advances rapidly from the ocean, wrapping in her extended shade both earth and heaven, and the wiles of the Myrmidons. The Trojans, dispersed about the walls, were hushed: deep sleep fast binds them weary in his embraces. And now the Grecian host, in their equipped vessels, set out for Tenedos, making towards the well-known shore, by the friendly silence of the quiet moonshine, as soon as the royal galley stern had exhibited the signal fire; and Sinon, preserved by the will of the adverse gods, in a stolen hour unlocks the wooden prison to the Greeks shut up in its tomb: the horse, from his expanded caverns, pours them forth to the open air. They assault the city buried in sleep, and wine. The sentinels are beaten down; and with opened gates they receive all their friends, and join the conquering bands.

Meanwhile the city is filled with mingled scenes of woe; and though my father's house stood retired and enclosed with trees, louder and louder the sounds rise on the ear, and the horrid din of arms assails. I start from sleep and, by hasty steps, gain the highest battlement of the palace, and stand with erect ears: as when a flame is driven by the furious south winds on standing corn; or as a torrent impetuously bursting in a mountain-flood desolates the fields, desolates the rich crops of corn and the labours of the ox.

Then, indeed, the truth is confirmed and the treachery of the Greeks disclosed. Now Deiphosus' spacious house tumbles down, overpowered by the conflagration; now, next to him, Ucalegon blazes: the straits of Sigaeum shine far and wide with the flames. The shouts of men and clangour of trumpets arise. My arms I snatch in mad haste: nor is there in arms enough of reason: but all my soul burns to collect a troop for the war and rush into the citadel with my fellows: fury and rage hurry on my mind, and it occurs to me how glorious it is to die in arms.

The towering horse, planted in the midst of our streets, pours forth armed troops; and Sinon victorious, with insolent triumph scatters the flames. Others are pressing at our wide-opened gates, as many thousands as ever came from populous Mycenae: others with arms have blocked up the lanes to oppose our passage; the edged sword, with glittering point, stands unsheathed, ready for dealing death: hardly the foremost wardens of the gates make an effort to fight and resist in the blind encounter. By the impulse of the gods, I hurry away into flames and arms, whither the grim Fury, whither the din and shrieks that rend the skies, urge me on. Ripheus and Iphitus, mighty in arms, join me; Hypanis and Dymas come up with us by the light of the moon, and closely adhere to my side. Whom, close united, soon as I saw resolute to engage, to animate them the more I thus begin: "Youths, souls magnanimous in vain! If it is your determined purpose to follow me in this last attempt, you see what is the situation of our affairs. All the gods, by whom this empire stood, have deserted their shrines and altars to the enemy: you come to the relief of the city in flames: let us meet death, and rush into the thickest of our armed foes. The only safety for the vanquished is to throw away all hopes of safety." Thus the courage of each youth is kindled into fury. Then, like ravenous wolves in a gloomy fog, whom the fell rage of hunger hath driven forth, blind to danger, and whose whelps left behind long for their return with thirsting jaws; through arms; through enemies, we march up to imminent death, and advance through the middle of the city: sable Night hovers around us with her hollow shade.

Who can describe in words the havoc, who the death of that night? or who can furnish tears equal to the disasters? Our ancient city, having borne sway for many years, falls to the ground: great numbers of sluggish carcasses are strewn up and down, both in the streets, in the houses, and the sacred thresholds of the gods. Nor do the Trojans alone pay the penalty with their blood: the vanquished too at times resume courage in their hearts, and the victorious Grecians fall: everywhere is cruel sorrow, everywhere terror and death in a thousand shapes.

We march on, mingling with the Greeks, but not with heaven on our side; and in many a skirmish we engage during the dark night: many of the Greeks we send down to Hades. Some fly to the ships, and hasten to the trusty shore; some through dishonest fear, scale once more the bulky horse, and lurk within the well-known womb.

Ye ashes of Troy, ye expiring flames of my country! witness, that in your fall I shunned neither darts nor any deadly chances of the Greeks. Thence we are forced away, forthwith to Priam's palace called by the outcries. Here, indeed, we beheld a dreadful fight, as though this had been the only seat of the war, as though none had been dying in all the city besides; with such ungoverned fury we see Mars raging and the Greeks rushing forward to the palace, and the gates besieged by an advancing testudo. Scaling ladders are fixed against the walls, and by their steps they mount to the very door-posts, and protecting themselves by their left arms, oppose their bucklers to the darts, while with their right hands they grasp the battlements. On the other hand, the Trojans tear down the turrets and roofs of their houses; with these weapons, since they see the extremity, they seek to defend themselves now in their last death-struggle, and tumble down the gilded rafters; others with drawn swords beset the gates below; these they guard in a firm, compact body. I mount up to the roof of the highest battlement, whence the distressed Trojans were hurling unavailing darts. With our swords assailing all around a turret, situated on a precipice, and shooting up its towering top to the stars, (whence we were wont to survey all Troy, the fleet of Greece, and all the Grecian camp,) where the topmost story made the joints more apt to give way, we tear it from its deep foundation, and push it on our foes. Suddenly tumbling down, it brings thundering desolation with it, and falls with wide havoc on the Grecian troops. But others succeed: meanwhile, neither stones, nor any sort of missile weapons, cease to fly. Just before the vestibule, and at the outer gate, Pyrrhus exults, glittering in arms and gleamy brass. At the same time, all the youth from Scyros advance to the wall, and toss brands to the roof. Pyrrhus himself in the front, snatching up a battleaxe, beats through the stubborn gates, and labours to tear the brazen posts from the hinges; and now, having hewn away the bars, he dug through the firm boards, and made a large, wide-mouthed breach. The palace within is exposed to view, and the long galleries are discovered: the sacred recesses of Priam and the ancient kings are exposed to view; and they see armed men standing at the gate.

As for the inner palace, it is filled with mingled groans and doleful uproar, and the hollow rooms all throughout howl with female yells: their shrieks strike the golden stars. Then the trembling matrons roam through the spacious halls, and in embraces hug the door-posts, and cling to them with their lips. Pyrrhus presses on with all his father's violence: nor bolts, nor guards themselves, are able to sustain. The gate, by repeated battering blows, gives way, and the door-posts, torn from their hinges, tumble to the ground. The Greeks make their way by force, burst a passage, and, being admitted, butcher the first they meet, and fill the places all about with their troops. Those fifty bedchambers, those doors, that proudly shone with barbaric gold and spoils, were leveled to the ground: where the flames relent, the Greeks take their place.

Perhaps, too, you are curious to hear what was Priam's fate. As soon as he beheld the catastrophe of the taken city, and his palace gates broken down, and the enemy planted in the middle of his private apartments, the aged monarch, with unavailing aim, buckles on his shoulders (trembling with years) arms long disused, girds himself with his useless sword, and rushes into the thickest of the foes, resolute on death. And lo! Polites, one of Priam's sons, who had escaped from the sword of Pyrrhus, through darts, through foes, flies along the long galleries, and wounded traverses the waste halls. Pyrrhus, all afire, pursues him with the hostile weapon, is just grasping him with his hand, and presses on him with the spear. Soon as he at length got into the sight and presence of his parents, he dropped down, and poured out his life with a stream of blood. Upon this, Priam, though now held in the very midst of death, yet did not forbear, nor spared his tongue and passion; and, without any force, threw a feeble dart: which was instantly repelled by the hoarse brass, and hung on the highest boss of the buckler without any execution. Pyrrhus made answer and dragged him to the very altar, trembling and sliding in the streaming gore of his son: and with his left hand grasped his twisted hair, and with his right unsheathed his glittering sword, and plunged it into his side up to the hilt. Such was the end of Priam's fate: this was the final doom allotted to him, having before his eyes Troy consumed, and its towers laid in ruins; once the proud monarch over so many nations and countries of Asia: now his mighty trunk lies extended on the shore, the head torn from the shoulders, and a nameless corpse.

# Invading Britain

[ J U L I U S   C A E S A R ]

During the short part of summer which remained, Cæsar, although in these countries, as all Gaul lies toward the north, the winters are early, nevertheless resolved to proceed into Britain, because he discovered that in almost all the wars with the Gauls succors had been furnished to our enemy from that country; and even if the time of year should be insufficient for carrying on the war, yet he thought it would be of great service to him if he only entered the island, and saw into the character of the people, and got knowledge of their localities, harbors, and landing-places, all which were for the most part unknown to the Gauls. For neither does anyone except merchants generally go thither, nor even to them was any portion of it known, except the sea-coast and those parts which are opposite to Gaul. Therefore, after having called up to him the merchants from all parts, he could learn neither what was the size of the island, nor what or how numerous were the nations which inhabited it, nor what system of war they followed, nor what customs they used, nor what harbors were convenient for a great number of large ships.

He sends before him Caius Volusenus with a ship of war, to acquire a knowledge of these particulars before he in person should make a descent into the island, as he was convinced that this was a judicious measure. He commissioned him to thoroughly examine into all matters, and then return to him as soon as possible. He himself proceeds to the Morini with all his forces. He orders ships from all parts of the neighboring countries, and the fleet which the preceding summer he had built for the war with the Veneti, to assemble in this place. In the meantime, his purpose having been discovered, and reported to the Britons by merchants, ambassadors come to him from several states of the island, to promise that they will give hostages, and submit to the government of the Roman people. Having given them an audience, he after promising liberally, and exhorting them to continue in that purpose, sends them back to their own country, and [dispatches] with them Commius, whom, upon subduing the Atrebates, he had created king there, a man whose courage and conduct he esteemed, and who he thought would be faithful to him, and whose influence ranked highly in those countries. He orders him to visit as many states as he could, and persuade them to embrace the protection of the Roman people, and apprize them that he would shortly come thither. Volusenus, having viewed the localities as far as means could be afforded one who dared not leave his ship and trust himself to barbarians, returns to Cæsar on the fifth day, and reports what he had there observed.

While Cæsar remains in these parts for the purpose of procuring ships, ambassadors come to him from a great portion of the Morini, to plead their excuse respecting their conduct on the late occasion; alleging that it was as men uncivilized, and as those who were unacquainted with our custom, that they had made war upon the Roman people, and promising to perform what he should command. Cæsar, thinking that this had happened fortunately enough for him, because he neither wished to leave an enemy behind him, nor had an opportunity for carrying on a war, by reason of the time of year, nor considered that employment in such trifling matters was to be preferred to his enterprise on Britain, imposes a large number of hostages; and when these were brought, he received them to his protection. Having collected together, and provided about eighty transport ships, as many as he thought necessary for conveying over two legions, he assigned such [ships] of war as he had besides to the quæstor, his lieutenants, and officers of cavalry. There were in addition to these eighteen ships of burden which were prevented, eight miles from that place, by winds, from being able to reach the same port. These he distributed among the horse; the rest of the army, he delivered to Q. Titurius Sabinus and L. Aurunculeius Cotta, his lieutenants, to lead into the territories of the Menapii and those cantons of the Morini from which ambassadors had not come to him. He ordered P. Sulpicius Rufus, his lieutenant, to hold possession of the harbor, with such a garrison as he thought sufficient.

These matters being arranged, finding the weather favorable for his voyage, he set sail about the third watch, and ordered the horse to march forward to the further port, and there embark and follow him. As this was performed rather tardily by them, he himself reached Britain with the first squadron of ships, about the fourth hour of the day, and there saw the forces of the enemy drawn up in arms on all the hills. The nature of the place was this: the sea was confined by mountains so close to it that a dart could be thrown from their summit upon the shore. Considering this by no means a fit place for disembarking, he remained at anchor till the ninth hour, for the other ships to arrive there. Having in the meantime assembled the lieutenants and military tribunes, he told them both what he had learned from Volusenus, and what he wished to be done; and enjoined them (as the principle of military matters, and especially as maritime affairs, which have a pre-cipitate and uncertain action, required) that all things should be performed by them at a nod and at the instant. Having dismissed them, meeting both with wind and tide favorable at the same time, the signal being given and the anchor weighed, he advanced about seven miles from that place, and stationed his fleet over against an open and level shore.

But the barbarians, upon perceiving the design of the Romans, sent forward their cavalry and chario-teers, a class of warriors of whom it is their practice to make great use in their battles, and following with the rest of their forces, endeavored to prevent our men landing. In this was the greatest difficulty, for the following reasons, namely, because our ships, on account of their great size, could be stationed only in deep water; and our soldiers, in places unknown to them, with their hands embarrassed, oppressed with a large and heavy weight of armor, had at the same time to leap from the ships, stand amid the waves, and encounter the enemy; whereas they, either on dry ground, or advancing a little way into the water, free in all their limbs, in places thoroughly known to them, could confidently throw their weapons and spur on their horses, which were accustomed to this kind of service. Dismayed by these circumstances and altogether untrained in this mode of battle, our men did not all exert the same vigor and eagerness which they had been wont to exert in engagements on dry ground.

When Cæsar observed this, he ordered the ships of war, the appearance of which was somewhat strange to the barbarians and the motion more ready for service, to be withdrawn a little from the transport vessels, and to be propelled by their oars, and be stationed toward the open flank of the enemy, and the enemy to be beaten off and driven away, with slings, arrows, and engines: which plan was of great service to our men; for the barbarians being startled by the form of our ships and the motions of our oars and the nature of our engines, which was strange to them, stopped, and shortly after retreated a little. And while our men were hesitating [whether they should advance to the shore], chiefly on account of the depth of the sea, he who carried the eagle of the tenth legion, after supplicating the gods that the matter might turn out favorably to the legion, exclaimed, "Leap, fellow soldiers, unless you wish to betray your eagle to the enemy. I, for my part, will perform my duty to the commonwealth and my general." When he had said this with a loud voice, he leaped from the ship and proceeded to bear the eagle toward the enemy. Then our men, exhorting one another that so great a disgrace should not be incurred, all leaped from the ship. When those in the nearest vessels saw them, they speedily followed and approached the enemy.

The battle was maintained vigorously on both sides. Our men, however, as they could neither keep their ranks, nor get firm footing, nor follow their standards, and as one from one ship and another from another assembled around whatever standards they met, were thrown into great confusion. But the enemy, who were acquainted with all the shallows, when from the shore they saw any coming from a ship one by one, spurred on their horses, and attacked them while embarrassed; many surrounded a few, others threw their weapons upon our collected forces on their exposed flank. When Cæsar observed this, he ordered the boats of the ships of war and the spy sloops to be filled with soldiers, and sent them up to the succor of those whom he had observed in distress. Our men, as soon as they made good their footing on dry ground, and all their comrades had joined them, made an attack upon the enemy, and put them to flight, but could not pursue them very far, because the horse had not been able to maintain their course at sea and reach the island. This alone was wanting to Cæsar's accustomed success.

The enemy being thus vanquished in battle, as

soon as they recovered after their flight, instantly sent ambassadors to Cæsar to negotiate about peace. They promised to give hostages and perform what he should command. Together with these ambassadors came Commius the Altrebatian, who, as I have above said, had been sent by Cæsar into Britain. Him they had seized upon when leaving his ship, although in the character of ambassador he bore the general's commission to them, and thrown into chains: then after the battle was fought, they sent him back, and in suing for peace cast the blame of that act upon the common people, and entreated that it might be pardoned on account of their indiscretion. Cæsar, complaining, that after they had sued for peace, and had voluntarily sent ambassadors into the continent for that purpose, they had made war without a reason, said that he would pardon their indiscretion, and imposed hostages, a part of whom they gave immediately; the rest they said they would give in a few days, since they were sent for from remote places. In the meantime they ordered their people to return to the country parts, and the chiefs assembled from all quarters, and proceeded to surrender themselves and their states to Cæsar.

A peace being established by these proceedings four days after we had come into Britain, the eighteen ships, to which reference has been made above, and which conveyed the cavalry, set sail from the upper port with a gentle gale, when, however, they were approaching Britain and were seen from the camp, so great a storm suddenly arose that none of them could maintain their course at sea; and some were taken back to the same port from which they had started;—others, to their great danger, were driven to the lower part of the island, nearer to the west; which, however, after having cast anchor, as they were getting filled with water, put out to sea through necessity in a stormy night, and made for the continent.

It happened that night to be full moon, which usually occasions very high tides in that ocean; and that circumstance was unknown to our men. Thus, at the same time, the tide began to fill the ships of war which Cæsar had provided to convey over his army, and which he had drawn up on the strand; and the storm began to dash the ships of burden which were riding at anchor against each other; nor was any means afforded our men of either managing them or of rendering any service. A great many ships having been wrecked, inasmuch as the rest, having lost their cables, anchors, and other tackling, were unfit for sailing, a great confusion, as would neces-sarily happen, arose throughout the army; for there were no other ships in which they could be con-veyed back, and all things which are of service in repairing vessels were wanting, and, corn for the winter had not been provided in those places, because it was understood by all that they would certainly winter in Gaul.

On discovering these things the chiefs of Britain, who had come up after the battle was fought to perform those conditions which Cæsar had imposed, held a conference, when they perceived that cavalry, and ships, and corn were wanting to the Romans, and discovered the small number of our soldiers from the small extent of the camp (which, too, was on this account more limited than ordinary, because Cæsar had conveyed over his legions without baggage), and thought that the best plan was to renew the war, and cut off our men from corn and provisions and protract the affair till winter; because they felt confident, that, if they were vanquished or cut off from a return, no one would afterward pass over into Britain for the purpose of making war. Therefore, again entering into a conspiracy, they began to depart from the camp by degrees and secretly bring up their people from the country parts.

But Cæsar, although he had not as yet discovered their measures, yet, both from what had occurred to his ships, and from the circumstance that they had neglected to give the promised hostages, suspected that the thing would come to pass which really did happen. He therefore provided remedies against all contingencies; for he daily conveyed corn from the

country parts into the camp, used the timber and
brass of such ships as were most seriously damaged
for repairing the rest, and ordered whatever things
besides were necessary for this object to be brought
to him from the continent. And thus, since that business was executed by the soldiers with the greatest
energy, he effected that, after the loss of twelve ships,
a voyage could be made well enough in the rest.

While these things are being transacted, one
legion had been sent to forage, according to custom,
and no suspicion of war had arisen as yet, and some
of the people remained in the country parts, others
went backward and forward to the camp, they who
were on duty at the gates of the camp reported to
Cæsar that a greater dust than was usual was seen in
that direction in which the legion had marched.
Cæsar, suspecting that which was [really the case],—
that some new enterprise was undertaken by the
barbarians, ordered the two cohorts which were on
duty, to march into that quarter with him, and two
other cohorts to relieve them on duty; the rest to be
armed and follow him immediately. When he had
advanced some little way from the camp, he saw that
his men were overpowered by the enemy and
scarcely able to stand their ground, and that, the
legion being crowded together, weapons were being
cast on them from all sides. For as all the corn was
reaped in every part with the exception of one, the

enemy, suspecting that our men would repair to that, had concealed themselves in the woods during the night. Then attacking them suddenly, scattered as they were, and when they had laid aside their arms, and were engaged in reaping, they killed a small number, threw the rest into confusion, and surrounded them with their cavalry and chariots.

Their mode of fighting with their chariots is this: firstly, they drive about in all directions and throw their weapons and generally break the ranks of the enemy with the very dread of their horses and the noise of their wheels; and when they have worked themselves in between the troops of horse, leap from their chariots and engage on foot. The charioteers in the meantime withdraw some little distance from the battle, and so place themselves with the chariots that, if their masters are overpowered by the number of the enemy, they may have a ready retreat to their own troops. Thus they display in battle the speed of horse, [together with] the firmness of infantry; and by daily practice and exercise attain to such expertness that they are accustomed, even on a declining and steep place, to check their horses at full speed, and manage and turn them in an instant and run along the pole, and stand on the yoke, and thence betake themselves with the greatest celerity to their chariots again.

Under these circumstances, our men being dismayed by the novelty of this mode of battle, Cæsar most seasonably brought assistance; for upon his arrival the enemy paused, and our men recovered from their fear; upon which thinking the time unfavorable for provoking the enemy and coming to an action, he kept himself in his own quarter, and, a short time having intervened, drew back the legions into the camp. While these things are going on, and all our men engaged, the rest of the Britons, who were in the fields, departed. Storms then set in for several successive days, which both confined our men to the camp and hindered the enemy from attacking us. In the meantime the barbarians dispatched messengers to all parts, and reported to their people the small number of our soldiers, and how good an opportunity was given for obtaining spoil and for liberating themselves forever, if they should only drive the Romans from their camp. Having by these means speedily got together a large force of infantry and of cavalry, they came up to the camp.

Although Cæsar anticipated that the same thing which had happened on former occasions would then occur—that, if the enemy were routed, they would escape from danger by their speed; still, having got about thirty horse, which Commius the Atrebatian, of whom mention has been made, had brought over with him [from Gaul], he drew up the legions in order of battle before the camp. When the action commenced, the enemy were unable to sustain the attack of our men long, and turned their backs; our men pursued them as far as their speed and strength permitted, and slew a great number of them; then, having destroyed and burned everything far and wide, they retreated to their camp.

The same day, ambassadors sent by the enemy came to Cæsar to negotiate a peace. Cæsar doubled the number of hostages which he had before demanded; and ordered that they should be brought over to the continent, because, since the time of the equinox was near, he did not consider that, with his ships out of repair, the voyage ought to be deferred till winter. Having met with favorable weather, he set sail a little after midnight, and all his fleet arrived safe at the continent, except two of the ships of burden which could not make the same port which the other ships did, and were carried a little lower down.

When our soldiers, about 300 in number, had been drawn out of these two ships, and were marching to the camp, the Morini, whom Cæsar, when setting forth for Britain, had left in a state of peace, excited by the hope of spoil, at first surrounded them with a small number of men, and ordered them to lay down their arms, if they did not wish to be slain; afterward however, when they, forming a circle, stood on their defense, a shout was raised and about 6000 of the enemy soon assembled; which being reported, Cæsar sent all the cavalry in the camp as a relief to his men. In the meantime our soldiers sustained the attack of the enemy, and fought most valiantly for more than four hours, and, receiving but few wounds themselves, slew several of them. But after our cavalry came in sight, the enemy, throwing away their arms, turned their backs, and a great number of them were killed.

The day following Cæsar sent Labienus, his lieutenant, with those legions which he had brought back from Britain, against the Morini, who had revolted; who, as they had no place to which they might retreat, on account of the drying up of their marshes (which they had availed themselves of as a place of refuge the preceding year), almost all fell into the power of Labienus. In the meantime Cæsar's lieutenants, Q. Titurius and L. Cotta, who had led the legions into the territories of the Menapii, having laid waste all their lands, cut down their corn and burned their houses, returned to Cæsar because the Menapii had all concealed themselves in their thickest woods. Cæsar fixed the winter quarters of all the legions among the Belgæ. Thither only two British states sent hostages; the rest omitted to do so. For these successes, a thanksgiving of twenty days was decreed by the senate upon receiving Cæsar's letter.

# An Occurrence at Owl Creek Bridge

[ AMBROSE BIERCE ]

A man stood upon a railroad bridge in northern Alabama, looking down into the swift water twenty feet below. The man's hands were behind his back, the wrists bound with a cord. A rope closely encircled his neck. It was attached to a stout cross-timber above his head and the slack fell to the level of his knees. Some loose boards laid upon the sleepers supporting the metals of the railway supplied a footing for him and his executioners—two private soldiers of the Federal army, directed by a sergeant who in civil life may have been a deputy sheriff. At a short remove upon the same temporary platform was an officer in the uniform of his rank, armed. He was a captain. A sentinel at each end of the bridge stood with his rifle in the position known as "support," that is to say, vertical in front of the left shoulder, the hammer resting on the forearm thrown straight across the chest—a formal and unnatural position, enforcing an erect carriage of the body. It did not appear to be the duty of these two men to know what was occurring at the centre of the bridge; they merely blockaded the two ends of the foot planking that traversed it.

Beyond one of the sentinels nobody was in sight; the railroad ran straight away into a forest for a hundred yards, then, curving, was lost to view. Doubtless there was an outpost farther along. The other bank of the stream was open ground—a gentle activity topped with a stockade of vertical tree trunks, loopholed for rifles, with a single embrasure through which protruded the muzzle of a brass cannon commanding the bridge. Midway of the slope between bridge and fort were the spectators—a single company of infantry in line, at "parade rest," the butts of the rifles on the ground, the barrels inclining slightly backward against the right shoulder, the hands crossed upon the stock. A lieutenant stood at the right of the line, the point of his sword upon the ground, his left hand resting upon his right. Excepting the group of four at the centre of the bridge, not a man moved. The company faced the bridge, staring stonily, motionless. The sentinels, facing the banks of the stream, might have been statues to adorn the bridge. The captain stood with folded arms, silent, observing the work of his subordinates, but making no sign. Death is a dignitary who when he comes announced is to be received with formal manifestations of respect, even by those most familiar with him. In the code of military etiquette silence and fixity are forms of deference.

The man who was engaged in being hanged was apparently about thirty-five years of age. He was a civilian, if one might judge from his habit, which was that of a planter. His features were good—a straight nose, firm mouth, broad forehead, from which his long, dark hair was combed straight back, falling behind his ears to the collar of his well-fitting frock-coat. He wore a mustache and pointed beard, but no whiskers; his eyes were large and dark gray, and had a kindly expression which one would hardly have expected in one whose neck was in the hemp. Evidently this was no vulgar assassin. The liberal military code makes provision for hanging many kinds of persons, and gentlemen are not excluded.

The preparations being complete, the two private soldiers stepped aside and each drew away the plank upon which he had been standing. The sergeant turned to the captain, saluted and placed himself immediately behind that officer, who in turn moved apart one pace. These movements left the condemned man and the sergeant standing on the two ends of the same plank, which spanned three of the cross-ties of the bridge. The end upon which the civilian stood almost, but not quite, reached a fourth. This plank had been held in place by the weight of the captain; it was now held by that of the sergeant. At a signal from the former the latter would step aside, the plank would tilt and the condemned man go down between two ties. The arrangement commended itself to his judgment as simple and effective. His face had not been covered nor his eyes bandaged. He looked a moment at his "unsteadfast footing," then let his gaze wander to the swirling water of the stream racing madly beneath his feet. A piece of dancing driftwood caught his attention and his eyes followed it down the current. How slowly it appeared to move! What a sluggish stream!

He closed his eyes in order to fix his last thoughts upon his wife and children. The water, touched to gold by the early sun, the brooding mists under the banks at some distance down the stream, the fort, the soldiers, the piece of drift—all had distracted him. And now he became conscious of a new disturbance. Striking through the thought of his dear ones was a sound which he could neither ignore nor understand, a sharp, distinct, metallic percussion like the stroke of a blacksmith's hammer upon the anvil; it had the same ringing quality. He wondered what it was, and whether immeasurably distant or near by—it seemed both. Its recurrence was regular, but as slow as the tolling of a death knell. He awaited each stroke with impatience and—he knew not why—apprehension. The intervals of silence grew progressively longer; the delays became maddening. With their greater infrequency the sounds increased in strength and sharpness. They hurt his ear like the thrust of a knife; he feared he would shriek. What he heard was the ticking of his watch.

He unclosed his eyes and saw again the water below him. "If I could free my hands," he thought, "I might throw off the noose and spring into the stream. By diving I could evade the bullets and, swimming vigorously, reach the bank, take to the woods and get away home. My home, thank God, is as yet outside their lines; my wife and little ones are still beyond the invader's farthest advance."

As these thoughts, which have here to be set down in words, were flashed into the doomed man's brain rather than evolved from it the captain nodded to the sergeant. The sergeant stepped aside.

## II

Peyton Farquhar was a well-to-do planter, of an old and highly respected Alabama family. Being a slave owner and like other slave owners a politician he was naturally an original secessionist and ardently devoted to the Southern cause. Circumstances of an imperious nature, which it is unnecessary to relate here, had prevented him from taking service with the gallant army that had fought the disastrous campaigns ending with the fall of Corinth, and he chafed under the inglorious restraint, longing for the release of his energies, the larger life of the soldier, the opportunity for distinction. That opportunity, he felt, would come, as it comes to all in war time. Meanwhile he did what he could. No service was too humble for him to perform in aid of the South, no adventure too perilous for him to undertake if consistent with the character of a civilian who was at heart a soldier, and who in good faith and without too much qualification assented to at least a part of the frankly villainous dictum that all is fair in love and war.

One evening while Farquhar and his wife were sitting on a rustic bench near the entrance to his grounds, a gray-clad soldier rode up to the gate and asked for a drink of water. Mrs. Farquhar was only too happy to serve him with her own white hands. While she was fetching the water her husband approached the dusty horseman and inquired eagerly for news from the front.

"The Yanks are repairing the railroads," said the man, "and are getting ready for another advance. They have reached the Owl Creek bridge, put it in order and built a stockade on the north bank. The commandant has issued an order, which is posted everywhere, declaring that any civilian caught interfering with the railroad, its bridges, tunnels or trains will be summarily hanged. I saw the order."

"How far is it to the Owl Creek bridge?" Farquhar asked.

"About thirty miles."

"Is there no force on this side the creek?"

"Only a picket post half a mile out, on the railroad, and a single sentinel at this end of the bridge."

"Suppose a man—a civilian and student of hanging—should elude the picket post and perhaps get the better of the sentinel," said Farquhar, smiling, "what could he accomplish?"

The soldier reflected. "I was there a month ago," he replied. "I observed that the flood of last winter had lodged a great quantity of driftwood against the wooden pier at this end of the bridge. It is now dry and would burn like tow."

The lady had now brought the water, which the soldier drank. He thanked her ceremoniously, bowed to her husband and rode away. An hour later, after nightfall, he repassed the plantation, going northward in the direction from which he had come. He was a Federal scout.

### III

As Peyton Farquhar fell straight downward through the bridge he lost consciousness and was as one already dead. From this state he was awakened—ages later, it seemed to him—by the pain of a sharp pressure upon his throat, followed by a sense of suffocation. Keen, poignant agonies seemed to shoot from his neck downward through every fibre of his body and limbs. These pains appeared to flash along well-defined lines of ramification and to beat with an inconceivably rapid periodicity. They seemed like streams of pulsating fire heating him to an intolerable temperature. As to his head, he was conscious of nothing but a feeling of fulness—of congestion. These sensations were unaccompanied by thought. The intellectual part of his nature was already effaced; he had power only to feel, and feeling was torment. He was conscious of motion. Encompassed in a luminous cloud, of which he was now merely the fiery heart, without material substance, he swung through unthinkable arcs of oscillation, like a vast pendulum. Then all at once, with terrible suddenness, the light about him shot upward with the noise of a loud plash; a frightful roaring was in his ears, and all was cold and dark. The power of thought was restored; he knew that the rope had broken and he had fallen into the stream. There was no additional strangulation; the noose about his neck was already suffocating him and kept the water from his lungs. To die of hanging at the bottom of a river!—the idea seemed to him ludicrous. He opened his eyes in the darkness and saw above him a gleam of light, but how distant, how inaccessible! He was still sinking, for the light became fainter and fainter until it was a mere glimmer. Then it began to grow and brighten, and he knew that he was rising toward the surface—knew it with reluctance, for he was now very comfortable. "To be hanged and drowned," he thought, "that is not so bad; but I do not wish to be shot. No; I will not be shot; that is not fair."

He was not conscious of an effort, but a sharp pain in his wrist apprised him that he was trying to free his hands. He gave the struggle his attention, as an idler might observe the feat of a juggler, without interest in the outcome. What splendid effort!—what magnificent, what superhuman strength! Ah, that was a fine endeavor! Bravo! The cord fell away; his arms parted and floated upward, the hands dimly seen on each side in the growing light. He watched them with a new interest as first one and then the other pounced upon the noose at his neck. They

tore it away and thrust it fiercely aside, its undulations resembling those of a water-snake. "Put it
back, put it back!" He thought he shouted these
words to his hands, for the undoing of the noose had
been succeeded by the direst pang that he had yet
experienced. His neck ached horribly; his brain was
on fire; his heart, which had been fluttering faintly,
gave a great leap, trying to force itself out at his
mouth. His whole body was racked and wrenched
with an insupportable anguish! But his disobedient
hands gave no heed to the command. They beat the
water vigorously with quick, downward strokes,
forcing him to the surface. He felt his head emerge;
his eyes were blinded by the sunlight; his chest
expanded convulsively, and with a supreme and
crowning agony his lungs engulfed a great draught
of air, which instantly he expelled in a shriek!

He was now in full possession of his physical
senses. They were, indeed, preternaturally keen and
alert. Something in the awful disturbance of his
organic system had so exalted and refined them that
they made record of things never before perceived.
He felt the ripples upon his face and heard their
separate sounds as they struck. He looked at the forest on the bank of the stream, saw the individual
trees, the leaves and the veining of each leaf—saw
the very insects upon them: the locusts, the
brilliant-bodied flies, the gray spiders stretching

their webs from twig to twig. He noted the pris-
matic colors in all the dewdrops upon a million
blades of grass. The humming of the gnats that
danced above the eddies of the stream, the beating
of the dragon-flies' wings, the strokes of the water-
spiders' legs, like oars which had lifted their boat—
all these made audible music. A fish slid along
beneath his eyes and he heard the rush of its body
parting the water.

He had come to the surface facing down the
stream; in a moment the visible world seemed to
wheel slowly round, himself the pivotal point, and he
saw the bridge, the fort, the soldiers upon the bridge,
the captain, the sergeant, the two privates, his executioners. They were in silhouette against the blue sky.
They shouted and gesticulated, pointing at him. The
captain had drawn his pistol, but did not fire; the others were unarmed. Their movements were grotesque
and horrible, their forms gigantic.

Suddenly he heard a sharp report and something
struck the water smartly within a few inches of his
head, spattering his face with spray. He heard a second report, and saw one of the sentinels with his
rifle at his shoulder, a light cloud of blue smoke rising from the muzzle. The man in the water saw the
eye of the man on the bridge gazing into his own
through the sights of the rifle. He observed that it
was a gray eye and remembered having read that

gray eyes were keenest, and that all famous marks-men had them. Nevertheless, this one had missed.

A counter-swirl had caught Farquhar and turned him half round; he was again looking into the forest on the bank opposite the fort. The sound of a clear, high voice in a monotonous singsong now rang out behind him and came across the water with a dis-tinctness that pierced and subdued all other sounds, even the beating of the ripples in his ears. Although no soldier, he had frequented camps enough to know the dread significance of that deliberate, drawling, aspirated chant; the lieutenant on shore was taking a part in the morning's work. How coldly and pitilessly—with what an even, calm into-nation, presaging, and enforcing tranquillity in the men—with what accurately measured intervals fell those cruel words:

"Attention, company! . . . Shoulder arms! . . . Ready! . . . Aim! . . . Fire!"

Farquhar dived—dived as deeply as he could. The water roared in his ears like the voice of Niagara, yet he heard the dulled thunder of the volley and, rising again toward the surface, met shining bits of metal, singularly flattened, oscillating slowly downward. Some of them touched him on the face and hands, then fell away, continuing their descent. One lodged between his collar and neck; it was uncomfortably warm and he snatched it out.

[ 262 ]

As he rose to the surface, gasping for breath, he saw that he had been a long time under water; he was perceptibly farther down stream—nearer to safety. The soldiers had almost finished reloading; the metal ramrods flashed all at once in the sunshine as they were drawn from the barrels, turned in the air, and thrust into their sockets. The two sentinels fired again, independently and ineffectually.

The hunted man saw all this over his shoulder; he was now swimming vigorously with the current. His brain was as energetic as his arms and legs; he thought with the rapidity of lightning.

"The officer," he reasoned, "will not make that martinet's error a second time. It is as easy to dodge a volley as a single shot. He has probably already given the command to fire at will. God help me, I cannot dodge them all!"

An appalling plash within two yards of him was followed by a loud, rushing sound, *diminuendo*, which seemed to travel back through the air to the fort and died in an explosion which stirred the very river to its deeps! A rising sheet of water curved over him, fell down upon him, blinded him, strangled him! The cannon had taken a hand in the game. As he shook his head free from the commotion of the smitten water he heard the deflected shot humming through the air ahead, and in an instant it was cracking and and smashing the branches in the forest beyond.

"They will not do that again," he thought; "the next time they will use a charge of grape. I must keep my eye upon the gun; the smoke will apprise me—the report arrives too late; it lags behind the missile. That is a good gun."

Suddenly he felt himself whirled round and round—spinning like a top. The water, the banks, the forests, the now distant bridge, fort and men—all were commingled and blurred. Objects were represented by their colors only; circular horizontal streaks of color—that was all he saw. He had been caught in a vortex and was being whirled on with a velocity of advance and gyration that made him giddy and sick. In a few moments he was flung upon the gravel at the foot of the left bank of the stream—the southern bank—and behind a projecting point which concealed him from his enemies. The sudden arrest of his motion, the abrasion of one of his hands on the gravel, restored him, and he wept with delight. He dug his fingers into the sand, threw it over himself in handfuls and audibly blessed it. It looked like diamonds, rubies, emeralds; he could think of nothing beautiful which it did not resemble. The trees upon the bank were giant garden plants; he noted a definite order in their arrangement, inhaled the fragrance of their blooms. A strange, roseate light shone through the spaces among their trunks and the wind made in their

branches the music of æolian harps. He had no wish
to perfect his escape—was content to remain in that
enchanting spot until retaken.

A whiz and rattle of grapeshot among the
branches high above his head roused him from his
dream. The baffled cannoneer had fired him a ran-
dom farewell. He sprang to his feet, rushed up the
sloping bank, and plunged into the forest.

All that day he traveled, laying his course by the
rounding sun. The forest seemed interminable;
nowhere did he discover a break in it, not even a
woodman's road. He had not known that he lived in
so wild a region. There was something uncanny in
the revelation.

By night fall he was fatigued, footsore, famishing.
The thought of his wife and children urged him on.
At last he found a road which led him in what he
knew to be the right direction. It was as wide and
straight as a city street, yet it seemed untraveled. No
fields bordered it, no dwelling anywhere. Not so
much as the barking of a dog suggested human
habitation. The black bodies of the trees formed a
straight wall on both sides, terminating on the horizon in a point, like a diagram in a lesson in perspective. Overhead, as he looked up through this rift in
the wood, shone great golden stars looking unfamiliar and grouped in strange constellations. He was
sure they were arranged in some order which had a

secret and malign significance. The wood on either side was full of singular noises, among which—once, twice, and again, he distinctly heard whispers in an unknown tongue.

His neck was in pain and lifting his hand to it he found it horribly swollen. He knew that it had a circle of black where the rope had bruised it. His eyes felt congested; he could no longer close them. His tongue was swollen with thirst; he relieved its fever by thrusting it forward from between his teeth into the cold air. How softly the turf had carpeted the untraveled avenue—he could no longer feel the roadway beneath his feet!

Doubtless, despite his suffering, he had fallen asleep while walking, for now he sees another scene—perhaps he has merely recovered from a delirium. He stands at the gate of his own home. All is as he left it, and all bright and beautiful in the morning sunshine. He must have traveled the entire night. As he pushes open the gate and passes up the wide white walk, he sees a flutter of female garments; his wife, looking fresh and cool and sweet, steps down from the veranda to meet him. At the bottom of the steps she stands waiting, with a smile of ineffable joy, an attitude of matchless grace and dignity. Ah, how beautiful she is! He springs forward with extended arms. As he is about to clasp her he feels a stunning blow upon the back of the neck; a blinding white light blazes all about him with a sound like the shock of a cannon—then all is darkness and silence!

Peyton Farquhar was dead; his body, with a broken neck, swung gently from side to side beneath the timbers of the Owl Creek bridge.

# The Pass of Thermopylae 430 B.C.

## [ CHARLOTTE YONGE ]

"Stranger, bear this message to the Spartans, that we lie here obedient to their laws."[1]

There was trembling in Greece. "The Great King," as the Greeks called the chief potentate of the East, whose domains stretched from the Indian Caucasus to the Ægæus, from the Caspian to the Red Sea, was marshalling his forces against the little free states that nestled amid the rocks and gulfs of the Eastern Mediterranean. Already had his might devoured the cherished colonies of the Greeks on the eastern shore of the Archipelago, and every traitor to home institutions

---

[1]Simonides: Epitaph on the tomb of the Spartans who fell at Thermopylae.

found a ready asylum at that despotic court, and tried to revenge his own wrongs by whispering incitements to invasion. "All people, nations, and languages," was the commencement of the decrees of that monarch's court; and it was scarcely a vain boast, for his satraps ruled over subject kingdoms, and among his tributary nations he counted the Chaldean, with his learning and old civilization, the wise and steadfast Jew, the skilful Phœnician, the learned Egyptian, the wild freebooting Arab of the desert, the dark-skinned Ethiopian, and over all these ruled the keen-witted, active native Persian race, the conquerors of all the rest, and led by a chosen band proudly called the Immortal. His many capitals—Babylon the great, Susa, Persepolis, and the like—were names of dreamy splendour to the Greeks, described now and then by Ionians from Asia Minor who had carried their tribute to the king's own feet, or by courtier slaves who had escaped with difficulty from being all too serviceable at the tyrannic court. And the lord of this enormous empire was about to launch his countless host against the little cluster of states the whole of which together would hardly equal one province of the huge Asiatic realm! Moreover, it was a war not only on the men, but on their gods. The Persians were zealous adorers of the sun and of fire; they abhorred the idol-worship of the Greeks, and defiled and plundered every temple that fell in their way. Death and desolation were almost the best that could be looked for at such hands; slavery and torture from cruelly barbarous masters would only too surely be the lot of numbers should their land fall a prey to the conquerors.

True it was that ten years back the former Great King had sent his best troops to be signally defeated upon the coast of Attica; but the losses at Marathon had but stimulated the Persian lust of conquest, and the new King Xerxes was gathering together such myriads of men as should crush down the Greeks and overrun their country by mere force of numbers.

The muster-place was at Sardis, and there Greek spies had seen the multitudes assembling and the state and magnificence of the king's attendants. Envoys had come from him to demand earth and water from each state in Greece, as emblems that land and sea were his; but each state was resolved to be free, and only Thessaly, that which lay first in his path, consented to yield the token of subjugation. A council was held at the Isthmus of Corinth, and attended by deputies from all the states of Greece, to consider of the best means of defence. The ships of the enemy would coast round the shores of the Ægean Sea, the land army would cross the Hellespont on a bridge of boats lashed together, and march southwards into Greece. The only hope of averting the danger lay in defending such passages as, from the nature of the ground, were so narrow that only a few persons could fight hand to hand at once, so that courage would be of more avail than numbers.

The first of these passes was called Tempe, and a body of troops was sent to guard it; but they found that this was useless and impossible, and came back again. The next was at Thermopylæ. Look in your map of the Archipelago, or Ægean Sea, as it was then called, for the great island of Negropont, or by its old name, Eubœa. It looks like a piece broken off from the coast, and to the north is shaped like the head of a bird, with the beak running into a gulf, that would fit over it, upon the mainland, and between the island and the coast is an exceedingly narrow strait. The Persian army would have to march round the edge of the gulf. They could not cut straight across the country, because the ridge of mountains called Œta rose up and barred their way. Indeed, the woods, rocks, and precipices came down so near the seashore that in two places there was only room for one single wheel track between the steeps and the impassable morass that formed the border of the gulf on its south side. These two very narrow places were called the gates of the pass, and were about a mile apart. There was a little more width left in the intervening space; but in this there were a number of springs of warm mineral water, salt and sulphurous, which were used for the sick to bathe in, and thus the place was called Thermopylæ, or the Hot Gates. A wall had once been built across the westernmost of these narrow places, when the Thessalians and Phocians, who lived on either side of it, had been at war with one another; but it had been allowed to go to decay, since the Phocians had found out that there was a very steep, narrow mountain path along the bed of a torrent by which it was possible to cross from one territory to the other without going round this marshy coast road.

This was therefore an excellent place to defend. The Greek ships were all drawn up on the farther side of Eubœa to prevent the Persian vessels from getting into the strait and landing men beyond the pass, and a division of the army was sent off to guard the Hot Gates. The council at the Isthmus did not know of the mountain pathway, and thought that all would be safe as long as the Persians were kept out of the coast path.

The troops sent for this purpose were from different cities, and amounted to about 4,000, who were to keep the pass against two millions. The leader of them was Leonidas, who had newly become one of the two kings of Sparta, the city that above all in Greece trained its sons to be hardy soldiers, dreading death infinitely less than shame. Leonidas had already made up his mind that the expedition would probably be his death, perhaps because a prophecy had been given at the Temple at Delphi that Sparta should be saved by the death of one of her kings of the race of Hercules. He was allowed by law to take with him 300 men, and these he chose most carefully, not merely for their strength and courage, but selecting those who had sons, so that no family might be altogether destroyed. These Spartans, with their helots or slaves, made up his own share of the numbers, but all the army was under his generalship. It is even said that the 300 celebrated their own funeral rites before they set out, lest they should be deprived of them by the enemy, since, as we have already seen, it was the Greek belief that the spirits of the dead found no rest till their obsequies had been performed. Such preparations did not daunt the spirits of Leonidas and his men; and his wife, Gorgo, was not a woman to be faint-hearted or hold him back. Long before, when she was a very little girl, a word of hers had saved her father from listening to a traitorous message from the King of Persia; and every Spartan lady was bred up to be able to say to those she best loved that they must come home from battle "with the shield or on it"—either carrying it victoriously or borne upon it as a corpse.

When Leonidas came to Thermopylæ, the Phocians told him of the mountain path through the chestnut woods of Mount Œta, and begged to have the privilege of guarding it on a spot high up on the mountain side, assuring him that it was very hard to find at the other end, and that there was every probability that the enemy would never discover it. He consented, and encamping around the warm springs, caused the broken wall to be repaired and made ready to meet the foe.

The Persian army were seen covering the whole country like locusts, and the hearts of some of the southern Greeks in the pass began to sink. Their homes in the Peloponnesus were comparatively secure: had they not better fall back and reserve themselves to defend the Isthmus of Corinth? But Leonidas, though Sparta was safe below the Isthmus, had no intention of abandoning his northern allies, and kept the other Peloponnesians to their posts, only sending messengers for further help.

Presently a Persian on horseback rode up to reconnoitre the pass. He could not see over the wall, but in front of it and on the ramparts he saw the Spartans, some of them engaged in active sports, and others in combing their long hair. He rode back to the king, and told him what he had seen. Now, Xerxes had in his camp an exiled Spartan prince, named Demartus, who had become a traitor to his country, and was serving as counsellor to the enemy. Xerxes sent for him, and asked whether his countrymen were mad to be thus employed instead of fleeing away; but Demartus made answer that a hard fight was no doubt in preparation, and that it was the custom of the Spartans to array their hair with especial care when they were about to enter upon any great peril. Xerxes would, however, not believe that so petty a force could intend to resist him, and waited four days, probably expecting his fleet to assist him; but as it did not appear, the attack was made.

The Greeks, stronger men and more heavily armed, were far better able to fight to advantage than the Persians with their short spears and wicker shields, and beat them off with great ease. It is said that Xerxes three times leapt off his throne in despair at the sight of his troops being driven backwards; and thus for two days it seemed as easy to force a way through the Spartans as through the rocks themselves. Nay, how could slavish troops, dragged from home to spread the victories of an ambitious king, fight like freemen who felt that their strokes were to defend their homes and children?

But on that evening a wretched man, named Ephialtes, crept into the Persian camp, and offered, for a great sum of money, to show the mountain path that would enable the enemy to take the brave defenders in the rear. A Persian general, named Hydarnes, was sent off at nightfall with a detachment to secure this passage, and was guided through the thick forests that clothed the hillside. In the stillness of the air, at daybreak, the Phocian guards of the path were startled by the crackling of the chestnut leaves under the tread of many feet. They started up, but a shower of arrows was discharged on them, and forgetting all save the present alarm, they fled to a higher part of the mountain, and the enemy, without waiting to pursue them, began to descend.

As day dawned, morning light showed the watchers of the Grecian camp below a glittering and shimmering in the torrent bed where the shaggy forests opened; but it was not the sparkle of water, but the shine of gilded helmets and the gleaming of silvered spears! Moreover, a Cimmerian crept over to the wall from the Persian camp with tidings that the path had been betrayed; that the enemy were climbing it, and would come down beyond the Eastern Gate. Still, the way was rugged and circuitous, the Persians would hardly descend before midday, and there was ample time for the Greeks to escape before they could thus be shut in by the enemy.

There was a short council held over the morning sacrifice. Megistias, the seer, on inspecting the entrails of the slain victim, declared, as well he might, that their appearance boded disaster. Him Leonidas ordered to retire, but he refused, though he sent home his only son. There was no disgrace to an ordinary tone of mind in leaving a post that could not be held, and Leonidas recommended all the allied troops under his command to march away while yet the way was open. As to himself and his Spartans, they had made up their minds to die at their post, and there could be no doubt that the example of such a resolution would do more to save Greece than their best efforts could ever do if they were careful to reserve themselves for another occasion.

All the allies consented to retreat, except the eighty men who came from Mycæne and the 700 Thespians, who declared that they would not desert Leonidas. There were also 400 Thebans who remained; and thus the whole number that stayed with Leonidas to confront two million of enemies were fourteen hundred warriors, besides the helots or attendants on the 300 Spartans, whose number is not known, but there was probably at least one to each. Leonidas had two kinsmen in the camp, like himself claiming the blood of Hercules, and he tried to save them by giving them letters and messages to Sparta; but one answered that "he had come to fight, not to carry letters," and the other that "his deeds would tell all that Sparta wished to know." Another Spartan, named Dienices, when told that the enemy's archers were so numerous that their arrows darkened the sun, replied, "So much the better: we shall fight in the shade." Two of the 300 had been sent to a neighbouring village, suffering severely from a complaint in the eyes. One of them, called Eurytus, put on his armour, and commanded his helot to lead him to his place in the ranks; the other, called Aristodemus, was so overpowered with illness that he allowed himself to be carried away with the retreating allies. It was still early in the day when all were gone, and Leonidas gave the word to his men to take their last meal. "To-night," he said, "we shall sup with Pluto."

Hitherto he had stood on the defensive, and had husbanded the lives of his men; but he now desired to make as great a slaughter as possible, so as to inspire the enemy with dread of the Grecian name. He therefore marched out beyond the wall, without waiting to be attacked, and the battle began. The Persian captains went behind their wretched troops and scourged them on to the fight with whips! Poor wretches! they were driven on to be slaughtered, pierced with the Greek spears, hurled into the sea, or trampled into the mud of the morass; but their inexhaustible numbers told at length. The spears of the Greeks broke under hard service, and their swords alone remained; they began to fall, and Leonidas himself was among the first of the slain. Hotter than ever was the fight over his corpse, and two Persian princes, brothers of Xerxes, were there killed; but at length word was brought that Hydarnes was over the pass, and that the few remaining men were thus enclosed on all sides. The Spartans and Thespians made their way to a little hillock within the wall, resolved to let this be the place of their last stand; but the hearts of the Thebans failed them, and they came towards the Persians holding out their hands in entreaty for mercy. Quarter was given to them, but they were all branded with the king's mark as untrustworthy deserters. The helots probably at this time escaped into the mountains; while the small desperate band stood side by side on the hill still fighting to the last, some with swords, others with daggers, others even with their hands and teeth, till not one living man remained amongst them when the sun went down. There was only a mound of slain, bristled over with arrows.

Twenty thousand Persians had died before that handful of men! Xerxes asked Demaratus if there were many more at Sparta like these, and was told there were 8,000. It must have been with a somewhat failing heart that he invited his courtiers from the fleet to see what he had done to the men who dared to oppose him, and showed them the head and arm of Leonidas set up upon a cross; but he took care that all his own slain, except 1,000, should first be put out of sight. The body of the brave king was buried where he fell, as were those of the other dead. Much envied were they by the unhappy Aristodemus, who found himself called by no name but the "Coward," and was shunned by all his fellow-citizens. No one would give him fire or water, and after a year of misery he redeemed his honour by perishing in the forefront of the battle of Platæa, which was the last blow that drove the Persians ingloriously from Greece.

# The 'Brigade' Classics

## [ ALFRED TENNYSON ]

## THE CHARGE OF
## THE LIGHT BRIGADE

I

Half a league, half a league
Half a league onward,
All in the valley of Death
    Rode the six hundred.
Forward the Light Brigade!
Charge for the guns!' he said.
Into the valley of Death
    Rode the six hundred.

II

'Forward, the Light Brigade!'
Was there a man dismay'd?

Not tho' the soldier knew
  Some one had blunder'd.
Theirs not to make reply,
Theirs not to reason why,
Theirs but to do and die.
Into the valley of Death
  Rode the six hundred.


III
Cannon to right of them,
Cannon to left of them,
Cannon in front of them
  Volley'd and thunder'd;
Storm'd at with shot and shell,
Boldly they rode and well,
Into the jaws of Death,
Into the mouth of hell
  Rode the six hundred.


IV
Flash'd all their sabres bare,
Flash'd as they turn'd in air
Sabring the gunners there,
Charging an army, while
  All the world wonder'd.
Plunged in the battery-smoke
Right thro' the line they broke;
Cossack and Russian

Reel'd from the sabre-stroke
   Shatter'd and sunder'd.
Then they rode back, but not,
   Not the six hundred.

V

Cannon to right of them,
Cannon to left of them,
Cannon behind them
   Volley'd and thunder'd;
Storm'd at with shot and shell,
While horse and hero fell,
They that had fought so well
Came thro' the jaws of Death,
Back from the mouth of hell,
All that was left of them,
   Left of six hundred.

VI

When can their glory fade?
O the wild charge they made!
   All the world wonder'd.
Honor the charge they made!
Honor the Light Brigade,
   Noble six hundred!

# THE CHARGE OF THE HEAVY BRIGADE AT BALACLAVA

## OCTOBER 25, 1854

I

The charge of the gallant three hundred, the Heavy
    Brigade!

Down the hill, down the hill, thousands of Russians,

Thousands of horsemen, drew to the valley—and stay'd;

For Scarlett and Scarlett's three hundred were riding by

When the points of the Russian lances arose in the sky;

And he call'd, 'Left wheel into line!' and they wheel'd
    and obey'd.

Then he look'd at the host that had halted he knew not
    why,

And he turn'd half round, and he bade his trumpeter
    sound

To the charge, and he rode on ahead, as he waved his
    blade

To the gallant three hundred whose glory will never
    die—

'Follow,' and up the hill, up the hill, up the hill,

Follow'd the Heavy Brigade.

II

The trumpet, the gallop, the charge, and the might of the
    fight!
Thousands of horsemen had gather'd there on the
    height,
With a wing push'd out to the left and a wing to the
    right,
And who shall escape if they close? but he dash'd up
    alone
Thro' the great gray slope of men,
Sway'd his sabre, and held his own
Like an Englishman there and then.
All in a moment follow'd with force
Three that were next in their fiery course,
Wedged themselves in between horse and horse,
Fought for their lives in the narrow gap they had made—
Four amid thousands! and up the hill, up the hill,
Gallopt the gallant three hundred, the Heavy Brigade.


III

Fell like a cannon-shot,
Burst like a thunderbolt,
Crash'd like a hurricane,
Broke thro' the mass from below,
Drove thro' the midst of the foe,
Plunged up and down, to and fro,
Rode flashing blow upon blow,
Brave Inniskillens and Greys

Whirling their sabres in circles of light!
And some of us, all in amaze,
Who were held for a while from the fight,
And were only standing at gaze,
When the dark-muffled Russian crowd
Folded its wings from the left and the right,
And roll'd them around like a cloud,—
O, mad for the charge and the battle were we,
When our own good redcoats sank from sight,
Like drops of blood in a dark-gray sea,
And we turn'd to each other, whispering, all dismay'd,
'Lost are the gallant three hundred of Scarlett's Brigade!'

IV
'Lost one and all' were the words
Mutter'd in our dismay;
But they rode like victors and lords
Thro' the forest of lances and swords
In the heart of the Russian hordes,
They rode, or they stood at bay—
Struck with the sword-hand and slew,
Down with the bridle-hand drew
The foe from the saddle and threw
Underfoot there in the fray—
Ranged like a storm or stood like a rock
In the wave of a stormy day;
Till suddenly shock upon shock
Stagger'd the mass from without,

Drove it in wild disarray,
For our men gallopt up with a cheer and a shout,
And the foeman surged, and waver'd, and reel'd
Up the hill, up the hill, up the hill, out of the field,
And over the brow and away.

V
Glory to each and to all, and the charge that they made!
Glory to all the three hundred, and all the Brigade!

Note.—The 'three hundred' of the 'Heavy Brigade'
who made this famous charge were the Scots Greys and
the 2d squadron of Inniskillens; the remainder of the
'Heavy Brigade' subsequently dashing up to their support.

The 'three' were Scarlett's aide-de-camp, Elliot, and the
trumpeter, and Shegog the orderly, who had been close
behind him.

# The Battle of Hastings

[ CHARLES OMAN ]

As the last great example of an endeavour to use the old infantry tactics of the Teutonic races against the now fully-developed cavalry of feudalism, we have to describe the battle of Hastings, a field which has been fought over by modern critics almost as fiercely as by the armies of Harold Godwineson and William the Bastard.

About the political and military antecedents of the engagement we have no need to speak at length. Suffice it to say that the final defeat of the old English thegnhood was immediately preceded by its most striking victory. In the summer of 1066 the newly-chosen King Harold was forced to watch two enemies at once. The Norman Duke William had openly protested against the election that had taken place in January, and was known to be gathering a great army and fleet at St. Valery. Harold knew him well, and judged him a most formidable enemy; he had called out the available naval strength of his realm, and a strong squadron was waiting all through June, July, and August, ranging between the Isle of Wight and Dover, ready to dispute the passage of the Channel. At the same time the earls and sheriffs had been warned to have the land forces of the realm ready for mobilisation, and the king with his house-carles lay by the coast in Sussex waiting for news. Duke William came not, for many a week; his host took long to gather, and when his ships were ready, August turned out a month of persistent storm and northerly winds, unsuited for the sailing of a great armament.

Meanwhile there was danger from the North also. King Harold's rebel brother, Earl Tostig, had been hovering off the coast with a small squadron, and had made a descent on the Humber in May, only to be driven away by the Northumbrian Earl Edwin. But Tostig had leagued himself with Harald Hardrada, the warlike and greedy King of Norway, and a Norse invasion was a possibility, though it seemed a less immediate danger than the Norman threat to the South Coast. September had arrived before either of the perils materialised.

By a most unlucky chance the crisis came just when the English fleet had run out of provisions, after keeping the sea for three months. On September 8, Harold ordered it round to London to revictual, and to refit, for it had suffered in the hard weather. It was to resume its cruising as soon as possible. Seven days later came the news that a Norwegian fleet of three hundred sail had appeared off the Yorkshire coast, and had ravaged Cleveland and taken Scarborough. Harold was compelled to commit the guard of the Channel to the winds, which had hitherto served him well, and to fly north with his housecarles to face Hardrada's invasion. On his way he got the disastrous message that the two Earls Edwin of Northumbria and Morkar of Mercia had been beaten in a pitched battle at Fulford, in front of York (September 20), and that the city was treating for surrender. Pressing on with all possible speed, the English king arrived at York in 'time to prevent this disaster, and the same afternoon he brought the Norsemen to action at Stamford Bridge on the Derwent, seven miles from the city. Here he inflicted on them an absolutely crushing defeat—Hardrada was slain, so was the rebel Earl Tostig, and the invading host was so nearly exterminated that the survivors fled on only twenty-four ships, though they had brought three hundred into the Humber.

The details of the fight are absolutely lost—we cannot unfortunately accept one word of the spirited narrative of the *Heimskringla*, for all the statements in it that can be tested are obviously incorrect. Harold *may* have offered his rebel brother pardon and an earldom, and have promised his Norse ally no more than the famous "seven feet of English earth, since his stature is greater than that of other men." The Vikings *may* have fought for long hours in their shieldring, and have failed at evening only, when their king had been slain by a chance arrow. But we cannot trust a saga which says that Morkar was King Harold Godwineson's brother, and fell at Fulford; that Earl Waltheof (then a child) took part in the fight, and that the English army was mostly composed of cavalry and archers. The whole tale of the *Heimskringla* reads like a version of the battle of Hastings transported to Stamford Bridge by some incredible error. The one detail about it recorded in the Anglo-Saxon Chronicle, namely, that the fighting included a desperate defence of a bridge against the pursuing English, does *not* appear in the Norse narrative at all. We can only be sure that both sides must have fought on foot in the old fashion of Viking and Englishman, "hewing at each other across the war-linden" till the beaten army was well-nigh annihilated.

Meanwhile, on September 28—two days after Stamford Bridge—William of Normandy had landed at Pevensey, unhindered either by the English fleet, which was refitting at London, or by the king's

army, which had gone north to repel the Norwe-
gians. The invaders began to waste the land, and met
with little resistance, since the king and his chosen
warriors were absent. Only at Romney, as we are
told, did the landsfolk stand to their arms and beat
off the raiders.

Meanwhile, the news of William's landing was
rapidly brought to Harold at York, and reached
him—as we are told—at the very moment when he
was celebrating by a banquet his victory over the
Northmen. The king received the message on October 1 or October 2: he immediately hurried southward to London with all the speed that he could
make. The victorious army of Stamford Bridge was
with him, and the North Country levies of Edwin
and Morkar were directed to follow as fast as they
were able. Harold reached London on the 7th or 8th
of October, and stayed there a few days to gather in
the fyrd of the neighbouring shires of the South
Midlands. On the 11th he marched forth from the
city to face Duke William, though his army was still
incomplete. The slack or treacherous earls of the
North had not yet brought up their contingents, and
the men of the western shires had not been granted
time enough to reach the mustering place. But
Harold's heart had been stirred by the reports of the
cruel ravaging of Kent and Sussex by the Normans,
and he was resolved to put his cause to the arbitra-

ment of battle as quickly as possible, though the delay of a few days would perhaps have doubled his army. A rapid march of two days brought him to the outskirts of the Andredsweald, within touch of the district on which William had for the last fortnight been exercising his cruelty.

Harold took up his position at the point where the road from London to Hastings first leaves the woods, and comes forth into the open land of the coast. The chosen ground was the lonely hill above the marshy bottom of Senlac, on which the ruins of Battle Abbey stand, but then marked to the chronicler only by "the hoar apple tree" on its ridge, just as Ashdown had been marked two centuries before by its aged thorn.

The Senlac position consists of a hill some 1100 yards long and 150 yards broad, joined to the main bulk of the Wealden Hills by a sort of narrow isthmus with steep descents on either side. The road from London to Hastings crosses the isthmus, bisects the hill at its highest point, and then sinks down into the valley, to climb again the opposite ridge of Telham Hill. The latter is considerably the higher of the two, reaching 441 feet above the sea-level, while Harold's hill is but 275 at its summit. The English hill has a fairly gentle slope towards the south, the side which looked towards the enemy, but on the north the fall on either side of the isthmus is so steep as to be almost precipitous. The summit of the position, where it is crossed by the road, is the highest point. Here it was that King Harold fixed his two banners, the Dragon of Wessex, and his own standard of the Fighting Man.

The position was very probably one that had served before for some army of an older century, for we learn from the best authorities that there lay about it, especially on its rear, ancient banks and ditches, in some places scarped to a precipitous slope. Perhaps it may have been the camp of some part of Alfred's army in 893–894, when, posted in the east end of the Andredsweald, between the Danish fleet which had come ashore at Lymne and the other host which had camped at Middleton, he endeavoured from his central position to restrain their ravages in Kent and Sussex. No place indeed could have been more suited for a force observing newly-landed foes. It covers the only road from London which then pierced the Andredsweald, and was so close to its edge that the defenders could seek shelter in the impenetrable woods if they wished to avoid a battle.

The hill above the Senlac bottom, therefore, being the obvious position to take, for an army whose tactics compelled it to stand upon the defensive, Harold determined to offer battle there. We need not believe the authorities who tell us that the King had been thinking of delivering a night attack upon the

Normans, if he should chance to find them scattered abroad on their plundering, or keeping an inefficient lookout. It was most unlikely that he should dream of groping in the dark through eight miles of rolling ground, to assault a camp whose position and arrangements must have been unknown. His army had marched hard from London, had apparently only reached Senlac at nightfall, and must have been tired out. Moreover, Harold knew William's capacities as a general, and could not have thought it likely that he would be caught unprepared. It must have seemed to him a much more possible event that the Norman might refuse to attack the strong Senlac position, and offer battle in the open and nearer the sea. It was probably in anticipation of some such chance that Harold ordered his fleet, which had run back into the mouth of the Thames in very poor order some four weeks back, to refit itself and sail round the North Foreland, to threaten the Norman vessels now drawn ashore under the cover of a wooden castle at Hastings. He can scarcely have thought it likely that William would retire over seas on the news of his approach, so the bringing up of the fleet must have been intended either to cut off the Norman retreat in the event of a great English victory on land, or to so molest the invader's stranded vessels that he would be forced to return to the shore in order to defend them.

The English position is said by one narrator of the battle to have been entrenched. According to Wace, the latest and the most diffuse of our authorities, Harold ordered his men to rear a fence of plaited woodwork from the timber of the forest which lay close at their backs. But the earlier chroniclers, without exception, speak only of the shield-wall of the English, of their dense mass covering the crest of the hill, and of relics of ancient fortifications, the *antiquus agger* and *frequentia fossarum*, and *fovea magna* mentioned above. There is nothing inconceivable in the idea of Harold's having used the old Danish device of palisading a camp, save that he had arrived only on the preceding night, and that his army was weary. In the morning hours of October 14 little could have been done, though between daybreak and the arrival of the Norman host there were certainly three long hours. But it is difficult to suppose that if any serious entrenching had been carried out, the earlier Norman narrators of the fight would have refrained from mentioning it, since the more formidable the obstacles opposed to him, the more notable and creditable would have been the triumph of their duke. And the Bayeux Tapestry, which (despite all destructive criticism) remains a primary authority for the battle, appears to show no traces of any breastwork covering the English front. Probably Wace, writing from oral tradition ninety years after the battle, had heard something of the *frequentia fossarum* by William of Poictiers, and the *agger* described by Orderic, and translated them into new entrenchments, which he described as works of the best military type of his day.

From end to end of the crest of the hill the English host was ranged in one great solid mass. Probably its line extended from the high road, which crosses the summit nearer to its eastern than to its western side, for some 200 yards to the left, as far as the head of the small steep combe (with a rivulet at its bottom) which lies 200 yards to the due east of the modern parish church; while on the other, or western, side of the high road, the battle-front was much longer, running from the road as far as the upper banks of the other ravine (with a forked brook flowing out of it from two sources) which forms the western flank of the hill. From the road to this ravine there must have been a front of 800 or 850 yards. Harold's two standards were, as we know, set up on the spot which was afterwards marked by the high altar of Battle Abbey. His standing-place must therefore have been in the left-centre rather than in the absolute middle-front of the line. But the spot was dictated by the lie of the ground—here is the actual highest point of the hill, 275 feet above sea-level, while the greater part of the position is along the 250 feet contour. It was the obvious place for the planting of standards to be visible all around, and a commander standing by them could look down from a slight vantage-ground on the whole front of his host.

In this array, the English centre being slightly curved forward, its flank slightly curved back, the army looked to the Normans more like a circular mass than a deployed line. Although the Northumbrian and West-country levies were still missing, the army must have numbered many thousands, for the fyrd of south and central England was present in full force, and stirred to great wrath by the ravages of the Normans. It is impossible to guess at the strength of the host: the figures of the chroniclers, which sometimes swell up to hundreds of thousands, are wholly useless. As the position was about 1100 yards long, and the space required by a single warrior swinging his axe or hurling his javelin was some three feet, the front rank must have been at least some eleven hundred or twelve hundred strong. The hilltop was completely covered by the English, whose spear-shafts appeared to the Normans like a wood, so that they cannot have been a mere thin line: if they were some eight or ten deep, the total must have reached ten or eleven thousand men. Of these the smaller part must have been composed of the fully-armed warriors, the king's housecarles, the thegnhood, and the wealthier and better-equipped freemen, the class owning some five hides of land. The rudely-armed levies of the fyrd must have constituted the great bulk of the army: they bore, as the Bayeux Tapestry shows, the most miscellaneous arms—swords, javelins, clubs, axes, a few bows, and probably even rude instruments of husbandry turned to warlike uses. Their only defensive armour was the round or kite-shaped shield: body and head were clothed only in the tunic and cap of everyday wear.

In their battle array we know that the well-armed housecarles—perhaps two thousand chosen and veteran troops—were grouped in the centre around the king and the royal standards. The fyrd, divided no doubt according to its shires, was ranged on either flank. Presumably the thegns and other fully-armed men formed its front ranks, while the peasantry stood behind and backed them up, though at first only able to hurl their weapons at the advancing foe over the heads of their more fully-equipped fellows.

We must now turn to the Normans. Duke William had undertaken his expedition not as the mere feudal head of the barons of Normandy, but rather as the managing director of a great joint-stock company for the conquest of England, in which not only his own subjects, but hundreds of adventurers, poor and rich, from all parts of western Europe had taken shares. At the assembly of Lillebonne the Norman baronage had refused in their corporate capacity to undertake the vindication of their duke's claims on England. But all, or nearly all, of them had consented to serve under him as volunteers, bringing not merely their usual feudal contingent, but as many men as they could get together. In return they were to receive the spoils of the island kingdom if the enterprise went well. On similar terms William had accepted offers of help from all quarters: knights and sergeants flocked in, ready, "some for land and some for pence," to back his claim. It seems that, though the native Normans were the core of the invading army, yet the strangers considerably outnumbered them on the muster-rolls. Great nobles like Eustace Count of Boulogne, the Breton Count Alan Fergant, and Haimar of Thouars were ready to risk their lives and resources on the chance of an ample profit. French, Bretons, Flemings, Angevins, knights from the more distant regions of Aquitaine and Lotharingia, even—if Guy of Amiens speaks truly—stray fighting men from among the Norman conquerors of Naples and Sicily, joined the host.

Many months had been spent in the building of a fleet at the mouth of the Dive. Its numbers, exaggerated to absurd figures by many chroniclers, may possibly have reached the six hundred and ninety-six vessels given to the duke by the most moderate estimate. What was the total of the warriors which it carried is as uncertain as its own numbers. If any analogies may be drawn from contemporary hosts, the cavalry must have formed a very heavy proportion of the whole. In continental armies the foot-soldiery were so despised that an experienced general devoted all his attention to increasing the numbers of his horse. If we guess that there may have been three thousand or even four thousand mounted men, and eight thousand or nine thousand foot-soldiers, we are going as far as probability carries us, and must confess that our estimate is wholly arbitrary. The most modest figure given by the chroniclers is sixty thousand fighting men; but, considering their utter inability to realise the meaning of high numbers, we are dealing liberally with them if we allow a fifth of that estimate.

After landing at Pevensey on September 28, William had moved to Hastings and built a wooden castle there for the protection of his fleet. It was then in his power to have moved on London unopposed, for Harold was only starting on his march from York. But the duke had resolved to fight near his base, and spent the fortnight which was at his disposal in the systematic harrying of Kent and Sussex. When his scouts told him that Harold was at hand, and had pitched his camp by Senlac hill, he saw that his purpose was attained; he would be able to fight at his own chosen moment, and at only a few miles' distance from his ships. At daybreak on the morning of October 14, William bade his host get in array, and marched over the eight miles of rolling ground which separate Hastings and Senlac. When they reached the summit of the hill at Telham, the English position came in sight, on the opposite hill, not much more than a mile away.

On seeing the hour of conflict at hand, the duke and his knights drew on their mail-shirts, which, to avoid fatigue, they had not yet assumed, and the host was arrayed in battle order. The form which William had chosen was that of three parallel corps, each containing infantry and cavalry. The centre was composed of the native contingents of Normandy; the left mainly of Bretons and men from Maine and Anjou; the right, of French and Flemings. But there seem to have been some Normans in the flanking divisions also. The duke himself, as was natural, took command in the centre, the wings fell respectively to the Breton Count Alan Fergant and to Eustace of Boulogne: with the latter was associated Roger of Montgomery, a great Norman baron.

In each division there were three lines: the first was composed of bowmen mixed with arbalesters: the second was composed of foot-soldiery armed not with missile weapons but with pike and sword. Most of them seem to have worn mail-shirts, unlike the infantry of the English fyrd. In the rear was the really important section of the army, the mailed knights. We may presume that William intended to harass and thin the English masses with his archery, to attack them seriously with his heavy infantry, who might perhaps succeed in getting to close quarters and engaging the enemy hand to hand; but evidently the crushing blow was to be given by the great force of horsemen who formed the third line of each division.

The Normans deployed on the slopes of Telham, and then began their advance over the rough valley which separated them from the English position.

When they came within range, the archery opened upon the English, and not without effect; at first there must have been little reply to the showers of arrows, since Harold had but very few bowmen in his ranks. The shieldwall, moreover, can have given but a partial protection, though it no doubt served its purpose to some extent. When, however, the Normans advanced farther up the slope, they were received with a furious discharge of missiles of every kind, javelins, lances, taper-axes, and even—if William of Poictiers is to be trusted—rude weapons more appropriate to the neolithic age than to the eleventh century, great stones bound to wooden handles and launched in the same manner that was used for the casting-axe. The archers were apparently swept back by the storm of missiles, but the heavy armed foot pushed up to the front of the English line and got to hand-to-hand fighting with Harold's men. They could, however, make not the least impression on the defenders, and were perhaps already recoiling when William ordered up his cavalry. The horsemen rode up the slope already strewn with corpses, and dashed into the fight. Foremost among them was a minstrel named Taillefer, who galloped forward cheering on his comrades, and playing like a *jougleur* with his sword, which he kept casting into the air and then catching again. He burst right through the shieldwall and into the English line, where he was slain after cutting down several opponents. Behind him came the whole Norman knighthood, chanting their battle-song, and pressing their horses up the slope as hard as they could ride. The foot-soldiery dropped back—through the intervals between the three divisions, as we may suppose—and the duke's cavalry dashed against the long front of the shield-wall, whose front rank men they may have swept down by their mere impetus. Into the English mass, however, they could not break: there was a fearful crash, and a wild interchange of blows, but the line did not yield at any point. Nay, more, the assailants were ere long abashed by the fierce resistance that they met; the English axes cut through shield and mail, lopping off limbs and felling even horses to the ground. Never had the continental horsemen met such infantry before.

After a space the Bretons and Angevins of the left wing felt their hearts fail, and recoiled down the hill in wild disorder, many men unhorsed and overthrown in the marshy bottom at the foot of the slope. All along the line the onset wavered, and the greater part of the host gave back, though the centre and right did not fly in wild disorder like the Bretons. A rumour ran along the front that the duke had fallen, and William had to bare his head and to ride down the ranks, crying that he lived, and would yet win the day, before he could check the retreat of his warriors. His brother Odo aided him to rally the waverers, and the greater part of the host was soon restored to order.

As it chanced, the rout of the Norman left wing was destined to bring nothing but profit to William. A great mass of the shire-levies on the English right, when they saw the Bretons flying, came pouring after them down the hill. They had forgotten that their sole chance of victory lay in keeping their front firm till the whole strength of the assailant should be exhausted. It was mad to pursue when two-thirds of the hostile army was intact, and its spirit still unbroken. Seeing the tumultuous crowd rushing after the flying Bretons, William wheeled his centre and threw it upon the flank of the pursuers. Caught in disorder, with their ranks broken and scattered, the rash peasantry were ridden down in a few moments. Their light shields, swords, and javelins availed them nothing against the rush of the Norman horse, and the whole horde, to the number of several thousands, were cut to pieces. The great bulk of the English host, however, had not followed the routed Bretons, and the duke saw that his day's work was but begun. Forming up his disordered squadrons, he ordered a second general attack on the line. Then followed an encounter even more fierce than the first. It would appear that the fortune of the Normans was somewhat better in this than in the earlier struggle: one or two temporary breaches were made in the English mass, probably in the places where it had been weakened by the rash onset of the shire-levies an hour before. Gyrth and Leofwine, Harold's two brothers, fell in the forefront of the fight, the former by William's own hand, if we may trust one good contemporary authority. Yet, on the whole, the duke had got little profit by his assault: the English had suffered severe loss, but their long line of shields and axes still crowned the slope, and their cries of "Out! out!" and "Holy Cross!" still rang forth in undaunted tones.

A sudden inspiration then came to William, suggested by the disaster which had befallen the English right in the first conflict. He determined to try the expedient of a feigned flight, a stratagem not unknown to Bretons and Normans of earlier ages.

By his orders a considerable portion of the assailants suddenly wheeled about and retired in seeming disorder. The English thought, with more excuse on this occasion than on the last, that the enemy was indeed routed, and for the second time a great body of them broke the line and rushed after the retreating squadrons. When they were well on their way down the slope, William repeated his former procedure. The intact portion of his host fell upon the flanks of the pursuers, while those who had simulated flight faced about and attacked them in front. The result was again a foregone conclusion: the disordered men of the fyrd were hewn to pieces, and few or none of them escaped back to their comrades on the height. But the slaughter in this period of the fight did not fall wholly on the English; a part of the Norman troops who had carried out the false flight suffered some loss by falling into a deep ditch,—perhaps the remains of old entrenchments, perhaps the "rhine" which drained the Senlac bottom,—and were there smothered or trodden down by the comrades who rode over them. But the loss at this point must have been insignificant compared with that of the English.

Harold's host was now much thinned and somewhat shaken, but, in spite of the disasters which had befallen them, they drew together their thinned ranks, and continued the fight. The struggle was still

destined to endure for many hours, for the most daring onsets of the Norman chivalry could not yet
burst into the serried mass around the standards. The
bands which had been cut to pieces were mere shire-
levies, and the well-armed house-carles had refused
to break their ranks, and still formed a solid core for
the remainder of the host.

The fourth act of the battle consisted of a series
of vigorous assaults by the duke's horsemen, alter-
nating with volleys of arrows poured in during the
intervals between the charges. The Saxon mass was
subjected to exactly the same trial which befell the
British squares in the battle of Waterloo—incessant
charges by a gallant cavalry mixed with a destructive
hail of missiles. Nothing could be more maddening
than such an ordeal to the infantry-soldier, rooted
to the spot by the necessities of his formation. The
situation was frightful: the ranks were filled with
wounded men unable to retire to the rear through
the dense mass of their comrades, unable even to
sink to the ground for the hideous press. The enemy
was now attacking on both flanks: shields and mail
had been riven: the supply of missile spears had
given out: the English could but stand passive, waiting for the night or for the utter exhaustion of the
enemy. The cavalry onsets must have been almost a
relief compared with the desperate waiting between
the acts, while the arrow-shower kept beating in on

the thinning host. We have indications that, in spite of the disasters of the noon, some of the English made yet a third sally to beat off the archery. Individuals worked to frenzy by the weary standing still, seem to have occasionally burst out of the line to swing axe or sword freely in the open and meet a certain death. But the mass held firm—"a strange manner of battle," says William of Poictiers, "where the one side works by constant motion and ceaseless charges, while the other can but endure passively as it stands fixed to the sod. The Norman arrow and sword worked on: in the English ranks the only movement was the dropping of the dead: the living stood motionless." Desperate as was their plight, the English still held out till evening; though William himself led charge after charge against them, and had three horses killed beneath him, they could not be scattered while their king still survived and their standards still stood upright. It was finally the arrow rather than the sword that settled the day: the duke is said to have bade his archers shoot not point–blank, but with a high trajectory, so that the shafts fell all over the English host, and not merely on its front ranks. One of these chance shafts struck Harold in the eye and gave him a mortal wound. The arrow-shower, combined with the news of the king's fall, at last broke up the English host: after a hundred ineffective charges, a band of Norman knights burst into the midst of the mass, hewed Harold to pieces as he lay wounded at the foot of his banners, and cut down both the Dragon of Wessex and the Fighting Man.

The remnant of the English were now at last constrained to give ground: the few thousands—it may rather have been the few hundreds—who still clung to the crest of the bloodstained hill turned their backs to the foe and sought shelter in the friendly forest in their rear. Some fled on foot through the trees, some seized the horses of the thegns and housecarles from the camp and rode off upon them. But even in retreat they took some vengeance on the conquerors. The Normans, following in disorder, swept down the steep slope at the back of the hill, scarped like a glacis and impassable for horsemen,— the back defence, as we have conjectured, of some ancient camp of other days. Many of the knights, in the confused evening light, plunged down this trap, lost their footing, and lay floundering, man and horse, in the ravine at the bottom. Turning back, the last of the English swept down on them and cut them to pieces before resuming their flight. The Normans thought for a moment that succours had arrived to join the English—and, indeed, Edwin and Morkar's Northern levies were long overdue. The duke himself had to rally them, and to silence the fainthearted counsels of Eustace of Boulogne, who bade him draw back when the victory was won. When the Normans came on more cautiously, following, no doubt, the line of the isthmus and not plunging down the slopes, the last of the English melted away into the forest and disappeared. The hard day's work was done.

The stationary tactics of the phalanx of axemen had failed decisively before William's combination of archers and cavalry, in spite of the fact that the ground had been favourable to the defensive. The exhibition of desperate courage on the part of the English had only served to increase the number of the slain. Of all the chiefs of the army, only Esegar the Staller and Leofric, Abbot of Bourne, are recorded to have escaped, and both of them were dangerously wounded. The king and his brothers, the stubborn housecarles, and the whole thegnhood of Southern England had perished on the field. The English loss was never calculated; practically it amounted to the entire army. Nor is it possible to guess that of the Normans: one chronicle gives twelve thousand,— the figure is absurd, and the authority is not a good or a trustworthy one for English history. But whatever was the relative slaughter on the two sides, the lesson of the battle was unmistakable. The best of infantry, armed only with weapons for close fight and destitute of cavalry support, were absolutely helpless before a capable general who knew how to combine the horseman and the archer. The knights, if unsupported by the bowmen, might have surged for ever against the impregnable shield-wall. The archers, unsupported by the knights, could easily have been driven off the field by a general charge. United by the skilful hand of William, they were invincible.

# The View From a Hill

[ JOHN BUCHAN ]

We were standing by the crumbling rails of what had once been the farm sheep-fold. I looked at Archie and he smiled back at me, for he saw that my face had changed. Then he turned his eyes to the billowing clouds.

I felt my arm clutched.

'Look there!' said a fierce voice, and his glasses were turned upward.

I looked, and far up in the sky saw a thing like a wedge of wild geese flying towards us from the enemy's country. I made out the small dots which composed it, and my glasses told me they were planes. But only Archie's practised eye knew that they were enemy.

'Boche?' I asked.

'Boche,' he said. 'My God, we're for it now.'

My heart had sunk like a stone, but I was fairly cool. I looked at my watch and saw that it was ten minutes to eleven.

'How many?'

'Five,' said Archie. 'or there may be six—no, only five.'

'Listen!' I said. 'Get on to your headquarters. Tell them that it's all up with us if a single plane gets back. Let them get well over the line, the deeper in the better, and tell them to send up every machine they possess and down them all. Tell them it's life or death. Not one single plane goes back. Quick!'

Archie disappeared, and as he went our anti-aircraft guns broke out. The formation above opened and zigzagged, but they were too high to be in much danger. But they were not too high to see that which we must keep hidden or perish.

The roar of our batteries died down as the invaders passed westwards. As I watched their progress they seemed to be dropping lower. Then they rose again and a bank of cloud concealed them.

I had a horrid certainty that they must beat us, that some at any rate would get back. They had seen our thin lines and the roads behind us empty of sup-ports. They would see, as they advanced, the blue columns of the French coming up from the south-west, and they would return and tell the enemy that a blow now would open the road to Amiens and the sea. He had plenty of strength for it, and presently he would have overwhelming strength. It only needed a spearpoint to burst the jerry-built dam and let the flood through. . . . They would return in twenty minutes, and by noon we would be broken. Unless—unless the miracle of miracles happened, and they never returned.

Archie reported that his skipper would do his damnedest and that our machines were now going up. 'We've a chance, sir,' he said, 'a good sportin' chance.' It was a new Archie, with a hard voice, a lean face, and very old eyes.

Behind the jagged walls of the farm buildings was a knoll which had once formed part of the high-road. I went up there alone, for I didn't want any-body near me. I wanted a view-point, and I wanted quiet, for I had a grim time before me. From that knoll I had a big prospect of country. I looked east to our lines on which an occasional shell was falling, and where I could hear the chatter of machine-guns. West there was peace, for the woods closed down on the landscape. Up to the north, I remember, there was a big glare as from a burning dump, and heavy guns seemed to be at work in the Ancre valley. Down in the south there was the dull murmur of a great battle. But just around me, in the gap, the dead-liest place of all, there was an odd quiet. I could pick out clearly the different sounds. Somebody down at the farm had made a joke and there was a short burst of laughter. I envied the humorist his composure. There was a clatter and jingle from a battery changing position. On the road a tractor was jolting along—I could hear its driver shout and the screech of its un-oiled axle.

My eyes were glued to my glasses, but they shook in my hands so that I could scarcely see. I bit my lip to steady myself, but they still wavered. From time to time I glanced at my wrist-watch. Eight minutes gone—ten—seventeen. If only the planes would come into sight! Even the certainty of failure would be better than this harrowing doubt. They should be back by now unless they had swung north across the salient, or unless the miracle of miracles—

Then came the distant yapping of an anti-aircraft gun, caught up the next second by others. While smoke patches studded the distant blue of the sky. The clouds were banking in mid-heaven, but to the west there was a big clear space now woolly with shrapnel bursts. I counted them mechanically— one—three—five—nine—with despair beginning to take the place of my anxiety. My hands were steady now, and through the glasses I saw the enemy.

Five attenuated shapes rode high above the bombardment, now sharp against the blue, now lost in a film of vapour. They were coming back, serenely, contemptuously, having seen all they wanted.

The quiet had gone now and the din was monstrous. Anti-aircraft guns, singly and in groups, were firing from every side. As I watched it seemed a futile waste of ammunition. The enemy didn't give a tinker's curse for it. . . . But surely there was one down. I could only count four now. No, there was the fifth coming out of a cloud. In ten minutes they would be all over the line. I fairly stamped in my vexation. Those guns were no more use than a sick headache. Oh, where in God's name were our own planes?

At that moment they came, streaking down into sight, four fighting scouts with the sun glinting on their wings and burnishing their metal cowls. I saw clearly the rings of red, white, and blue. Before their downward drive the enemy instantly spread out.

I was watching with bare eyes now, and I wanted companionship, for the time of waiting was over. Automatically I must have run down the knoll, for the next instant I knew I was staring at the heavens with Archie by my side. The combatants seemed to couple instinctively. Diving, wheeling, climbing, a pair would drop out of the melee or disappear behind a cloud. Even at that height I could hear the methodical rat-tattat of the machine-guns. Then there was a sudden flare and wisp of smoke. A plane sank, turning and twisting, to earth.

'Hun!' said Archie, who had his glasses on it.

Almost immediately another followed. This time the pilot recovered himself while still a thousand feet from the ground, and started gliding for the enemy lines. Then he wavered, plunged sickeningly, and fell headlong into the wood behind La Bruyère.

Farther east, almost over the front trenches, a two-seater Albatross and a British pilot were having a desperate tussle. The bombardment had stopped, and from where we stood every movement could be followed. First one, then another, climbed uppermost, and dived back, swooped out and wheeled in again, so that the two planes seemed to clear each other only by inches. Then it looked as if they closed and interlocked. I expected to see both go crashing, when suddenly the wings of one seemed to shrivel up, and the machine dropped like a stone.

'Hun,' said Archie. 'That makes three. Oh, good lads! Good lads!'

Then I saw something which took away my breath. Sloping down in wide circles came a German machine, and, following, a little behind and a little above, a British. It was the first surrender in mid-air I had seen. In my amazement I watched the couple right down to the ground, till the enemy landed in a big meadow across the highroad and our own man in a field nearer the river.

When I looked back into the sky, it was bare.

North, South, east, and west, there was not a sign of aircraft, British or German.

A violent trembling took me. Archie was sweeping the heavens with his glasses and muttering to himself. Where was the fifth man? He must have fought his way through, and it was too late.

But was it? From the toe of a great rolling cloud bank a flame shot earthwards, followed by a V-shaped trail of smoke. British or Boche? British or Boche? I didn't wait long for an answer. For, riding over the far end of the cloud, came two of our fighting scouts.

I tried to be cool, and snapped my glasses into their case, though the reaction made me want to shout. Archie turned to me with a nervous smile and a quivering mouth. 'I think we have won on the post,' he said.

He reached out a hand for mine, his eyes still on the sky, and I was grasping it when it was torn away. He was staring upwards with a white face.

We were looking at a sixth enemy plane.

It had been behind the others and much lower, and was making straight at a great speed for the east. The glasses showed me a different type of machine—a big machine with short wings, which looked menacing as a hawk in a covey of grouse. It was under the cloud bank, and above, satisfied, easing down after their fight, and unwitting of this enemy, rode the two British craft.

A neighbouring anti-aircraft gun broke out into a sudden burst, and I thanked Heaven for its inspiration. Curious as to this new development, the two British turned, caught sight of the Boche, and dived for him.

What happened in the next minutes I cannot tell. The three seemed to be mixed up in a dogfight, so that I could not distinguish friend from foe. My hands no longer trembled; I was too desperate. The patter of machine-guns came down to us, and then one of the three broke clear and began to climb. The others strained to follow, but in a second he had risen beyond their fire, for he had easily the pace of them. Was it the Hun?

Archie's dry lips were talking.

'It's Lensch,' he said.

'How d'you know?' I gasped angrily.

'Can't mistake him. Look at the way he slipped out as he banked. That's his patent trick.'

In that agonizing moment hope died in me. I was perfectly calm now, for the time for anxiety had gone. Farther and farther drifted the British pilots behind, while Lensch in the completeness of his triumph looped more than once as if to cry an insulting farewell. In less than three minutes he would be safe inside his own lines, and he carried the knowledge which for us was death.

Some one was bawling in my ear, and pointing upward. It was Archie and his face was wild. I looked and gasped—seized my glasses and looked again.

A second before Lensch had been alone; now there were two machines.

I heard Archie's voice. 'My God, it's the Gladas—the little Gladas.' His fingers were digging into my arm and his face was against my shoulder. And then his excitement sobered into an awe which choked his speech, as he stammered, 'It's old—'

But I did not need him to tell me the name, for I had divined it when I first saw the new plane drop from the clouds. I had that queer sense that comes sometimes to a man that a friend is present when he cannot see him. Somewhere up in the void two heroes were fighting their last battle—and one of them had a crippled leg.

I had never any doubt about the result. Lensch was not aware of his opponent till he was almost upon him, and I wonder if by any freak of instinct he recognized his greatest antagonist. He never fired a shot, nor did Peter. . . . I saw the German twist and side-slip as if to baffle the fate descending upon him. I saw Peter veer over vertically and I knew that the end had come. He was there to make certain of victory and he took the only way. . . . The machines closed, there was a crash which I felt though I could not hear it, and next second both were hurtling down, over and over, to the earth.

They fell in the river just short of the enemy lines, but I did not see them, for my eyes were blinded and I was on my knees.

After that it was all a dream. I found myself being embraced by a French General of Division, and saw the first companies of the cheerful bluecoats for whom I had longed. With them came the rain, and it was under a weeping April sky that early in the night I marched what was left of my division away from the battlefield. The enemy guns were starting to speak behind us, but I did not heed them. I knew that now there were warders at the gate, and I believed that by the grace of God that gate was barred for ever.

They took Peter from the wreckage with scarcely a scar except his twisted leg. Death had smoothed out some of the age in him, and left his face much as I remembered it long ago in the Mashonaland hills. In his pocket was his old battered *Pilgrim's Progress*. It lies before me as I write, and beside it—for I was his only legatee—the little case which came to him

weeks later, containing the highest honour that can
be bestowed upon a soldier of Britain.

It was from the *Pilgrim's Progress* that I read next
morning, when in the lee of an apple orchard Mary
and Blenkiron and I stood in the soft spring rain
beside his grave. And what I read was the tale of the
end, not of Mr. Standfast whom he had singled out
for his counterpart, but of Mr. Valiant-for-Truth
whom he had not hoped to emulate. I set down the
words as a salute and a farewell:

'Then said he, "I am going to my Father's; and though
with great difficulty I am got hither, yet now I do not repent
me of all the trouble I have been at to arrive where I am.
My sword I give to him that shall succeed me in my pil-
grimage, and my courage and skill to him that can get it.
My marks and scars I carry with me, to be a witness for me
that I have fought His battles who now will be my
rewarder.'

'So he passed over, and all the trumpets sounded for him
on the other side.'

# The Taking of Lungtungpen

[ RUDYARD KIPLING ]

So we loosed a bloomin' volley,
   An' we made the beggars cut,
An' when our pouch was emptied out,
   We used the bloomin' butt,
     Ho! My!
     Don't yer come anigh,
When Tommy is a playin' with the
     bayonit an' the butt.

*-Barrack Room Ballad.*

**M**y friend Private Mulvaney told me this, sitting on the parapet of the road to Dagshai, when we were hunting butter-flies together. He had theories about the Army, and colored clay pipes perfectly. He said that the young soldier is the best to work with, "on account av the surpassing innocinse av the child."

"Now, listen!" said Mulvaney, throwing himself full length on the wall in the sun. "I'm a born scutt av the barrick room! The Army's mate an' dhrink to me, bekaze I'm wan av the few that can't quit ut. I've put in sivinteen years, an' the pipeclay's in the marrow av me. Av I cud have kept out av wan big dhrink a month, I wud have been a Hon'ry Lift'nint by this time—a nuisance to my betthers, a laughin' shtock to my equils, an' a curse to meself. Bein' fwhat I am, I'm Privit Mulvaney, wid no good-conduc' pay an' a devourin' thirst. Always barrin' me little frind Bobs Bahadur, I know as much about the Army as most men."

I said something here.

"Wolseley be shot! Betune you an' me an' that butterfly net, he's a ramblin', incoherent sort av a divil, wid wan oi on the Quane an' the Coort, an' the other on his blessed silf—everlastin'ly playing Saysar an' Alexandrier rowled into a lump. Now Bobs is a sinsible little man. Wid Bobs an' a few three-year-olds, I'd swape any army av the earth into a towel, an' throw it away aftherward. Faith, I'm not jokin'! 'Tis the bhoys—the raw bhoys—that don't know fwhat a bullet manes, an' wudn't care av they did—that dhu the work. They're crammed wid bull-mate till they fairly *ramps* wid good livin'; and thin, av they don't fight, they blow each other's hids off. 'Tis the trut' I'm tellin' you. They shud be kept on water an' rice in the hot weather; but ther'd be a mut'ny av 'twas done.

"Did ye iver hear how Privit Mulvaney tuk the town av Lungtungpen? I thought not! 'Twas the Lift'nint got the credit; but 'twas me planned the schame. A little before I was inviladed from Burma, me an' four-an'-twenty young wans undher a Lift'nint Brazenose, was ruinin' our dijeshins thryin' to catch dacoits. An' such double-ended divils I niver knew! 'Tis only a *dah* an' a Snider that makes a dacoit. Widout thim, he's a paceful cultiva-tor, an' felony for to shoot. We hunted, an' we hunted, an' tuk fever an' elephints now an' again; but no dacoits. Evenshually, we *puckarowed* wan man. 'Trate him tinderly,' sez the Lift'nint. So I tuk him away into the jungle, wid the Burmese Inter-prut'r an' my clanin'-rod. Sez I to the man, 'My paceful squireen,' sez I, 'you shquot on your hunkers an' dimonstrate to *my* frind here, where *your* frinds are whin they're at home?' Wid that I introjuced him to the clanin'-rod, an' he comminst to jabber; the Interprut'r interprutin' in betweens, an' me helpin' the Intilligence Departmint wid my clanin'-rod whin the man misremembered.

"Prisintly, I learn that, acrost the river, about nine miles away, was a town just dhrippin' wid *dahs*, an' bohs an' arrows, an' dacoits, an' elephints, an' *jingles*. 'Good!' sez I; 'this office will now close!'

"That night, I went to the Lift'nint an' communicates my information. I never thought much of Lift'nint Brazenose till that night. He was shtiff wid books an' the-ouries, an' all manner av thrimmin's no manner av use. 'Town did ye say?' sez he. 'Accordin' to the the-ouries av War, we shud wait for reinforcemints.'—'Faith!' thinks I, 'we'd betther dig our graves thin;' for the nearest throops was up to their shtocks in the marshes out Mimbu way. 'But,' says the Lift'nint, 'since 'tis a speshil case, I'll make an excepshin. We'll visit this Lungtungpen tonight.'

"The bhoys was fairly woild wid deloight whin I tould 'em; an', by this an' that, they wint through the jungle like buck-rabbits. About midnight we come to the shtrame which I had clane forgot to minshin to my orficer. I was on, ahead, four bhoys, an' I thought that the Lift'nint might want to the-ourise. 'Shtrip bhoys!' sez I. 'Shtrip to the buff, an' shwim in where glory waits!'—'But I *can't* shwim!' sez two of thim. 'To think I should live to hear that from a bhoy wid a board-school edukashin!' sez I. 'Take a lump av timber, an' me an' Conolly here will ferry ye over, ye young ladies!'

"We got an ould tree-trunk, an' pushed off wid the kits an' the rifles on it. The night was chokin' dhark, an' just as we was fairly embarked, I heard the Lift'nint behind av me callin' out. 'There's a bit av a *nullah* here, sorr,' sez I, 'but I can feel the bottom already.' So I cud, for I was not a yard from the bank.

"'Bit av a *nullah*! Bit av an eshtuary!' sez the Lift'nint. 'Go on, ye mad Irishman! Shtrip bhoys!' I heard him laugh; an' the bhoys begun shtrippin' an' rollin' a log into the wather to put their kits on. So me an' Conolly shtruck out through the warm wather wid our log, an' the rest come on behind.

"That shtrame was miles woide! Orth'ris, on the rear-rank log, whispers we had got into the Thames below Sheerness by mistake. 'Kape on shwimmin', ye little blayguard,' sez I, 'an' Irriwaddy.'—'Silence, men!' sings out the Lift'nint. So we shwum on into the black dhark, wid our chests on the logs, trustin' in the Saints an' the luck av the British Army.

"Evenshually, we hit ground—a bit av sand—an' a man. I put my heel on the back av him. He skreeched an' ran.

"'*Now* we've done it!' sez Lift'nint Brazenose. 'Where the Divil *is* Lungtungpen?' There was about a minute and a half to wait. The bhoys laid a hould av their rifles an' some thried to put their belts on; we was marchin' wid fixed baynits av coorse. Thin we knew where Lungtungpen was; for we had hit the river-wall av it in the dhark, an' the whole town blazed wid thim messin' *jingles* an' Sniders like a cat's back on a frosty night. They was firin' all ways at wanst; but over our heads into the shtrame.

" 'Have you got your rifles?' sez Brazenose. 'Got 'em!' sez Orth'ris. 'I've got that thief Mulvaney's for all my back-pay, an' she'll kick my heart sick wid that blunderin' long shtock av hers.'—'Go on!' yells Brazenose, whippin' his sword out. 'Go on an' take the town! An' the Lord have mercy on our sowls!'

"Thin the bhoys gave wan divastatin' howl, an' pranced into the dhark, feelin' for the town, an' blindin' an' stiffin' like Cavalry Ridin' Masters whin the grass pricked their bare legs. I hammered wid the butt at some bamboo-thing that felt wake, an' the rest come an' hammered contagious, while the *jingles* was jingling, an' feroshus yells from inside was shplittin' our ears. We was too close under the wall for thim to hurt us.

"Evenshually, the thing, whatever ut was, bruk; an' the six-an'-twenty av us tumbled, wan after the other, naked as we was borrun, into the town of Lungtungpen. There was a *melly* av a sumpshus kind for a whoile; but whether they tuk us, all white an' wet, for a new breed av divil, or a new kind av dacoit, I don't know. They ran as though we was both, an' we wint into thim, baynit an' butt, shriekin' wid laughin'. There was torches in the shtreets, an' I saw little Orth'ris rubbin' his showlther ivry time he loosed my long-shtock Martini; an' Brazenose walkin' into the gang wid his sword, like Diarmid av the Gowlden Collar—barring he hadn't a stitch av clothin' on him. We diskivered elephints wid dacoits under their bellies, an', what wid wan thing an' other, we was busy till mornin' takin' possession av the town of Lungtungpen.

"Then we halted an' formed up, the wimmen howlin' in the houses an' the Lift'nint blushin' pink in the light av the mornin' sun. 'Twas the most ondasint p'rade I iver tuk a hand in. Foive-an'-twinty privits an' a orficer av the Line in review ord-her, an' not as much as wud dust a fife betune 'em all in the way of clothin'! Eight av us had their belts an' pouches on; but the rest had gone in wid a handful av cartridges an' the skin God gave them. *They* was as nakid as Vanus.

"'Number off from the right!' sez the Lift'nint. 'Odd numbers fall out to dress; even numbers pathrol the town till relieved by the dressing party.' Let me tell you, pathrollin' a town wid nothin' on is an ex*pay*rience. I pathrolled for tin minutes, an' begad, before 'twas over, I blushed. The women laughed so. I niver blushed before or since; but I blushed all over my carkiss thin. Orth'ris didn't pathrol. He sez only, 'Portsmouth Barricks an' the 'Ard av a Sunday!' Thin he lay down an' rolled any ways wid laughin'.

"Whin we was all dhressed, we counted the dead—sivinty-foive dacoits besides the wounded. We tuk five elephints, a hunder' an' sivinty Sniders, two hunder' dahs, and a lot of other burglarious thruck. Not a man av us was hurt—excep' maybe the Lift'nint, an' he from the shock of his dasincy.

"The Headman av Lungtungpen, who surrinder'd himself asked the Interprut'r—'Av the English fight like that wid their clo'es off, what in the wurruld do they do wid their clo'es on?' Orth'ris began rowlin' his eyes an' crackin' his fingers an' dancin' a step-dance for to impress the Headman. He ran to his house; an' we spint the rest av the day carryin' the Lift'nint on our showlthers round the town, an' playin' wid the Burmese babies—fat, little, brown little divils, as pretty as picturs.

"Whin I was inviladed for the dysent'ry to India, I sez to the Lift'nint, 'Sorr,' sez I, 'you've the makin' in you av a great man; but, av you'll let an ould sodger spake, you're too fond of the-ourisin'.' He shuk hands wid me and sez, 'Hit high, hit low, there's no plazin' you, Mulvaney. You've seen me waltzin' through Lungtungpen like a Red Injin widout the war-paint, an' you say I'm too fond av the-ourisin'?'—'Sorr,' sez I, for I loved the bhoy; 'I wud waltz wid you in that condishin through *Hell*, an' so wud the rest av the men!' Thin I went downshtrame in the flat an' left him my blessin'. May the Saints carry ut where ut shud go, for he was a fine upstandin' young orficer.

"To reshume. Fwhat I've said jist shows the use av three-year-olds. Wud fifty seasoned sodgers have taken Lungtungpen in the dhark that way? No! They'd know the risk av fever an' chill. Let alone the shootin'. Two hunder' might have done ut. But the three-year-olds know little an' care less; an' where there's no fear, there's no danger. Catch thim young, feed thim high, an' by the honor av that great, little man Bobs, behind a good orficer, 'tisn't only dacoits they'd smash wid their clo'es off—'tis Con-ti-nental Ar-r-r-mies! They tuk Lungtungpen nakid; an' they'd take St. Pethersburg in their dhrawers! Begad, they would that!"

So saying, Mulvaney took up his butterfly-net, and returned to the barracks.

# Sources

"Carrying the Flag," from *The Red Badge of Courage,*
Stephen Crane, 1895.

"Waterloo," from *Les Miserables*, Victor Hugo, 1862.

"Fort William Henry 1757," from *Fort William Henry 1757*,
Francis Parkman, 1884.

"Trenches," from *The Fighting Men*, Alden Brooks, 1917.

"Gunda Din," from *Ballads and Barrack Room Ballads*, Rudyard Kipling, 1892.

"Andrey and Bagration: A Rearguard Action," from *War and
Peace*, Leo Tolstoy, 1868.

"The Trojan Horse," from *The Aeneid*, Virgil, 19 B.C.

"Invading Britain," from *Caesar's Commentaries*, Julius Caesar, 58 B.C.

"An Occurrence at Owl Creek Bridge," from *The Collected
Works of Ambrose Bierce*, 1911.

"The Pass at Thermoplylae 430 B.C.," from *A Book of
Golden Deeds*, Charlotte Yonge, 1864.

"The Brigade Classics," *Charge of the Light Brigade* and
*Charge of the Heavy Brigade*, Alfred Tennyson.

"The Battle of Hastings," from *A History of the Art of War in
the Middle Ages*, Charles Oman, 1898.

"The View from a Hill," from *Mr Standfast*, John Buchan, 1919.

"The Taking of Lungtungpen," Rudyard Kipling, 1888.